The Touch of Magic

The Story of My Life

The Touch of Magic by Lorena A. Hickok was first published in 1961.
The Story of My Life by Helen Keller was first published in 1903.
Cover design by Elle Staples
Cover illustration by Dan Burr
This unabridged version has updated grammar and spelling.
© 2020 The Good and the Beautiful, LLC
goodandbeautiful.com

Contents

THE TOUCH OF MAGIC

1. The Unwanted 1
2. Jimmie 9
3. Interlude 17
4. Rescue 24
5. New World 32
6. Valedictorian 41
7. Groping 49
8. Breakthrough 57
9. Wonder Child 65
10. Triumph and Despair 73
11. New Plans 82
12. Happy Days 91
13. Radcliffe 99
14. Enter Romance 108
15. Wanderers 113
16. Winter in the Sun 122
17. Hollywood Adventure 130
18. Behind the Footlights 138
19. New Career 146

THE STORY OF MY LIFE

Chapter 1 165
Chapter 2 170
Chapter 3 177
Chapter 4 180
Chapter 5 184
Chapter 6 187
Chapter 7 191
Chapter 8 198
Chapter 9 200
Chapter 10 204
Chapter 11 207
Chapter 12 212
Chapter 13 215
Chapter 14 220
Chapter 15 228
Chapter 16 232
Chapter 17 234
Chapter 18 237
Chapter 19 243
Chapter 20 248
Chapter 21 255
Chapter 22 266
Chapter 23 276

THE TOUCH OF MAGIC

by Lorena A. Hickok

CHAPTER 1

The Unwanted

THE DAY was Washington's Birthday. The year, 1876. Through the cold February twilight, an ugly black conveyance jolted and rattled on high iron-rimmed wheels over a frozen dirt road through the outskirts of Tewksbury, Massachusetts.

It had only one small window, covered with iron bars, in the padlocked rear door. Along the sides, up near the top, were narrow slits, presumably to let in a little light and air. It was drawn by two dejected-looking horses.

Housewives, cleaning up after their children's Washington's Birthday parties, frowned as they glanced out their windows and saw it go by. For it was called the "Black Maria," and it was used to haul criminals off to jail.

The passengers on this trip, however, were not under arrest. There were two of them, a small boy and girl huddled together on one of the long wooden benches that ran along the sides. The Black Maria was borrowed to take people to the place where they were going. It belonged to the town, and it was the only conveyance available.

The bench was worn and slippery, and the children clung desperately to each other to keep from falling off. The boy had a crutch, and he whimpered and sometimes cried out in pain as the cumbersome vehicle swayed and lurched in the frozen ruts.

Outside the town, the Black Maria turned into a driveway, passed through a big gate and stopped in front of a large building that looked run-down and rickety even in the dim wintry dusk. A man who had brought them out from Boston on a train climbed down from the front seat, where he had ridden with the driver, and led the tired, half-frozen passengers up some creaking steps, across a sagging porch, and into a big hall dimly lighted with kerosene lamps. Nine-year-old Annie Sullivan and her little brother Jimmie had arrived at their new home.

It was called the Massachusetts State Infirmary. But there were no nurses about, in starched white uniforms. When doctors came there—and they seldom came unless called in an emergency—they received no pay. Although its name implied that it was a hospital, this was actually the state almshouse, grudgingly supported by the legislature at a cost of $1.88 per week for each patient.

The patients were people whom nobody wanted around. Some were insane; some were alcoholics. Some were foundlings, born out of wedlock. Most of the babies did not live long, for there was not enough money to give them proper food and care. Many of the inmates were old people, no longer able to work, without money and with nobody to support them. Here they were sent to die, out of sight and forgotten. In their misery, some of them welcomed death as a release.

Annie and Jimmie were sent there because they had no other place to go. Their mother was dead, and their father had deserted them. Annie's eyes were bad, and Jimmie had a lump on his hip which the doctor said was tuberculous. He was unable to walk without a crutch. Nobody wanted a nine-year-old girl who was going blind or a little boy who was a cripple.

The trouble with Annie's eyes had started before she was three years old. They became badly inflamed as little lumps began to form on the insides of her eyelids. The disease was trachoma, which is most apt to occur where sanitary conditions are bad. It is a bacteria that can be carried by flies, and window screens were a luxury beyond the means of families situated as the Sullivans were. When a person has trachoma, the lumps inside the eyelids, soft and fuzzy at first, eventually become hard, like calluses. These keep scratching the eyeballs, causing ulcers and scar tissue. Gradually the scar tissue covers the eyes, and blindness results.

With proper care and treatment in the beginning, Annie's sight might have been saved. But her father, working as a day laborer on farms around Feeding Hills, Massachusetts, where Annie was born, spent most of his meager pay on cheap whiskey. There was little enough left to buy food, let alone to pay doctor bills. Her mother, crippled and ill herself, did not know what was wrong with Annie's eyes. A neighbor woman told her to wash them with "geranium water." So she would pluck leaves off a scrawny plant that somehow managed to survive in a tin can on her kitchen window. These she cooked up into a brew that smarted and made Annie howl with pain when it was applied to her sore, inflamed eyes. It did no good. Annie's father, who would sometimes be in an amiable mood when he came home drunk on payday, said her eyes could be cured with drops of water from the River Shannon. But Feeding Hills was a long, long way from Ireland and the River Shannon.

Annie was not quite nine and Jimmie three when their mother died of tuberculosis. Of the three little Sullivans left motherless, only one was healthy and attractive. Mary, less than a year old, was a sweet, cuddly baby, and she was promptly adopted by relatives. They took Jimmie, too, but on a temporary basis.

For several months, Annie lived on with her father in a wretched, tumble-down cabin. While the memory of her mother's death was still fresh, the neighbors frequently sent in leftover dishes, and now and then one of the women would come in and help Annie clean house. But the neighbors had many mouths to feed, money was scarce, and the women were busy looking after their own families. A child, nearly blind, trying to keep house for a father who came home on payday drunk and with empty pockets, was in a hopeless situation. Finally her father did not come home at all, and the Sullivan relatives had to get together and decide what to do about Annie.

Annie, just turning nine, was strong, well developed and healthy, except for her eyes. She had thick, soft brown hair, a lovely Irish complexion and beautifully curved lips that gave her face, in repose, a wistful expression. But her blue eyes were scarred and cloudy, the lids red and inflamed. All through her girlhood, people would say of her, "She'd be pretty if it weren't for her eyes."

Finding a home for Annie would have been difficult enough because she was going blind. She also had a very bad disposition, was subject to violent outbursts of temper, and had never in her short life shown the slightest trace of love or affection for anyone. A child psychologist would have understood that a child in her predicament would be apt to develop into a little lone wolf fighting the world. But her Sullivan relatives knew nothing of child psychology. She was simply not a nice little girl, and nobody wanted her.

She was finally taken into the home of her father's cousin John, the most prosperous of the Sullivans. John and his wife, Anastasia, whom the relatives called "Statia," did not want her, but since they were better off than the others, they could not very well get out of it. John was a tobacco farmer, and he and Statia lived in a big white house, the cleanest, most comfortable house Annie had ever seen. They had several children, and Statia may have consoled herself with the thought that at least Annie could earn her keep by helping with the housework. If she had any such hope, however, she was soon disillusioned. Annie could not see well enough to do much, and she was so rude and at times so violent that Statia was a little afraid of her. Before long, Annie was left pretty much to her own devices, so long as she did not break anything in one of her tantrums. When autumn came, the other children went to school. Annie wanted to go, too, but when she asked Statia about it she was told harshly, "Don't be a fool. With your eyes, you could never learn to read or write." So Annie wandered out to the big red tobacco sheds to play by herself.

"She's a queer one," John remarked. "She can't get along with people, but with animals and birds she gets along fine. This afternoon she was lying out there on the ground, so quiet that sparrows were hopping all around her, even lighting on her hands. They weren't the least bit afraid of her."

"Well, I am when she starts throwing things," his wife replied. "I don't know what to do with her."

Annie's troubles came to a head on Christmas morning. For several days, packages had been carried into the front parlor, which was hardly ever used except for weddings and wakes. From the other children, she learned that these were Christmas presents, and that each child, including Annie, would get some on Christmas morning. The children were forbidden to go in there. So, naturally, Annie went.

Several of the packages had been unwrapped, and among them Annie found, to her amazement and delight, a beautiful doll. Even with her bad eyes she could see that it had golden curls—"Just like real hair!" she told herself in wonder. It wore a lovely blue dress, and it had arms and legs that moved. Almost afraid to touch it, Annie picked it up and cradled it in her arms, crooning to it softly. Never before had she known such ecstasy. This was going to be her Christmas present! It had to be! It was her doll. Nobody could take it away from her. Whenever she had a chance, she would slip into the parlor and hold the doll in her arms.

Early Christmas morning, the parlor doors were opened, and the children trooped in. Cousin John played Santa Claus, and Annie waited tensely as he started distributing the presents. There were two for her, but she dropped them on the floor without looking at them. Frowning because she couldn't see very well, she stared at the doll. Finally Cousin John picked it up—her doll—and smilingly handed it to one of the other children, who squealed with delight as it was placed in her arms.

For an instant Annie stood frozen as the realization dawned on her that her doll had been given to someone else. Then she flew into a rage the like of which even Cousin John and Statia had never seen before. First she tried to grab the doll from her little cousin, but Cousin John seized her roughly and pushed her away. Then she stamped on her own presents and started smashing everything she could reach—toys, Christmas tree ornaments, and a vase which Statia had received as a wedding gift.

"She's just a wild animal," Statia said after they had finally quieted her down and had cleaned up the debris. "I can't have her around any longer. I won't!"

A few days later, the Sullivans held another family council. Something would have to be done with Annie, and with Jimmie, too. The lump on Jimmie's hip was as big as a teacup. He would never be anything but a sickly little boy, a burden. The children's father was contributing nothing to their support. Most of the time, nobody knew where he was.

There was one place to go for help—the town. When the village authorities were consulted, they said the children were paupers and wards of the state. The place for them was the State Infirmary, at Tewksbury. The Sullivans had no idea what the place was like. Even if they had known, it might not have made any difference. Their one concern was to get rid of the two troublesome burdens.

Annie, of course, knew nothing about the family council or the arrangements. She was excited and felt very important that cold February morning when a horse-drawn hack, with Jimmie inside, pulled up in front of Cousin John's house. With Jimmie was a strange man, one of the town officials. The "nice man," the children were told, was going to take them to Springfield, where they would go for a ride on a train. Neither Annie nor Jimmie had ever ridden on a train. Only once had they ridden in a carriage—to their mother's funeral.

Jubilant at the prospect of these treats, Annie could hardly wait while Statia packed her few belongings in a cardboard box. When they were ready to leave, Statia tried to kiss Annie, something she had never done before.

"You might at least try to be a good girl at a time like this!" she said resentfully as Annie jerked herself away. There were no more goodbyes, and Annie did not look back as the hack rattled off down the road.

From Springfield they took a train to Boston, where they would change for Tewksbury. At first Annie and Jimmie were delighted with the journey—the elegant red plush seats; the passing landscape outside the windows; the conductor in a uniform with brass buttons who punched their tickets with a little nickel-plated "gun"; the boy selling peanuts, apples, crackerjack, and magazines, who, the man said, was a "news butcher." Their companion bought a magazine for himself and some crackerjack for the children.

Long before they reached Boston, however, the novelty of their first train ride had worn off. Watching the scenery go by hurt Annie's eyes and made her feel sick at her stomach. She did not even enjoy the crackerjack—a rare treat to a child who never had candy and who took her annual spring dose of sulfur and molasses with relish because it tasted sweet. Each time the train lurched to a stop and started up with a jerk, Jimmie bounced on the seat and hurt the lump on his hip.

In Boston, the man bought them some milk and sandwiches, but they were too tired and too confused by the noise and the crowds to eat. And Annie was still very carsick. Their second train trip, from Boston to Tewksbury, was no novelty and no fun. They were exhausted and half frozen after their ride in the Black Maria when they were led into the big dark hall in the state almshouse.

They were told to sit down on a bench and wait. Behind a desk, a man wearing a green eyeshade began to make notes, talking with the man who had brought them there. Annie and Jimmie paid little attention until they heard the man with the green eyeshade say, "We'll put the girl in with the women. The boy will have to go in the men's ward."

Jimmie caught it first; they were going to be separated. He began to cry and frantically clutched Annie's arm.

Then in a flash something happened to Annie, something wild, fierce, and desperate. For the first time in her life she knew she loved another human being. She threw her arms around her little brother and held him close, glaring over his head at the men.

"No! No! No! You can't!" she cried, in a voice that was half-scream and half-growl. "He's my brother!"

Alarmed, the man with the green eyeshade jumped up and came over to them. "There, there, don't cry!" he said, clumsily patting Annie's head. "Don't cry! We'll leave you together."

Looking up at the man who had brought them, he said in a whisper, barely moving his lips, "For tonight, at least."

CHAPTER 2

Jimmie

Aftera skimpy supper, which they were too tired to eat, Annie and Jimmie were taken to a small room at one end of the women's ward.

There was a narrow iron bed. They crawled in and seconds later were sound asleep, Annie with a protecting arm around her brother. Nobody tucked them in or offered to hear their prayers, but since nobody ever had, they would have been bewildered by such attention.

In the room was a small altar. Whenever one of the old women died out in the ward, the body would be wheeled in to lie there until the men came with a pine box, in which it would be carried out to the potter's field. Sometimes, if there was a clergyman available, there would be a brief funeral service. The room was called "the dead house."

Had Annie and Jimmie known about it, they would not have been disturbed. Death was no mystery to them. They were used to it. Their mother had taken a long time dying. She herself and everyone around her knew that she was dying, and the children had watched her finger with satisfaction the shroud in which she was to be buried. Most of her life she had worn rags. In death, she would be decently dressed. A neighbor woman had made the shroud for her own eventual use, but Mrs. Sullivan's need was more immediate, so the neighbor gave it to her.

Annie remembered her mother's funeral as an event both exciting and beautiful. In the carriage, she and Jimmie had fought for the best vantage point from which to watch the horses until their father soundly slapped them both. In the church, she could not look at the candles long, for it hurt her eyes, but the soft light through the stained glass windows was lovely. There had been other deaths in the Sullivan family, a little sister and a baby brother. There had been no funerals for them. Each time their father rode away in a hack alone, holding a small pine box on his knees.

After breakfast the following morning, Annie and Jimmie waited on a bench in the big dark hall a long time while the superintendent decided what to do with them. Because the foundlings in the maternity ward, in another part of the building, never lived very long, there were no other children in the institution. Finally one of the attendants came to them with a girl's apron—for Jimmie. He started to squirm and howl in protest as they tied it on him, but Annie hurriedly quieted him. If they were to remain together, this was the price he must pay.

Annie and Jimmie settled down happily in the women's ward. They were given adjoining beds, and the dead house was their playroom. Nobody paid much attention to them, and, since she was seldom interfered with, Annie had few tantrums. Whenever she did start to get out of hand, an attendant had only to threaten to send Jimmie to the men's ward—a most effective way of teaching her to control her temper.

The old women in the ward were bedridden, most of them badly crippled with arthritis. There was one exception: a tall woman with white hair, who would pace up and down the ward for hours at a time, usually in the night, muttering to herself. The other patients and the attendants could make out only one word of what she was saying. That word was "lost." So they nicknamed her "Lost," and nobody paid any attention to her.

The other old women did not talk much. They were past the stage where gossip interested them, and, anyway, there was little to gossip about in the dreary procession of these, their final days on earth. Some of them murmured prayers, but most of them just lay on their beds, quietly waiting to die. A groan, sometimes only a long, deep sigh, and it was over. Attendants would wheel the bed, its iron wheels creaking over the uneven wooden floor boards, into the dead house. The bed never remained empty very long. Times were bad, and there were many old women with no other place to go.

Annie and Jimmie had no toys, but they never had had any toys, so they did not miss them. One day they found a pile of dusty old magazines—copies of a women's fashion magazine called *Godey's Lady's Book* and *The Police Gazette,* forerunner of some of today's lurid tabloids. They looked them over, but they were not much interested in them until one day, rummaging in a closet that was supposed to be locked, they found a set of instruments stored there by one of the doctors. Handling the sharp knives and scissors gave Annie an idea. She had often watched Cousin John's children playing with paper dolls. The pictures in the magazines—especially the ladies in pretty colored dresses—would make fine paper dolls. Jimmie had to do most of the cutting, however, for Annie couldn't see well enough, and every now and then she would accidentally snip off a head or an arm.

Jimmie did not care much about playing with paper dolls, but Annie had another inspiration. At school her cousins had made paper chains, held together with flour paste. So Annie managed to wheedle a little flour out of the kitchen help, mixed it with water, and she and Jimmie pasted their paper dolls on the walls of the dead house. The attendants were amused and left them there. The game ended abruptly one day when the doctor found them cutting out paper dolls with his instruments.

"You little devils," he said, "if I ever catch you doing this again, I'll cut off your ears!"

Evenings in the women's ward, lighted by only one flickering, smoky kerosene lamp over the door into the dead house, were never dull for Annie and Jimmie. The place was alive with cockroaches and mice, and along the baseboards were some large rat holes. Cockroaches, mice, and even big, gray rats held no terror for Annie and Jimmie. They had lived with them most of their lives. Jimmie would make a long paper quill and poke it into the rat holes, shouting with glee when an infuriated rat would leap out and race madly around the ward. The bedridden old women would scream, and an attendant would come running to see what was causing the uproar. Annie and Jimmie would be scolded and sent to bed, but it was almost bedtime anyway. They might have sent Jimmie to the men's ward to punish him, but, if they had, they would have lost a convenient way of controlling Annie.

The days grew longer, the ice and snow melted, and spring arrived. On April 14, Annie was ten years old, but nobody took note of it. She did not even know it was her birthday. Since she had never had any birthday presents or a birthday cake, birthdays meant nothing to her. When anyone asked her when her birthday was, she would answer pertly, "The Fourth of July." That was a date to remember because of the fireworks.

As the days grew milder, Annie began to go outdoors to play, riding up and down the driveway in one of the rickety old wheelchairs that were kept on the porch. Sometimes she would talk with the old men who came out to sit on the benches in the sun. They were not so quiet or so resigned as the old women were. They blamed their plight on "the government," and "the government" was a man named Grant. Annie had never heard of the Civil War or of General U.S. Grant. She did not know he was president. But he was "the government," and she thought he must be a very bad man.

Jimmie never went outdoors to play with Annie. He was

content to remain in the women's ward, teasing the old women by making faces at them and mimicking them. It was becoming more difficult for him to walk, and the tapping of his small crutch on the wooden floor was heard less and less often. May had come, and the air outdoors was fragrant with lilacs, when one morning, as Annie was helping him to dress, he fell back on his bed, screaming with pain.

The old woman in the next bed said crossly, "Didn't you hear him crying in the night? He kept me awake."

Later that morning the doctor came, and Annie sat fearfully watching as he ran his hands over her brother's thin little body. The lump on Jimmie's hip had grown much larger. Whenever the doctor touched it, the little boy moaned, "It hurts! It hurts!"

Finally the doctor straightened up and turned to Annie. "Little girl," he said gently, "your brother will soon be going on a journey."

Annie was not sure what he meant. But whatever he meant, she and Jimmie would be separated. She flew at the doctor, kicking and screaming. An attendant came running and threatened to send her out of the ward. That quieted her instantly.

Jimmie did not get up again, and Annie spent the next few days sitting beside his bed, afraid that, if she left him, they would take him away. At night, after Jimmie was asleep, she would drop off herself into the deep sleep of exhaustion. It did not last through the night, however, for once or twice she would wake up with a start and reach out to touch Jimmie's bed. One night she reached out—and Jimmie's bed was gone.

Annie started to get out of bed, but for a second she was trembling so violently that she could not. When a bed was wheeled out of the ward, it was taken to one place only. Her heart pounding wildly, she stumbled to the door under the flickering light and opened it. Groping in the dark, she found the foot of the narrow iron bed and held onto it for support. Her legs were trembling so that she could hardly stand. She shook herself and felt her way along the side of the bed. There was a sheet, covering something. She lifted it and placed her hand on Jimmie's cold little body.

Her screams wakened everybody. An attendant rushed in and tried to pull her away, but Annie held Jimmie in her arms and would not let go. Another attendant came, and the two of them dragged her out into the ward and tried to put her to bed. But Annie fought them so hard, kicking, scratching, biting, that they finally dropped her on the floor and left her there. Annie became quiet, trying to hold her breath, hoping that if she held it long enough, she would die.

One of the old women crawled painfully out of her bed, hobbled over and tried to lift Annie up off the floor. The effort made her groan with pain. The groan roused the child, and she got up and helped the woman back to her bed. She had Annie sit beside her on the bed, stroked her tousled hair, and tried to comfort her. The tears came, and for a long time Annie sat there, weeping quietly, while the old woman whispered to her about God and Heaven.

As soon as it was light, Annie went back to the dead house, but the attendant would not let her in. "Go and get dressed," she directed. Annie dressed quickly and returned. But again the attendant turned her away, telling her to go and wash her hands and face.

"After breakfast," she said, "we'll let you see your brother if you'll be good and not make any trouble."

When they finally did let her in, they made her sit down in a chair before they turned back the sheet. The light in the dead house was dim; it had only one small window. But even Annie's clouded eyes did not need much light to see Jimmie's dark curls and his white face, thin and wizened, like the face of a little old man. Suddenly she jumped up, put her arms around him and covered his face with kisses.

The attendant put a firm hand on her shoulder. "Come away now," she said. "You can see him again later. You must control yourself. It doesn't do any good to make such a fuss."

The day matron found Annie huddled on her bed, her face buried in her arms.

"How would you like to go out with me and pick some lilacs for Jimmie?" the day matron asked.

Annie jumped up quickly, and together they went out into the bright, morning sunshine. "Pick all you want," the day matron said. Annie picked all she could carry and took them, fragrant and still wet with dew, into the dead house. There were enough to cover Jimmie's body.

She watched quietly when the men came in with the new, unpainted pine box and docilely followed the day matron out of the room when they told her she must leave for a moment. They had placed Jimmie in the box when she returned, but they had left the upper part open, so she could see his face once more, a spray of the lilac blossoms caressing his cheek. Then they closed the box, lifted it gently, and carried it out. For an instant Annie stood rigid, then began running into things, for her clouded eyes were blinded even more with tears.

The doctor found her down near the gate. "Would you like to go to the burying ground?" he asked.

Annie looked at him pleadingly and nodded.

They followed the men along a narrow path out to a barren, sand field, where there was an open grave. They lowered the box into it and started shoveling in the dirt. Annie dropped to the ground and lay with her face pressed against the earth, trying not to hear the scraping of the shovels, the rattle of the little stones as they dropped on the pine box.

Their work completed, the men stood talking quietly for a moment, then moved away. But one of them came back, and the doctor came over and spoke to Annie.

"Look, little girl," he said. "Tom has brought you some flowers for your little brother's grave."

Annie accepted them in silence—a small handful of shabby, dusty pink geraniums. She looked about and then knelt beside the grave and one by one stuck the stems into the soft earth. Around them, when she arose, were some small, dark splotches in the sand, made by her falling tears.

Quietly she followed the doctor back to the women's ward. Jimmie's bed had been returned to its place. It had been made up with fresh sheets. For a long time she sat staring at it, a lonely, desolate child, trying to make the hardest adjustment she would ever have to make in her whole life.

Ten years would have to pass before Annie Sullivan would find another human being to love her as she had loved Jimmie.

CHAPTER 3

Interlude

THERE WAS one patient in the women's ward at Tewksbury whom everyone respected and liked. She was Maggie Carroll, so badly crippled that she could not move her body at all and had to be strapped to a wooden board. She must have been in almost constant pain, but no one ever heard her complain.

Annie was drawn to her by her manner of speaking. She had a soft, well-modulated voice, and she spoke good English, which even to Annie's untrained ear sounded more pleasant than the coarse, vulgar, often profane speech of the others.

Some days Annie could see a little better than she could on others, and then she could dimly make out a pair of clear gray eyes and finely molded features. The attendants told each other that Maggie Carroll must have been a beautiful woman when she was young. But no one in the women's ward knew anything about her past. She never discussed it, just as she never complained. God had willed that she spend her last days on earth in this dreary place helpless and in pain, and Maggie Carroll accepted God's will with quiet resignation.

Because they were fond of her, the attendants tried to do more for Maggie Carroll than they did for the others. Maggie could read, and she had a little pile of books on the table by her bed. She could not move her arms and could not lift a book or hold it in her twisted hands. But the handyman made a small rack against which the book could be propped up by one of the attendants. Maggie managed to move one finger enough to turn the pages.

Before Jimmie died, Maggie Carroll would sometimes read aloud to the two children. Even the inattentive, mischievous Jimmie would be quiet, as if hypnotized by her voice. And Annie listened hungrily.

Maggie's books were all about religion, mostly the lives of the saints. The awful persecution, the physical torture inflicted upon the saints, appealed to Annie's sense of the dramatic. Annie herself was already becoming an accomplished storyteller. But she could not understand why the saints accepted all their suffering so willingly, even joyously, and never tried to break away.

"Anyway," she told herself, "Maggie Carroll is a saint herself, the best saint of all."

Not long after Jimmie's death, the old woman in the bed next to Maggie Carroll was finally wheeled into the dead house. "How would you like to move in next to Maggie Carroll?" the head matron asked Annie, and a lonely little girl became the new occupant of the empty bed.

Annie no longer played as she had when Jimmie was there. She never went into the dead house again after the morning he died. She would spend hours curled up on her bed while Maggie read aloud the lives of the saints—the same stories over and over until Annie knew them by heart.

She had one way of repaying Maggie. Every morning a tray was passed around the ward from bed to bed. On the tray was an assortment of pills—sedatives and pain killers. Some of them contained a little opium, and these were eagerly sought after by the patients. Sometimes the attendants would let Annie pass the tray. If they gave her any directions as to which patient was to get which pill, Annie paid no attention. She would offer the tray first to Maggie Carroll to take whatever she wanted. She would next take it to the bedside of a blind woman and give her what she asked for. The rest of the patients got what was left.

Sometimes Annie and Maggie Carroll would have long talks, but Annie got less satisfaction out of the talks than she got out of the reading. She could not accept Maggie's philosophy at all.

"We were all born in sin," Maggie would tell her. "You and I—everybody. That is why God has put us here. It is His will, and we must not fight against it."

Maggie seemed to think that God had placed little Annie Sullivan in Tewksbury for the rest of her life, with no hope of escape. But Annie did not feel like a sinner. And she had a dream—a great big, wonderful dream—although she had no idea how she could ever make it come true.

Sometime before Jimmie's death, one of the old women told her she had heard that there were places where blind children could be sent to school.

"I'm going to one of those schools," Annie promptly announced.

The old woman grunted disapprovingly and told Annie not to get "uppity." No one else paid any attention. One lone, castoff child, a pauper, ward of the state which did not care what became of her so long as she was out of sight! Her chances of getting out of Tewksbury and going to school were too remote to be worthy of any consideration at all.

But from that day on, Annie lived with her dream. She did not talk about it, because the others only scolded her and told her not to be a little fool. But the dream was always there. Someday, somehow, she would get away from Tewksbury. She would go to school and grow up to be a fine lady, wearing beautiful dresses like those worn by the paper dolls she and Jimmie cut out of *Godey's Lady's Book.*

A few months after Jimmie's death, something happened that made it look as though Annie's dreams might be coming true.

A new priest, Father Barbara, took over the pastoral duties at the institution. Unlike his predecessor, a French Canadian whom the women disliked and nicknamed "Frenchie," Father Barbara came regularly to hear confessions and say Mass and showed genuine interest in his forlorn little flock. The old women found comfort in his kindness and in the warmth of his personality, and they felt less lonely and rejected. Annie followed him about like a shadow.

One day as he was leaving he stopped to talk to Annie, gently stroking her unkempt head.

"This is no place for you, little lady," he said. "I'm going to take you away from here."

Annie's spirits leaped skyward. "Can I go to school?" she asked eagerly.

"Perhaps, after a while," Father Barbara replied. "But first we must see if something can be done about your eyes."

Annie pulled herself away from him and began to cry. Twice in the last few months a doctor at Tewksbury had tried to do something about her eyes. She had been placed on a table, with her hands and feet strapped down so she could not fight or kick. An attendant had held her head while the doctor scraped some of the small granules off the linings of her eyelids. The pain had been excruciating and the eyes were no better. Lately, as a matter of fact, they had grown worse, with bright specks and streaks dancing around in blinding confusion. Struggling to see through them or around them, Annie kept blinking and rubbing her eyes, which made them more inflamed. The linings of her eyelids were like coarse sandpaper.

"But I'm going to take you to another doctor," Father Barbara said. "He's a very good doctor, and he knows all about eyes. I think he'll be able to help you. You'd like to be able to see, wouldn't you?"

Annie nodded and wiped away her tears on her sleeve.

"Then you must be a brave girl and let the doctor help you," Father Barbara said. "I hope he'll be able to make you see, so that you can go to school as other children do and learn to read and write."

A few days later Father Barbara came for her and took her to a hospital operated by the Sisters of Charity in nearby Lowell. It was February, just about a year since Annie and Jimmie had arrived at Tewksbury.

Father Barbara was chaplain of the hospital, and he came to the ward to see Annie early in the morning before they took her to the operating room.

"You're not afraid anymore, are you, Annie?" he asked.

Annie managed to shake her head in apparent agreement. But she did not mean it.

In the gleaming, spotless operating room, the doctor in white went to work on her eyes. But before he started he put drops in them, "Cocaine," he said, "so it won't hurt."

Again her hands and feet were strapped down.

"If you started to thrash around and fight me, my hand might slip," the doctor said. "We can't let that happen. Now let the Sister hold your head perfectly still. This isn't going to hurt much."

The ordeal turned out to be less painful for Annie than the first two, back at Tewksbury, had been. The cocaine made her eyes feel numb, and she realized that the doctor was trying not to hurt her. Sometimes she would squirm a little, and the doctor would let her rest.

"Now," he would say softly, "just a little more there."

After what seemed like a year to Annie, he finished, and a very tired child was taken back to the ward with her eyes bandaged.

The operation might have been more successful had it not been for something that happened in the ward the next day. A woman, so badly burned that she died after a few hours, was brought in and placed in the bed next to Annie.

Annie could see nothing, of course, but she could smell the burned cloth and scorched flesh. The woman's screams and the uproar in the ward frightened her as she had never been frightened in her life before. She became hysterical and had managed to rip the bandages off her eyes before she was taken away, into another ward. At any rate, when the final bandages were removed, the specks and streaks were gone, but her vision was badly blurred, worse than it had ever been before.

Annie remained in the hospital all through the spring and early summer, while the doctor treated her eyes. It was the most pleasant time she had ever known. The sisters were kind to her, gentle and cheerful. They let her help them in little tasks around the wards, and they sometimes took her with them when they carried baskets to the poor.

Also, she spent a great deal of time with Father Barbara. Sometimes they would sit in a pew in the chapel, next to the hospital, and pretend they were listening to a sermon. Sometimes they would go around to the Stations of the Cross, Father Barbara describing each picture to her and chanting the story that went with it. Sometimes they would take long walks together along the nearby Merrimack River. And sometimes in the evening he would read to her the lives of the saints, as Maggie Carroll had.

Finally the day came when the doctor had finished his work. He could do no more for Annie. It was time for her to leave. Father Barbara, however, had not given up.

"There are some doctors in Boston who may be able to help you," he told Annie. "I'm taking you there. I have some friends in Boston, and you'll stay with them until the doctors are ready for you."

The prospects of more doctors and more operations filled Annie with misgivings. But at any rate she would not have to go back to Tewksbury. And always there was the hope that the next operation might be successful, that the frustrating curtain in front of her eyes would be rolled away.

She stayed only a few days with Father Barbara's friends, then was admitted to the Boston City Infirmary. The doctors there were optimistic, as the doctor in Lowell had been. They started to work on Annie's eyes on a hot day in July.

There were two operations this time, only a few days apart—two more ordeals for Annie. The first one was to remove more of the granules from her eyelids. The second one, longer and more nerve-racking, was to cut away some of the scar tissue from her eyeballs. Somehow Annie managed to get through them. She had no choice in the matter. Again she was taken back to the ward with bandaged eyes. And again she waited, and waited, building up a dream of the day when the bandages would come off and she could see.

But when that day came, and the bandages were taken off, her vision was no better than it had been before. The curtain was still there. Everything looked blurred. And now there were little ridges and scars on her eyeballs.

There followed more weeks in the hospital while the doctors treated her eyes. One day Father Barbara came to say goodbye. He had been called away to another part of the country.

It was autumn when the doctors finally told Annie that they had done all they could for her. It was time for her to leave the hospital.

Annie knew what this meant. She would have to go back to Tewksbury. She cried and clung desperately to one of the doctors, but he gently pushed her away. It was hopeless. He could do no more for her.

The autumn day was gray and gloomy when Annie Sullivan—alone this time—rode again through the streets of Tewksbury in the Black Maria. While she sat on the bench in the big dark hall, the man with the green eyeshade made a fresh notation on her record. It was: "Virtually blind."

But Annie Sullivan still could dream.

CHAPTER 4

Rescue

ANNIE WAS not put back into the old women's ward upon her return to Tewksbury, but was placed with a group in another part of the institution.

These were not bedridden old women, patiently waiting to die. They were young—some of them not much older than Annie who in April became eleven years old—and they had by no means lost interest in the outside world, which most of them would never see again.

They were there for the same reason the old women were there. They were human discards, cast off by a society that wanted them kept out of sight. There were mild lunatics among them, epileptics, and cripples. Some had cancer, some had venereal disease, and some were slowly dying of tuberculosis.

Across the hall was another ward, where the unwed mothers came to have their babies. After the babies were born and had lived out the few hours, days, or weeks they were destined to spend on this earth, the unwed mothers were sent to a workhouse, from which they would be released when jobs were found for them as maids or scrubwomen.

Annie found life in these surroundings much more interesting than it had been in the old women's ward. Daytimes she played with the unwanted babies, who were too weak to give anyone much trouble. Whenever they did become bothersome, the attendants would silence their feeble cries with laudanum or paregoric, thereby probably shortening their miserable little lives. When it was cold, the babies shivered under thin, shabby cotton quilts. In summertime they were covered with flies and bitten by mosquitoes. Tewksbury had no window screens.

In the evening, the unwed mothers would come across the hall and join Annie's group around a smoking kerosene lamp set on a post in the center of the room. Here they would regale one another with their life stories—accounts so exaggerated that only Annie and the lunatics believed them.

Out of all the talk, Annie got the impression that men were somehow responsible for the unwanted babies, although she did not know how. There was always a "he" involved. "He said we'd get married." Or, "The mistress was out, and he came home." Or, "He just went away—I don't know where."

Annie was curious, but whenever she asked questions, the women laughed and answered her with ribald remarks which she did not understand. Coarse and vile as they were in thought and speech, they were strangely prudish about explaining the mystery of creation to a child. Annie decided that men were creatures to be avoided, and that having a baby was always a disgrace—the worst thing that could happen to a woman.

Among her new companions, Annie had her favorites. One was a good-natured Irish girl who waited on tables in the superintendent's dining room. She wore a blue dress and white apron, which Annie thought were very elegant. Sometimes she would bring Annie a treat—biscuits, cake, and chicken salad, all crammed together in her apron pocket. Annie would eat the soggy mess greedily, licking her fingers. Compared with the lumpy oatmeal, water stews, rotten fish, and rancid corned beef to which she was accustomed, it was pure ambrosia.

In charge of the dark, dreary inmates' dining room was a huge, evil brute whom the women despised and nicknamed "Beefy." Whenever they complained about the food—which was not often, because they were afraid of him—Beefy would roar at them, calling them unprintable names and threatening to throw them out.

One day Sadie, one of the pregnant women, yelled back at him, "I dare you to throw me out, you dirty beast!" Infuriated, Beefy lunged across the table at her, slipped, and fell. Sadie threw her plate at him, but he regained his feet, seized her by the hair and beat her savagely about her head, chest, and stomach.

Bedlam broke loose, in shouts and flying plates, forks, and spoons. Annie managed to dump a bucket of hot tea on Beefy as he leaned across the table. Suddenly there was a piercing scream from Sadie.

A couple of days later, they placed Sadie and her premature baby in a pine box, which they carried out to the barren, sandy field where Jimmie was buried.

There might have been an investigation of the incident, but there apparently was none. The superintendent was toiling over a report to the state legislature, in which he humbly noted that, as the result of "careful economy in management and expenditure," the average cost per inmate per week was down to $1.75. It had been $1.88 when Annie first came there. Beefy remained in charge of the inmates' dining room.

In the midst of all the degradation and violence in Annie's surroundings, there was one gentle influence. Maggie Hogan, with a terribly twisted back, had been sent to Tewksbury when she was a small child, a cripple, and an orphan. Middle-aged now, she was in charge of Annie's group and the unwed mothers. Patiently and quietly, she mothered them all. When one of the unwanted babies died, and there was no priest available, Maggie Hogan baptized it herself, using candles and going through the ritual, which she knew by heart.

Maggie Hogan accepted her dreary fate with resignation, but, unlike Maggie Carroll, she did not attribute it to God's will. It was just one of the hard facts of life, and there was no use in fighting against it. In spirit, you could rise above it to a degree.

"You can't help being poor," she would say to Annie, "but you can keep poverty from eating the heart out of you."

Maggie Hogan was unable to give Annie any encouragement in her ambition to get out of Tewksbury and go to school. So far as she could see, Annie would spend her life there, as she herself had. But she did one thing which, instead of satisfying Annie's desire for an education, only made her want to go to school more than she had before.

In the superintendent's office there was a small shelf of books. Maggie introduced Annie to them and found someone to read them to her. This required some searching, for most of the inmates were illiterate. But there was one girl, Tilly Delaney, who could read, though poorly. Tilly was one of the mild lunatics. She was apparently an epileptic also, for every now and then she would fall down in a fit and foam at the mouth.

Tilly demanded a price for her services. In her disordered mind there was one spark of hope—a determination to escape from Tewksbury. At nights she would prowl around the grounds like a caged animal, furtively probing for a break in the high walls.

Annie made a bargain with her. If Tilly would read to her, Annie would help her to escape, and the two of them made the rounds night after night. Occasionally Tilly would become restless and dissatisfied and would accuse Annie of not really trying to help her. So Annie would persuade the night watchman to leave the big gate open a crack. Tilly would slip out, but before she had gone many steps, the night watchman would catch her and bring her back. She had almost made it, she thought, and she felt better. Next time, she would assure Annie, she would really get away.

Most of the books were sentimental trash, probably left behind by some inmate who had been carried out in a pine box to the desolate burial ground. There was, for instance, a gem called *Tempest and Sunshine,* about a violent and wicked brunette and a saccharine little blonde angel. The rest of the books were lives of the saints, which Maggie Carroll had read to Annie.

Tilly read in a bored monotone, stumbling over words of more than two syllables, skipping words, sentences, sometimes whole pages. Sometimes the reading would be interrupted by one of her seizures. These frightened Annie at first, but presently she got used to them and would sit patiently by until Tilly came out of her fit and could go on reading.

Whatever Tilly left out, Annie filled in from her own imagination, and evenings she would entertain the group around the kerosene lamp with renditions of *Tempest and Sunshine, Ten Nights in a Barroom,* or *Stepping Heavenward* that their authors would never have recognized. Her fellow inmates listened with relish, no doubt welcoming the change from their own familiar stories.

Sometimes Annie would get hold of a copy of *The Police Gazette* or one of the more sensational Boston newspapers. Crime, politics, scandals, she devoured them all via Tilly's halting recital. For anything printed on paper, Annie Sullivan had a hunger as avid as that of a starving man for food. And the more Tilly read to her, the more determined she became somehow to learn to read herself, as the blind were taught to read.

The weeks, the months, the years slipped by in shadowy procession. Annie was eleven years old when she was returned to Tewksbury. She did not know when her birthday was, but at intervals she was told that she was now twelve, thirteen, and fourteen.

Her eyes had grown worse. She could no longer distinguish one face from another and could recognize her fellow inmates only by the sizes and shapes of their bodies and by their voices.

Although her brief sojourn outside Tewksbury had given her an idea of what it would be like to live in clean and orderly surroundings, Annie was not bothered by the filth, the rats, the mice, and the cockroaches. She had lived with dirt and vermin most of her life. The vulgarity and the coarseness of her fellow inmates did not worry her. Most people in the world were like that, she thought. She had no sense of shame or degradation. Nobody paid much attention to her, and since she was undisciplined, she seldom had tantrums.

When she talked about her ambition to leave Tewksbury and go to school, the women laughed at her and told her she was putting on airs. They called her "the Empress of Penzance." Theater-going was hardly one of the privileges of women in their circumstances, but the Gilbert and Sullivan operettas were popular and much talked about. Apparently someone in the group had heard of *The Pirates of Penzance*. "The Emperor of Penzance" was a nickname they had given to one of the harmless lunatics, a boy whose job was to sweep the sidewalks. In his topsy-turvy dream world, he was a general leading his armies in defense of his realm. Annie rather liked the idea of being an empress, although she was not quite sure what it meant, but "the Emperor" had no place in her hopes for the future.

Annie Sullivan was fourteen years old and had been at Tewksbury for more than four years, except for the few months she had spent in hospitals, when the Massachusetts State Board of Charities decided to investigate the place. Some of the stories going around the state sounded incredible, but the board appointed a commission to look into them. F.B. Sanborn, a friend of Ralph Waldo Emerson, was its chairman.

Word of the impending visit was quickly picked up on the inmates' grapevine. They did not expect much of it. From time to time in the past, fashionably dressed lady do-gooders had come prying about. Nothing ever came of those visits.

"There's a man named Sanborn who's head of it," the women told her. "Maybe if you can get to him, he'll pat you on the head and call you a poor little girl."

Annie expected more from Mr. Sanborn. For days she went about in a dream, going over and over in her mind what she would say to him if she had a chance. Annie had never heard of King Arthur and his knights. If she had, she might have pictured herself as a princess imprisoned in a tower, with Mr. Sanborn a knight galloping to her rescue.

Black despair filled her heart at times. How could she, one lone child, virtually blind, apparently destined to spend the rest of her life at Tewksbury, expect Mr. Sanborn to do anything for her? In all the years she had been there, only one outsider, Father Barbara, had shown any interest in her. But Father Barbara had. And so Annie hoped.

On a morning in late September, word went around the wards that Mr. Sanborn had come. He was with a group of well-dressed gentlemen. From ward to ward they proceeded, looking around, asking questions.

They were followed by the worried superintendent, whose answer was always the same: "I know something should be done about it, but I can't get the money."

All day Annie followed them about, staying as close as she dared. She did not know which of the men was Mr. Sanborn. They were all just shadowy figures to her. And voices.

The day wore on. Finally it was late afternoon, and they were down by the gate, about to leave. Annie saw her one chance, her big dream about to slip away.

Suddenly she sprang into the middle of the startled group of men. "Mr. Sanborn!" she shouted desperately. "Mr. Sanborn! I want to go to school!"

"What is the matter with you?" a surprised voice asked.

"I can't see very well," Annie said timidly, frightened now that she was the center of attention. She expected someone to grab her by the arm and pull her away.

"How long have you been here?" the voice asked.

Tongue-tied in her embarrassment, Annie could not answer,

and the men moved a few steps away, stopped, and talked in low voices with the superintendent.

Annie cried herself to sleep that night, convinced that she had failed. Her last hope was gone.

A couple of days later, however, Maggie Hogan came looking for her.

"Annie! Annie!" she cried. "You've got your wish. You're going away to school!"

Annie had to have some clothes. Somehow a little money was found to buy some cheap cotton cloth for two dresses, one red and one blue. One of the inmates, who did mending for the institution, made the dresses and a couple of coarse cotton chemises. Annie's new shoes were heavy, ugly, and too tight, but she would have walked on burning coals to get away to school. Her dream was coming true. Nothing else mattered.

Finally the morning of her departure arrived. The Black Maria was engaged to take her to the railroad station, where her escort, a man from the State Board of Charities, would meet her for the short train ride to Boston, where the school was located.

Annie wore her new red dress. Maggie Hogan wrapped the rest of her wardrobe—the other dress, the other chemise, and a couple of pairs of heavy black cotton stockings—in a newspaper and carried the bundle down to the Black Maria for her.

Nobody kissed Annie goodbye, although several of her fellow inmates went down to the gate to see her off. As she climbed up beside Tim, the driver, one of the unwed mothers shrilly advised her:

"Don't let any man fool you into thinking he's going to marry you. He won't mean what he says."

But the advice she would remember all the rest of her life was given her by Tim as they clattered along to the station.

"Don't you ever come back here," Tim said. "Forget this place, and you'll be alright."

CHAPTER 5
New World

IN THE late afternoon, Annie arrived at her school, the Perkins Institution for the Blind, in South Boston.

The trip from Tewksbury had not been a happy one, in spite of Annie's eager anticipation.

On the train a stylishly dressed woman noticed her and asked, "Where are you going, little girl?"

"I'm going to school," Annie replied, feeling very important.

"Where are you from?"

Annie did not answer. Although she could not see well enough to take in the details of the stranger's costume, she realized that this woman belonged in her dream world, the wonderful world of *Godey's Lady's Book*. Tewksbury did not belong in that world, and Annie no longer belonged in Tewksbury.

She could feel her cheeks burning with embarrassment as her escort proceeded to tell the stranger all about her, and she was not made any happier when the woman called her a "poor child" and gave her an apple. Her new dress, which had seemed perfectly satisfactory that morning—it was, in fact, the first new dress she had ever had—was all wrong, she felt. And she tried to hide her feet, in the ugly, ill-fitting new shoes, under the seat. Something happened to Annie at that moment that had never happened before. It hurt to be called a "poor child" by this elegant stranger. She was ashamed of her poverty.

Upon her arrival at the school, Annie was taken to a class already in session. It was a singing class, but the teacher had a harsh, unpleasant voice.

"What is your name?" the teacher asked.

"Annie Sullivan."

"Spell it."

"I can't spell."

A titter rippled around the class.

"How old are you?"

"Fourteen."

"Fourteen years old and can't spell?"

The whole class laughed.

It was not an auspicious entry into Annie's dream world, in which her first few months were to prove difficult and disappointing.

The Perkins Institution for the Blind, when Annie Sullivan entered it, was the most famous school for the blind in this country. It was founded by Dr. Samuel Gridley Howe, husband of Julia Ward Howe, who wrote *The Battle Hymn of the Republic.*

Dr. Howe had been dead several years when Annie arrived, and his place as head of the school had been taken by his son-in-law, a young Greek named Michael Anagnos.

Julia Ward Howe, for whom the American public had a kind of reverence, maintained her husband's interest in the school and spent a good deal of time there, giving it prestige that extended far beyond Boston and New England.

Since all the children and some of the teachers were blind, courses were taught in raised print and in braille, the "dot language" of the blind. In addition to reading, writing, English literature, arithmetic, geography, and history, all the girls learned to knit, crochet, and do fine needlework. Most of the students attended the school for six years.

The children came mostly from New England, sons and daughters of farmers, well-to-do businessmen, doctors, lawyers, clergymen. Only a few were charity pupils, as Annie was. Their sheltered backgrounds could hardly have been more unlike Annie's if she had landed in their midst from the planet Mars. Although she had come through the years at Tewksbury amazingly innocent, Annie knew more about the harsh realities of life than her schoolmates would ever learn in all their lives. Even the girls of her own age seemed as infantile to her as the unwanted babies at Tewksbury. And to them, her rough manners, her speech—often coarse, sometimes shocking—and her outlook on life were entirely alien. There was no common meeting ground.

One of Annie's major difficulties, although she did not know it at first, arose from the fact that her name was Sullivan, an Irish name. At the time when her parents had arrived in this country, there had been a famine in Ireland. Thousands of young Irish had come pouring into Boston with nothing but the clothes on their backs. Many of them had not even been able to raise the money for their passage and had to work it out after they got here.

Naturally they had to take work where they could get it, as day laborers and servants. Many of them were illiterate. In Ireland during those bad years, it was hard enough to keep body and soul together, let alone trying to get an education. Thrifty New Englanders found them a highly satisfactory source of cheap labor. Since they performed the most menial tasks, they were regarded as social inferiors. Italians, Portuguese, Eastern Europeans, and other immigrants coming later would be in the same situation.

Annie arrived at Perkins wholly unaware that there was any stigma attached to being Irish. Practically all the people she had ever known were Irish and proud of it. Poor and illiterate though they might be, they handed down to their children lofty tales of the ancient kings of Ireland. They carried in their hearts a fierce love and longing for their homeland. It took Annie some time to find out that being Irish made her socially unacceptable to the smug little New Englanders by whom she was surrounded.

Another source of her troubles was the fact that she was so far behind in her classes. She had to start way down at the bottom, weaving mats, which she loathed. A great big fourteen-year-old down among the first-graders. They called her "Big Annie," and the nickname stuck for a long time. Impatient as she was to get ahead, Annie's reach exceeded her grasp. She would make ridiculous mistakes in class, and the other children, and sometimes the teachers, would laugh at her.

The other girls practiced on Annie an exquisite kind of torture that girls have undoubtedly inflicted on girls since time began. It is called "having secrets." They would gather in little groups, whispering and giggling. Several times at first Annie confronted them, demanding to know what they were laughing at. Stifling their giggles, they replied with elaborate innocence, "Oh, nothing!"

Her resentment and frustration made Annie a problem for her teachers. Since nobody had ever really tried to discipline her before, she rebelled at taking orders from these austere, critical spinsters, so colorless compared to the women she had known at Tewksbury. She was rude, and she was disobedient. Several times during her first year, she would have been expelled from the school had there been any place to send her except back to Tewksbury. Even the most annoyed and discouraged among her teachers could not bear to do that to her.

The result of all her difficulties was that Annie withdrew into herself, a lonely, unhappy misfit. Her dream world was proving to be a cruel disappointment. Night after night she cried herself to sleep in the first nightgown she had ever owned. A teacher had borrowed one for her from one of the other girls the first night she was there. Annie Sullivan was homesick—homesick for Tewksbury.

The children at Perkins were housed in pleasant cottages, with a fine view of Boston Harbor, which of course none of them could see. Living in the cottage to which Annie was assigned was a silent middle-aged woman who rarely left her room. She was Laura Bridgman, blind, deaf, and dumb.

Many years before Annie was born, more than forty years before she entered the Perkins Institution, Dr. Samuel Gridley Howe and Laura Bridgman, then a child, were famous the world over. Dr. Howe had succeeded in communicating with little Laura, the first time anyone had ever been able to communicate with a person who was blind, deaf, and dumb.

Laura was seven when Dr. Howe discovered her, the child of a farmer in New Hampshire. Scarlet fever when she was three had left her imprisoned within an impenetrable wall of darkness and silence. She could communicate with no one. No one could communicate with her.

Dr. Howe took her to the Perkins Institution and set to work trying to find some way of getting through to her. The method he devised was by use of the manual alphabet, the "finger language" by which the deaf and dumb who are not blind talk to each other. Since Laura was blind, he spelled words with his fingers into the palm of her hand and taught her to spell them back to him.

At first, of course, the words had no meaning for her, and it took many months of careful, patient, tedious effort before the moment arrived when it dawned on Laura that the finger letters K-E-Y in her palm meant the object, a key, which she held in her other hand—that everything she touched had a name.

Laura learned to read and write as the other blind children did, and to do beautiful, intricate needlework, but she never progressed far beyond that point. Unable to cope with the outside world, she was unhappy away from the school, which had become her home. A fund was established to permit her to stay on at the school. She was fifty years old when Annie arrived there—a silent middle-aged woman all but forgotten by the public which had marveled at the "miracle child" forty years ago.

All the children were taught the manual alphabet so that they could communicate with Laura. Most of them were bored, for Laura had no knowledge of conversational, idiomatic English, and the sentences she spelled out with her fingers were stilted, the meaning sometimes obscure. But Annie was fascinated, and Laura Bridgman became the first friend she made after leaving Tewksbury.

For hours they would sit together in Laura's room, in silence, Annie spelling into Laura's palm the day's happenings, the school gossip, things she was reading, and stories that had been read to her, including the lives of the saints.

Laura, in her queer, stilted English, would spell out her thoughts and her troubles into Annie's hand: "I hate to go without my best friend. She kept weeping many times until she left me the ninth of November. She gave me a very beautiful and pure breast pin before I parted with her."

As the months went by, Annie concentrated most of her interest and energy on learning to read raised type with her fingers, and she did so easily and quickly. To be able to read was the thing she wanted most. Annie's teachers were discovering that she could master any subject with speed if it interested her, but could be exasperatingly slow if it did not. Arithmetic, for instance, and braille. She did not have the patience to learn the series of dots that make up the braille alphabet. She was never good at braille. She had to learn to sew, as all the girls did, but it took her two years to make an apron, which any of the others would have finished in a few hours.

The carefully selected books in raised letters, or braille, in the Perkins library were few in number—only about sixty—but they were good. As it became easier and easier for her to follow the raised print with her fingertips, Annie haunted the library. There she discovered *Silas Marner*, *The Vicar of Wakefield*, and a copy of *Old Curiosity Shop*, which Charles Dickens had had printed in raised type and presented to the school after he visited the place during his American tour many years before Annie was there. There was poetry, too, the poems of Lord Byron, Longfellow's *Evangeline*, and Milton's *Paradise Lost*. Even through her searching fingertips Annie got the rhythm, the beauty of the words, and began to acquire a taste for poetry and good English that would stay with her for the rest of her life.

What to do with Annie Sullivan became a problem as the summer vacation approached. The other children all went home for summer vacations, and the school was closed. Even Laura Bridgman returned to New Hampshire to stay with relatives. There seemed to be no place for Annie except Tewksbury, and even Tewksbury did not want her as a summer transient. The teachers were opposed to sending her back there, anyway. Finally one of the teachers found a summer job for her doing light work in a rooming house in Boston. It turned out to be a most fortunate experience for Annie.

One of the roomers, a young man, felt sorry for her at first, then discovered that she had an unusually alert and quick mind. Amused by her gift of storytelling, he talked with her and sometimes read the newspapers to her.

One day he remarked, "I think I know a place where they might be able to do something about your eyes."

Annie was not impressed. She had heard that sort of talk before. But she agreed to go along when the young man arranged for one of the servants at the rooming house to take her to see young Dr. Bradford, and the Carney Catholic Hospital.

"I'd like to operate on those eyes," Dr. Bradford said after he had examined them.

"But I've had operations before," Annie protested. "They didn't do one bit of good."

"But let's try again," Dr. Bradford urged. "I think I can help you."

In the late summer, toward the end of the vacation, Annie

entered the Massachusetts Eye and Ear Infirmary. As the others had done, Dr. Bradford went to work on the linings of her eyelids, cutting away the hard granules that kept scratching her eyeballs.

"You're not going to notice much difference now," he told her after the operation was over, "except that your eyes won't be so sore and inflamed as they have been. I want to treat them for a few months, and a year from now I'll go to work on that scar tissue that has built up on your corneas. If I succeed—well, that will be the operation that will make the difference."

A year passed, and Annie returned to the hospital for her second operation. Dr. Bradford was hopeful, and to Annie the passage of the days before the bandages could be removed was agonizingly slow. Finally one morning in the hospital ward, the bandages were cut away.

"Open your eyes, Annie," Dr. Bradford said.

Almost afraid to do so, Annie opened her eyes—and almost jumped out of bed.

"What can you see, Annie?" the doctor asked.

"I can see you!" Annie cried, almost shouting. "I can see you! I can see your eyes and your nose and your mouth and your hair! I can see!"

Her glance raced around the ward—to the window, no longer just a white space but definitely a window, through which she could see a patch of blue sky, to the other patients in their beds, back to Dr. Bradford and the smiling nurse in white at his elbow.

The pictures were a little blurred, but beautiful beyond description to a sixteen-year-old girl who had not seen them so clearly since she was a small child. Annie Sullivan had stepped into a new world—a world she had never hoped to enter back in the days at Tewksbury. In her dream world she had expected always to be blind, but able to go to school and learn to read as blind children are taught to read.

"That's enough—rest them a bit," Dr. Bradford cautioned. "They're weak. They'll have to get used to working. You must take good care of them."

By Dr. Bradford's standards, the operation was incomplete. There were still ridges of scar tissue on Annie's eyeballs. He would have to treat them and perhaps operate again sometime in the future.

But to Annie Sullivan, when she finally left the hospital—not with the slow, shuffling gait of the blind, but walking swiftly and confidently, with springs in her feet—it was the most wonderful operation in all medical history. Her respect for doctors amounted to veneration.

CHAPTER 6

Valedictorian

STRICTLY SPEAKING, Annie should not have been permitted to return to the Perkins Institution for the Blind following the successful operation on her eyes.

Only the hopelessly blind were eligible for admission. While her vision was by no means normal, Annie Sullivan could no longer be classified as "virtually blind."

Again, however, the old question of what to do with her arose. Annie, at sixteen, was still a minor, still a ward of the state, still a pauper, unequipped to earn her living. But nobody wanted to send her back to Tewksbury.

So at Perkins Annie remained, a charity pupil, arrayed in hand-me-downs which her teachers begged from philanthropic-minded ladies of Boston. She had been at the school two years and had four more to go.

Gradually a change was coming over Annie. She still had a fiercely independent spirit that would not readily accept discipline from her elders. The fact that a teacher said a thing was so did not make it so. She questioned everything. But she was learning to conform to the ways of her classmates. Her manners and her speech had improved. She was getting along better with both teachers and students.

In addition to her own gradual conformity, other factors contributed to making Annie's lot at the school happier than it had been at first. For one thing, the girls her own age, who had rejected her so mercilessly, had received their diplomas and left. Annie was several years older than the other students in her class, but they had grown used to her. They no longer called her "Big Annie."

Another reason undoubtedly was that, after she regained her sight, Annie was always willing to take her classmates on little excursions into Boston, something the teachers seldom had time to do. To get away for a few hours means as much to a blind child at boarding school as it does to a child who can see.

Annie had a way with the smaller children, especially the new arrivals. The sight of a woebegone, tearful little face brought back to her vividly a time when she, too, was homesick—homesick for Tewksbury. She played with them, and she comforted them. The teachers, observing this, sometimes asked her to assist them in the lower grades.

But a deeper, more important change was taking place in Annie. It could be attributed to the influence of wise, patient Miss Mary Moore, her English teacher.

Annie's friendship with Miss Moore began after an incident that almost sent her back to Tewksbury. It happened in spelling class during her second year. Annie did not have the patience to learn to spell. So long as she could make herself understood on paper, she could not see that it made any difference how the words were spelled!

Perhaps with the idea of shaming her into doing better, the teacher with sarcastic exaggeration would spell back the words as she had misspelled them. This would send the class off into squeals of laughter.

Finally one day Annie's temper exploded. "Laugh, you silly things!" she stormed at her classmates. "That's all you can do, to the queen's taste!"

Annie had not meant to refer to the teacher. "To the queen's taste" was just an expression she had picked up somewhere. But the teacher took it as an insult and ordered her to leave the room and sit on the stairs outside until the class was over.

Furious, Annie jumped up and banged into one of the desks. Whereupon the teacher indignantly directed her to come back and leave the room quietly.

But Annie rushed to the door and before she slammed it behind her, shrilly announced, "I will not sit on the stairs! And I will not come back to this class again!"

This precipitated a meeting of all the teachers with Mr. Anagnos, the principal. Mr. Anagnos sternly decreed that Annie would have to return to the class and apologize to the teacher or be expelled. This Annie stubbornly refused to do.

With Tewksbury in mind, some of the teachers intervened, and one of them, Miss Moore, volunteered to take Annie in hand and see if she could tame her. Once a week they had an hour's session together, all by themselves.

Ostensibly, Miss Moore was teaching Annie Sullivan to spell and to speak and write correct English. Actually she taught her much more—so much more that all the rest of her life Annie would consider her the best teacher and one of the best friends she ever had.

Miss Moore did not treat Annie as a problem child. In fact, she treated her more as an adult than as a child. Studying her carefully, she realized that, while superficially Annie was as immature as any other youngster in the second grade, she had a knowledge of the seamier side of life that made her adult far beyond her years. Miss Moore, with her sheltered background, could only guess at some of the things Annie had seen and heard at Tewksbury.

When Annie was rude, when she brashly expressed opinions that indicated she did not know what she was talking about, Miss Moore did not correct her. She merely changed the subject, leaving Annie feeling sheepish, and wondering if her ill behavior had been noticed. When Miss Moore, without laughing, pointed out her mistakes in spelling and grammar, Annie was fired with ambition to do better. And above all, Annie was brought to the realization that there were a great many things she did not know.

There were times when Annie had an uneasy feeling that Miss Moore was getting her under her thumb, but she was defenseless against her quiet good manners and matter-of-fact assumption that they were friends. Little by little, Miss Moore was disciplining Annie Sullivan's lawless mind.

Miss Moore taught a class in Shakespeare one hour a week. When Annie was far enough advanced to be admitted to that class, it became for her the high point in the week. She would soar out of the class on a magic carpet of romance, great poetry, beautiful words singing in her mind and heart. They read *The Tempest, King Lear, As You Like It, Macbeth*, and Annie Sullivan loved them all.

As a matter of fact, Annie loved everything she read. She loved the history and mythology of ancient Greece. It was her idea that a group of ten-year-olds, struggling with Greek history, take on the names of the heroes. Thus a girl named Eunice became Pericles, a girl named Lydia became Aristides, and so on. Mr. Anagnos, a Greek, was amused, but observed that Aristides applied to a girl should be Aristidena. The nickname clung to Lydia long after she was out of school and had become head of the Commission for the Blind in another state.

Annie never could remember just how long it took her to learn to read with her eyes, but it probably did not take very long, for her fingertips knew the shapes of the letters. And now she read everything she could get her hands on, from the classics to the most lurid crime stories in the newspapers. Any book that came her way she read, and the daylight hours were not long enough. One evening Miss Moore found Annie leaning far out of a window into the twilight, her nose literally buried in a trashy novel called *East Lynne.*

Annie Sullivan, blind no more, was entering her fourth year at Perkins when a new matron came to take charge of the cottage where she lived. She was Mrs. Sophia Hopkins, widow of a sea captain. Her home was on Cape Cod, but she had found the place unbearably empty following the death of her only child, a girl about Annie's age.

Wandering aimlessly along the beach one day near her home, Mrs. Hopkins had noticed some blind children, on a holiday from the Perkins Institution, playing in the sand. She applied at the school for a position, to the great good fortune of one untamed, unkempt youngster named Annie Sullivan. It was inevitable that Annie should appeal to her.

No two human beings could have been less alike. Prim, conventional Sophia Hopkins, with her sedate New England background. Willful, impulsive Annie Sullivan, child of Irish immigrants, with Tewksbury as her background. Sophia Hopkins, who needed to mother someone, and Annie, who had never been mothered in her life.

One of the first noticeable changes must have been in Annie's appearance. Mrs. Hopkins could sew, and those hand-me-downs Annie was obliged to wear were a challenge to her. They could at least be made to fit properly, even though the colors and materials might not be very becoming!

A big change took place at the end of Annie's third year at the school. She no longer had to look around for a summer job in a rooming house. Mrs. Hopkins took her home with her, to Cape Cod, as she did every summer thereafter.

There must have been times when Mrs. Hopkins was shocked and dismayed as some of the ideas Annie had picked up at Tewksbury slipped out. And undoubtedly there were times when Annie chafed a little at Mrs. Hopkins's gentle, but determined efforts to make her over into a "nice girl." But Sophia Hopkins needed Annie Sullivan, and Annie Sullivan needed Sophia Hopkins. Out of their need developed a friendship that would last as long as they both lived.

Gradually Annie Sullivan was tamed, and as she advanced into her fourth and fifth years at the school, she steadily became a better student. Nobody was surprised when in her sixth and final year she was chosen to be valedictorian of her class. She had earned the right.

As the important day approached, Mrs. Hopkins took charge. Annie's graduation dress, her shoes, everything she wore that day, Mrs. Hopkins gave to her. It was the first pretty dress Annie Sullivan ever owned. And with it, white shoes, which Annie in her childhood had thought were worn only by angels!

A few days before Annie's graduation, an event took place in the White House, in Washington, that sent feminine hearts fluttering all over the country. President Grover Cleveland married his beautiful young ward, Miss Frances Folsom. No other president was ever married in the White House.

Day after day photographs of the bride appeared in the newspapers, in Boston as well as everywhere else in the country. It was Mr. Anagnos who first noticed a resemblance between the White House bride and Annie Sullivan. Others could see it too, and Annie spent hours in front of her mirror, trying to copy Miss Folsom's hairdo.

Mrs. Hopkins decided that Annie's graduation dress should be a copy, not of Miss Folsom's wedding gown, but of the dress she had worn when she was graduated from college. The material was white muslin, with three deep ruffles on the skirt, edged with lace. On the morning of the graduation, she got out her curling iron and fashioned little ringlets, like Miss Folsom's around Annie's forehead.

Annie was standing in front of the mirror in Mrs. Hopkins's room, staring at herself in ecstasy, when Mrs. Hopkins came in with a beautiful pink sash. It had belonged to her daughter.

"I want you to wear it today," she said and tied it around Annie's waist.

Later, in Tremont Temple, as Annie was about to go up on the platform where she would deliver her address as valedictorian and receive her diploma, Miss Moore appeared with a corsage of pink roses to match the sash and pinned it to her blouse.

Because of the prestige enjoyed by the Perkins Institution, the graduation exercises each year were largely attended. The governor of Massachusetts presided and handed out the diplomas.

There was music, and there were other speeches, but Annie was hardly aware of them. Nothing seemed real to her as she sat on the platform awaiting her turn to speak. The governor had to call her name twice before she managed to get up and advance to the front of the platform. Her mouth was dry, and her feet did not feel as though they belonged to her. But after she had managed, in a trembling voice, to get out "Ladies and Gentlemen," she felt better.

The Boston newspapers the next day, with complimentary remarks, published little excerpts from her speech:

"Self-culture is a benefit, not only to the individual, but also to mankind. Every man who improves himself is aiding the progress of society, and everyone who holds still is holding it back."

There was a nagging worry in the back of Annie's mind that night, however, as she took off her pretty dress, lovingly fingering the lace and the little pearl buttons.

Annie Sullivan was now a graduate of the Perkins Institution for the Blind. She must go out on her own and earn her living. But how? She had come a long, long way from Tewksbury. But she had no training that would fit her for a job. And when she left Perkins, as she must, where would she go?

Miss Moore wanted her to go to a normal school and study to become a teacher. But money would be needed for that. One of the teachers knew someone who might hire her as nursery governess for some young children. But there was nothing definite. Where did people go when they had no home and could not support themselves?

"I won't go back there!" she told herself fiercely. "I won't! I won't!"

Shaking herself angrily, she began to put away her finery. With her face towel she wiped off her white shoes, wrapped them in tissue paper and put them back in their box. She put her corsage in a glass of water and carefully smoothed out the pink sash.

"I wonder if I'll ever have a chance to wear it again," she thought.

Annie was staying with Mrs. Hopkins on Cape Cod when a letter came from Mr. Anagnos, asking her to read an enclosed letter and let him know if she was interested. The enclosure was from a gentleman in Alabama. It was a sad letter about his six-year-old daughter, who was deaf, dumb, and blind. Could the Perkins Institution recommend a teacher who could help her?

The little girl's name was Helen Keller.

CHAPTER 7

Groping

IVY GREEN, the home of Captain Arthur Keller, Confederate veteran, newspaper editor, gentleman farmer, and leading citizen of Tuscumbia, Alabama, was set in spacious grounds, at the end of a long driveway.

The afternoon spring sunshine lay warm upon trees and grass and plowed fields, and the good smell of earth was in the air, as the Keller carriage turned into the driveway.

In the carriage with Mrs. Keller was a young woman wearing a gray woolen costume much too heavy for a mild March day in Alabama. Her eyes were red and swollen, as though she had been weeping. Her expression was anxious, tense. Miss Annie Sullivan had arrived to become Helen Keller's teacher.

Annie had not been weeping. Coal dust and cinders on the long train trip from Boston had left her eyes, still tender from a recent operation, badly inflamed. So impatient was she to meet her little pupil that she could hardly sit still in the carriage.

Captain Keller waited on the lawn with a flowery speech of welcome, but Annie scarcely heard him.

When he paused for breath, she interrupted: "Helen—where is Helen?"

"There on the porch, waiting," Mrs. Keller told her.

Annie's weak eyes made out a small figure in the shadow of a vine, and, almost running, she hurried toward it. As she drew near she slowed down, in order not to startle the child. Now she could see her more clearly.

She was surprised at Helen's forlorn, neglected appearance. Her light brown hair was unkempt, tangled, her face streaked with dirt and tears, her pinafore soiled. Annie would learn presently that on days when Helen was in a bad mood, as she had been that day, she would not let anyone comb her hair or wash her face.

From the bustle of preparation for Annie's arrival—the guest room aired and cleaned, extra cooking being done in the kitchen, her mother's departure in the carriage without her—Helen had sensed that something unusual was happening. Since she had no way of finding out what it was, she was resentful and badly behaved.

As Annie approached her with outstretched arms, Helen leaped at her with such force that she would have knocked her off the porch if Captain Keller had not caught her.

Snarling like a little wild animal, Helen wrenched herself loose from Annie's arms. These were not her mother's arms, as she had expected, but the arms of a stranger.

Her groping hands found Annie's handbag and jerked it out of her grasp. When Mrs. Keller tried to rescue it, Helen flew into a rage, kicking and scratching.

"She thinks there's candy in it," Mrs. Keller panted.

Annie intervened, handing Helen her precious watch, a graduation present from her teachers at the Perkins Institution. Examining this new toy with her fingers, Helen calmed down. Curious now, she followed Annie into the house and upstairs to her room.

As Annie started to unpack, Helen's grubby fingers were everywhere, into everything.

"Looking for candy," Annie decided.

She recalled having seen a trunk outside in the hall. She led Helen out to it, placed her small hands on it and tried to indicate by a series of pats that there would be candy in her trunk, which would be along later.

Helen seemed to understand, and Annie felt a glow of satisfaction at her first apparent success with her pupil. Had she realized at that moment what the next month would be like, she would have been tempted to repack her bags and go back to Boston.

With only six years of schooling, no training, no experience, and a childhood background that would have horrified the Kellers had they known about it, Annie Sullivan was taking on as difficult and complicated a job as was ever undertaken by any teacher. The date was March 5, 1887. Her twenty-first birthday was a month away.

Her own childhood, however, was really in Annie's favor. Annie had never been deaf, but she knew what it was like to be blind, frustrated, and resentful.

When the Kellers, in a recital of Helen's misdeeds, told how in a fit of anger she had nearly killed her baby sister by dumping her out of her cradle, there flashed into Annie's memory an incident out of her own childhood. She, too, in a fit of anger, had dumped her baby sister out of her cradle.

Thus was Annie Sullivan equipped to understand Helen Keller far better than her parents ever could.

She did not mention the incident to the Kellers. Mr. Anagnos had told them nothing about her background, and Annie would have died rather than have them know.

Annie's first task was to win the confidence of a miserable little soul who trusted no one because she knew no one. The people around her existed in her imprisoned mind only as hands—hands that were forever trying to restrain her.

Annie had hoped to win her with gentleness and affection. But almost immediately she realized that this would not work. She had been with the Kellers only a few days when Helen, in a sudden rage, knocked out two of her front teeth! Helen could be as dangerous as a ferocious dog.

At times Helen's tantrums were unpredictable, but in general they followed a pattern. Whenever she could not have her own way, Helen had a tantrum.

This tendency was aggravated by the fact that her parents, rather than fight with her, gave in to her, even to the extent of allowing her to go unwashed and uncombed for days at a time. She was an undisciplined little tyrant, ruling the household by physical force.

After a few encounters with her, Annie was forced to the realization that the only solution must be discipline. Understanding as she did the reason for Helen's violence, she set to work reluctantly, hoping that she would not break the child's spirit.

"If anyone had ever really cared enough about me when I was a child to discipline me," she told herself in justification, "I might have been a happier child."

Their longest and most violent battle occurred one morning at the breakfast table. No one had ever tried to teach Helen to sit at the table and eat from her own place with a spoon. Instead, she would run around the table, grabbing food off other people's plates and the dishes that were being passed while the family went on eating and talking as though nothing extraordinary was happening.

That morning Helen started to grab some food off Annie's plate. Annie pushed her greasy hands away. Helen tried it again, and Annie slapped her. Whereupon Helen threw herself on the floor, kicking and screaming. Annie lifted her up, set her down hard on a chair, forced a spoon into her hand and started to help her scoop up some food on it.

Helen threw the spoon on the floor. Annie dragged her down off the chair, made her pick up the spoon, set her back on the chair and started over again. But Helen hurled the spoon to the floor and threw herself on top of it.

At this point Captain and Mrs. Keller, who had been watching in horrified silence, got up and left the room, breakfast unfinished. Annie followed them to the door, locked it behind them, returned to the table, and went on eating her breakfast, although it nearly choked her.

Helen jumped up and tried to pull Annie's chair out from under her. When that didn't work, she pinched Annie, and Annie slapped her. This was repeated several times.

Finally, after another fit of kicking and screaming, Helen started feeling her way around the table. When she discovered that her parents' places were empty, she came back to Annie. She seemed puzzled and placed her hand on Annie's wrist. Raising her fork to her mouth, Annie indicated that she was eating. Helen hesitated for a moment, then climbed up on her chair and docilely permitted Annie to help her eat her breakfast with a spoon. Apparently hunger had won out.

But the battle was not yet over. As she finished eating, Helen tore off the napkin that had been tied around her neck, threw it on the floor, and ran over to the door. Finding it locked, she blazed with fury, pounding and kicking the door and howling.

Annie went over and, after a struggle that required every ounce of strength she could muster, dragged Helen back to the table, forced her to pick up the napkin and started to show her how to fold it. Helen managed to jerk the napkin away from her, threw it to the floor again and herself on top of it.

This time Annie left her alone. Helen's screams finally subsided into sobs, and she let Annie lift her up and show her how to fold her napkin. It was nearly lunchtime when Annie unlocked the door, and a subdued, quiet Helen wandered out into the garden to play.

Annie went upstairs to her room, threw herself on the bed, and cried herself to sleep.

A day or so later, when Helen again started to misbehave at the table, Annie seized her by the arm and dragged her toward the door. Before she had reached the door, however, Captain Keller ordered her back.

"No child of mine," he stormed, "is ever going to be sent away from my table hungry!"

From the beginning, there was difficulty with Helen's parents, especially with her father. She very quickly learned to run to her parents for sympathy whenever Annie corrected her.

"I know we shouldn't do it," Mrs. Keller said. "But we feel so sorry for her."

"If I could have her alone with me for a while, I think I could accomplish more," Annie replied in a discouraged tone. "She has got to learn to obey me before I can help her. I can't do anything with her the way she is."

Mrs. Keller came up with a solution. But she had a hard time convincing her husband. At this point, Captain Keller was going around saying he had a good mind to send that Yankee girl packing. And that Yankee girl would not have cared much if he had!

The Kellers, however, were really in desperate straits. Every day Helen was growing larger, stronger, and more dangerous. Unless she could be brought under control, she would have to be sent away. And the only place to send her would be to a home for the feeble-minded—and a strait jacket.

With this in mind, Captain Keller grudgingly gave his consent, and Annie and Helen moved into a cottage a short distance from the Keller home.

In the meantime, as she fought Helen's tantrums, Annie worked tirelessly, doggedly, unceasingly to communicate with her, using the manual alphabet, as Dr. Howe had used it with Laura Bridgman many years earlier. Before coming to Alabama, she had unmercifully abused her eyes, poring over and over the cramped, barely legible notes Dr. Howe and her teachers had made as they worked with Laura.

They had had one advantage she did not have. Laura had been a placid, docile child, who had never given them any trouble.

"But Helen is a much brighter child than Laura was," Annie told herself as she nursed her bruises. "I know she is! I've got to get through to her!"

She started using the manual alphabet with Helen the morning after her arrival. In her trunk was a doll for Helen. The blind children at Perkins had bought it with their pennies, and Laura Bridgman had dressed it.

Annie smiled wistfully as Helen delightedly cradled the doll in her arms. She was remembering another little girl, practically blind, who long ago had lovingly cradled a doll in her arms, thinking it was her Christmas present.

She took Helen's hand and slowly and carefully with her fingers spelled into her palm: D-O-L-L. She did it several times, then showed Helen how to form the letters with her own small fingers.

Presently, like an imitative monkey, Helen spelled the word back to her: D-O-L-L. Tears sprang to Annie's eyes as she patted her small pupil's shoulder.

In the cottage the finger-spelling—which Helen seemed to regard as an interesting new game—continued, along with other things Annie found for Helen to do with beads and a ball of yarn and a crochet hook. With these pastimes, Helen seemed more contented. She had fewer tantrums. Although the words as yet had no meaning for her, she learned to spell them with amazing ease and rapidity.

But Annie still had Helen's father to contend with. He was impatient and skeptical. He wanted his child at home. And after two weeks Annie had to give in.

It had been agreed that Captain Keller could look in on Helen every morning on his way to his office, provided she did not know he was there. One morning, a day or two before they moved out of the cottage, he brought Helen's dog Belle, a beautiful setter, with him.

Helen raised her head, sniffed, and ran eagerly to the dog. She dropped to her knees, took one of Belle's paws in her hands, and began moving her claws about while Captain Keller and Annie stared.

"What's she doing with that dog's paw?" Captain Keller demanded.

There was wonder in Annie's voice as she cried, "She's trying to teach her to spell! Look—she's trying to teach her to spell 'doll'!"

But Captain Keller shook his head. "What's the good of it?" he said bitterly. "She doesn't know what it means any more than the dog does!"

CHAPTER 8

Breakthrough

THEY APPEARED to be playing in the water on a warm spring day—Annie and Helen in the vine-covered pump house in the Kellers' backyard.

Helen held a cup in one hand. As Annie pumped water into the cup, she kept moving her fingers in the child's other hand.

They were not playing a game, however. Helen looked sullen, and Annie's expression was pleading, almost desperate, as she pressed her fingers into the unresponsive little palm.

The date was April 5, a month and two days since Annie's arrival to become Helen's teacher. Day after day through that month, Annie's fingers had moved in Helen's hand, spelling words—words—words.

Helen knew how to spell them back with her own small fingers, but they still had no meaning for her. And she was becoming bored with what at first had been a fascinating new game.

That April morning had been difficult. Annie was trying to teach Helen to distinguish between two words, "cup" and "water." Since she did not know what they meant, Helen kept mixing them up. She could not understand what she was supposed to do, and she had grown tired and cross. Finally her frustration drove her into a rage, and she smashed her favorite doll, the doll the blind children had sent her from Boston.

To give her a change, Annie led her out to the pump, a place where Helen loved to play. But still the lesson went on, Annie's determined fingers pressing insistently in her pupil's palm, spelling one word over and over again: W-A-T-E-R. W-A-T-E-R. W-A-T-E-R. The cool water overflowed the cup and ran down the child's hand and wrist.

Suddenly Helen dropped the cup. Her body stiffened. For an instant she stood transfixed, holding her breath. Like a bright probing sunbeam, a new thought had penetrated the curtain that had held her mind a prisoner within its dark folds.

She stumbled toward Annie, reaching for her hand. With trembling fingers she started to spell. W-A-T— she had not finished when she felt Annie's approving pat on her shoulder. The expression on Helen Keller's face was something Annie Sullivan would never forget.

Groping wildly Helen ran about touching things and back to Annie. The ground, the pump, the trellis, the honeysuckle vine. And as Annie's fingers moved swiftly in her hand, the child quickly spelled them back. She knew these words! They had been spelled in her hand dozens of times! This was it—the Big Secret that had been withheld from her so long! Everything had a name!

She stopped for a moment, looking thoughtful, then placed a questioning hand on Annie's arm. Tears ran down Annie's cheeks as her fingers moved in Helen's eager palm—slowly and carefully, for they had not spelled this word before.

In that shining moment, Annie Sullivan took on a new identity. Henceforth for the rest of her life, to Helen and to everyone they knew, she would be "Teacher." Her whole life would be wrapped up in that one word. And Annie was content to have it so.

The progress of Annie and Helen into the house that day was a slow march of triumph—slow because of interruptions as Helen found more objects to be identified.

She bumped into the nurse carrying her little sister, Mildred. B-A-B-Y? Of course! Teacher had been spelling into her hand for a month. Lovingly she patted her baby sister, toward whom she had previously felt only antagonism.

To Captain and Mrs. Keller was given the supreme joy of watching their daughter's fingers delightedly spelling: M-A-M-A! P-A-P-A!

By bedtime that evening, Helen Keller had learned the meaning of more than thirty words. And a contented, sleepy little girl snuggled against Teacher and kissed her goodnight. She had never kissed Annie before or permitted Annie to kiss her. A big hole in Annie Sullivan's heart was filled. Never again in her life would she feel that aching loneliness she had felt when Jimmie died.

The breakthrough had come at last. Annie's real job would now begin.

The first problem would be to teach Helen to express herself with those dancing fingers in conversational language, as other people did. Annie would have none of the stilted, awkward, copybook English of Laura Bridgman.

"How do babies learn to talk?" she asked herself as she tossed about that night, too excited and too happy to go to sleep. "By hearing the people about them of course. At first they don't understand a word. Then they pick up a word here and a word there. They keep learning more words until at last—well, they just talk, and that's all."

The following day she started in, keeping a constant stream of conversation flowing into Helen's hand. She encouraged the Kellers to do the same thing, and they were now learning the manual alphabet in earnest.

To her delight, Helen responded with enthusiasm. Her eagerness to learn was insatiable.

"Don't feel sorry for her anymore," Annie urged the child's parents. "She's not a poor little thing. She's brighter than most children. And I'm going to help her to be as normal a child as possible."

Helen was learning nouns with amazing speed. Next she must learn to make sentences. She would "hear" them of course as Teacher spelled them into her hand, but she must learn to use verbs, prepositions, adjectives, adverbs. Thus it happened that Helen Keller learned to read almost as soon as Teacher could communicate with her.

Annie had brought with her from Boston some cards on which words were printed in raised letters—names of objects, verbs "is," "come," "go," "run," and prepositions "in" and "on" and "to." Spelling was no problem. Helen learned to read as she learned the manual alphabet, not letter by letter, but whole words at a time.

They started with a box and a table. Helen knew these words, and it was not difficult for Teacher to make her understand that the bumps on the card meant the same thing as the word spelled into her hand.

Next Teacher placed the box on the table and on the box the card identifying it in raised letters. Next to it she placed the cards "is" and "on" and finally the card bearing the word "table."

She had Helen run her fingers over them. Helen hesitated, puzzled, over "is" and "on," but she recognized with satisfaction the words she knew.

Helen entered into this new game with delight, and they played it every day, Teacher introducing new words. Teacher had her reward a few days later. She found Helen standing in a closet, holding in her hand a card on which was printed "girl." Strung out beside her on the floor were cards bearing "is" and "in" and "closet." "Girl is in closet." Helen Keller had completed her first sentence without help.

Annie had also brought with her some little readers in raised print. She gave these to Helen, and the child would spend hours going through them looking for words she recognized. Almost every day she would run across new words, to her great pride.

Helen's lessons were not confined to learning to read and make sentences. In the lovely spring weather, she and Teacher spent most of the daytime hours outdoors. With a packet of seeds, Teacher took her to a plowed field and let her feel the warm, upturned earth. Then she leveled off a place and guided Helen's hands as they poked the seeds into the ground. When they returned later, and Helen felt the little plants that had poked their way up, she wriggled with pleasure.

There were little animals for her to meet. Puppies, kittens, colts, lambs, a baby pig which she held in her arms while Teacher pressed her hand against its throat so she could feel it squeal. One day Teacher placed an egg in her hands and let her hold it while a baby chick poked its way through the shell.

There was another aspect of Helen's training to which Annie gave considerable thought. Helen was a sturdy, active youngster, not timid as many blind children are.

Teacher encouraged her to run, romp, and play tomboy games. She even taught her to climb trees!

"We don't want her to go shuffling along, always afraid of running into things," she explained when Mrs. Keller expressed some misgivings. "She'll take some bumps, but I won't let her hurt herself badly."

Years later, when Helen Keller was a young woman, people marveled at her poise, the grace with which she moved.

Almost as soon as she started "talking" and reading with her fingers, Helen began to write. This was her own idea. One day she found Teacher laboriously writing a long letter to Mrs. Hopkins. Helen kept bothering her, indicating that whatever Teacher was doing she wanted to do, too.

Finally, to keep her occupied, Teacher brought out a writing board, used by the blind, a heavy piece of cardboard with grooved lines. She fitted a piece of paper into the grooved lines and let Helen run her fingers along them. Then she took a pencil and guided her small hand, printing several times, "Cat does drink milk." She used the "square letter" printing taught to the blind, every letter made with straight lines, including "o" and "q." It is apparently easier for a person who cannot see to make straight lines than circles.

By the time Teacher finished her letter, Helen had covered the page. Her printing was far from perfect, letters slanting in all directions, but she had kept them within the grooved lines. And her jubilant fingers informed Teacher that she, too, had written a letter.

Not so very long after that, Helen actually did write her first letter. It did not make much sense; she had simply strung together in sentences a lot of words she knew. But it was written only six weeks after Helen learned at the pump that words had meaning!

Preoccupied as she was with her pupil's amazing progress, Annie Sullivan did not pay as much attention to the people about her as she might have done under different circumstances. It was fortunate that this was so, for the old quick-tempered, rebellious Annie could have become involved in some heated arguments at the Keller dinner table.

With some surprise she did notice that the topic of conversation was always the same—the War Between the States and why the South should have won it. To Captain Arthur Keller, as Annie years later recalled it, "everything southern was desirable, noble, and eternal." Of course, in his opinion, the South had had the best generals, the finest armies, the only just cause. The fact that the North had won, which he never admitted, must have been to him a queer, inexplicable twist of fate.

But Annie, on her part, did not have the strong feeling many Northerners had about the Civil War. At the Perkins Institution, she had at first refused to believe it when they told her there had been a Civil War, and that General Grant, whom she had decided as a child at Tewksbury was "the government" and a bad man, was a great hero. Her inclination to argue with Captain Keller about the war was not so keen as it would have been in some of her Boston friends.

In Boston those days, southern aristocrats were referred to as "haughty Southrons," and her friends had given her an idea, albeit exaggerated, of what to expect from them. But she was a little startled when a southern gentleman at the Keller dinner table, ignoring her presence, declared that he would rather die than see his daughters working for a living!

Captain Keller had two sons by a previous marriage, thirteen-year-old Simpson and James, a young man. James' friends were in and out of the house all the time, but they never invited her to their parties and they ignored her completely. Annie probably would not have enjoyed herself much if they had included her. She was badly dressed, her eyes—over which most of the time she wore protecting dark glasses that Mrs. Hopkins had sent her—were scarred and inflamed, and she did not dance.

Whatever temptation she must have had at times to flare up was checked by her love and concern for Helen. In a way she was in the position she had been in at Tewksbury before Jimmie died. Whenever she started to have a tantrum, they would threaten to send Jimmie to the men's ward. Now she would have endured any insult rather than jeopardize her position as her adored Helen's teacher.

And the Kellers, whatever their opinion of Yankees—and they were never reticent about expressing it in front of Annie—obviously did not feel the same way about this particular Yankee. How they felt, Annie wrote Mrs. Hopkins, describing her first Christmas with them:

"When we came downstairs, Mrs. Keller said to me with tears in her eyes, 'Miss Annie, I thank God every day of my life for sending you to us, but I never realized until this morning what a blessing you have been to us.' Captain Keller took my hand, but could not speak. But his silence was more eloquent than words. My heart, too, was full of gratitude and solemn joy."

As the months sped by, so full that Annie hardly noticed their passage, the education of Helen proceeded. There was braille for her to learn to read and write. Annie detested braille herself and was never very good at it, but she taught it to Helen. More books for the blind were printed in braille than in raised letters.

The circus came to town, and Helen had a ride on an elephant, played with the monkeys, was lifted up to stroke the ears of a giraffe, and was taken inside the cage of a tame—and well-fed—young lion to "see" it by passing her hands over its great tawny body.

And there were long walks, with Teacher's fingers spelling sights and sounds into Helen's receptive palm. There were rabbits and there were pigeons, which Teacher tamed so that Helen could handle them.

There were books to be spelled to Helen, poetry and the tales of ancient Greece, which Annie Sullivan had loved when she was a schoolgirl at Perkins.

And there were lessons about the contours of the earth and its geography, taught in the sand on the shore of the Tennessee River! Helen first learned about mountains when Teacher built them for her in miniature out of sand, rivers when she dug channels in the sand, and lakes when she built little dams of rocks and poured water in behind them! Out of sand, relief maps of the five continents were built.

And always from Helen there were questions, questions, questions. Her capacity for learning seemed infinite!

In 1888, a little more than a year after her arrival in Tuscumbia, Annie decided with some misgivings and reluctance to accept the urgent request of Mr. Anagnos and take Helen to Boston.

It was time, she decided, for Helen to "see" the world. And there were braille books in the library at the Perkins Institution.

CHAPTER 9

Wonder Child

ANNIE'S MISGIVINGS about taking Helen to Boston were founded on highly exaggerated reports of her progress that had appeared in the press, due to the enthusiasm of Mr. Anagnos.

Less than five weeks after Helen had discovered that words had meaning, Annie read with indignation a report in a Boston newspaper that her pupil was already speaking fluent English.

"How perfectly absurd," Annie sputtered in a letter to Mrs. Hopkins, "to say that Helen is already speaking fluently. One might as well say that a two-year-old child speaks fluently when he says 'apple give' or 'baby walk go.'

"Then it is amusing to read of the elaborate preparation I underwent to fit me for the great task my friends entrusted to me. I am sorry that preparation did not include spelling. It would have saved me such a lot of trouble."

In a subsequent letter she thanked Mrs. Hopkins for the gift of a little red dictionary.

At the urgent request of Mr. Anagnos, she wrote a progress report on Helen after she had been with her seven months. Her factual, truthful report was published by the Perkins Institution, with some extravagant interpolations and comments by Mr.

Anagnos. Naturally the newspapers became even more interested in the "wonder child."

Their stories apparently did not worry Mr. Anagnos, who seemed to have greatly magnified Helen's achievements even to himself, but Annie was deeply disturbed. One account had Helen working out problems in algebra. Annie had not even started teaching her arithmetic yet!

"When people find out that those stories aren't true," Annie fumed to herself, "they won't believe she has made the amazing progress she really has made. They'll call me a liar."

Mrs. Hopkins then became Annie's only confidante.

"I shall write freely to you and tell you everything on one condition," she wrote Mrs. Hopkins. "You must promise never to show my letters to anyone."

From that time on Annie wrote a long weekly letter to Mrs. Hopkins. Fortunately Mrs. Hopkins kept those letters, for they constitute the only record of Annie's experiments, successes and failures during those first—and most important—months with Helen Keller. On that record is based much of the procedure which is used in teaching blind-deaf children today.

Despite the urging of Mr. Anagnos, Annie never kept any day-by-day record of her work with Helen, as Dr. Howe and her teachers had with Laura Bridgman. Her weak eyes made writing difficult; her weekly letter to Mrs. Hopkins was an ordeal. And Annie was much too engrossed with drawing out her young pupil and watching her personality unfold to bother with writing reports on how it was accomplished.

Annie only half understood Mr. Anagnos' point of view at first. It was important to Mr. Anagnos that the Perkins Institution receive its share of the glory of Annie's achievement. She was, after all, a graduate of the school. Prestige for the school, which welcomed gifts and bequests, was highly desirable.

Only when she could withstand the pressure no longer would Annie give in and write a report for Mr. Anagnos. It was hard to refuse him. Annie herself owed a debt of loyalty to the Perkins Institution, which had rescued her from Tewksbury and had given her a chance. And Mr. Anagnos had been a generous friend. It was Mr. Anagnos who advanced, out of his own pocket, the money for her railroad fare to Tuscumbia, and when Annie, out of her first month's salary, twenty-five dollars, started to pay him back, he returned the money, admonishing her to start a bank account first. After all other persuasive methods failed, Mr. Anagnos had a final trick. He would enlist the support of Captain Keller.

On a morning late in May 1888, Annie and Helen, Mrs. Keller, and little Mildred set out for Boston. Helen's eighth birthday was a month away.

En route they stopped in Washington to see Dr. Alexander Graham Bell. Dr. Bell had been indirectly responsible for bringing Annie and Helen together.

Months before they ever heard of Annie Sullivan, the Kellers did hear of a renowned eye specialist in Baltimore, and they hopefully took Helen to him. The eye specialist could do nothing for her, but he knew of a man in Washington who might be able to do something about her deafness.

That man was Dr. Bell, who throughout his career gave lavishly of his time and his money to efforts to help the deaf. As a matter of fact, he was trying to make a hearing aid when he invented the telephone.

Dr. Bell examined Helen's ears and shook his head. He took her on his lap and let her play with his watch while he sadly told her parents there was no hope. But he had heard of the Perkins Institution and of Dr. Howe's success with Laura Bridgman. So at his suggestion, Captain Keller wrote to the school, and Annie Sullivan became Helen Keller's teacher.

Captain Keller's grateful letter after Helen's release started a correspondence through which Dr. Bell had been kept informed of her progress. He had also read Annie's report, with Mr.

Anagnos' interpolations and comments, and the newspaper stories.

Annie's meeting with Dr. Bell was the beginning of a friendship that would last the rest of their lives. But it started somewhat awkwardly for Annie. Dr. Bell was charmed with Helen, who had developed into a most appealing, lovable child.

"What method do you use, Miss Sullivan?" he asked, smiling as he watched Helen's small fingers fluttering like birds as they spelled questions.

"M-m-method?" Annie stammered, her face red with embarrassment. "I—well, I don't really have any method. I just keep trying new things as I think of them. Some of them work. Some don't."

Method or no method, Dr. Bell was enthusiastic about what Annie had accomplished. One thing that amazed him was Helen's facility in the use of the article "the" and such abstract words as "love," "happy," "good," "bad," and so on. This was not difficult for Annie to explain.

"She learned to use the word 'the,'" she said, "by having it spelled constantly in her hand. I've always used complete sentences with her since her vocabulary became extensive enough to permit it. No baby talk. She learned to use 'the' from hearing it, as any normal child does.

"Other words she had learned from association. One day when she was crying, I put my arms around her and said, 'Teacher is sorry.' She has used the word ever since.

"One day I asked her a question she couldn't answer easily. While she was pondering, I tapped her on the forehead and spelled T-H-I-N-K. She got the idea and started using that word correctly, too."

So pleased was Dr. Bell that in an article published later, he wrote:

"The great problem that confronts us in this country is how to impart to a deaf child a knowledge of idiomatic English. It must be admitted by all who have come into contact with Helen Keller that this problem has been solved in the case of one deaf child."

Again and again in later years, Dr. Bell gave encouragement and staunch support to a beleaguered and heartsick Annie.

When a famous child visits a famous man, reporters find out about it. All the Washington newspapers carried stories about Helen. Everyone was interested in her, including President Cleveland, who invited Helen and Teacher to the White House to meet him. No record of their conversation was kept, but Helen's comment as they drove away may give an inkling.

"Mr. Cleveland was very glad to see me," her fingers spelled happily.

For Annie the visit was in one way disappointing. Mrs. Cleveland, heroine of her schoolgirl days, was not at home.

Helen's first visit to Boston was too brief for the full impact of her fame to hit Annie as hard as it would later. There was, of course, a great deal of publicity, and Helen was the star at the Perkins school commencement, where she read a poem with her fingers, Annie translating it simultaneously. People gushed over her, wept over her, and wrote poems about her.

Helen, however, was unaware of it and thoroughly enjoyed herself playing with the blind children, who knew the manual alphabet, and browsing in the school library, which added more volumes in braille each year. She was as eager to read as Annie had been when she was a blind child, and she would tackle any book, no matter how little of it she understood.

Annie learned on that visit that keeping Helen from getting spoiled by all the adulation that was heaped upon her was not going to be any problem. Since only those who knew the manual alphabet could communicate with her, and hardly anyone knew the manual alphabet, Helen heard only what Teacher chose to spell into her hand. That did not include any of the extravagant compliments. Fortunately, from Teacher's point of view, Mr. Anagnos did not know the manual alphabet!

After a brief stay in Boston, Annie and Helen spent the summer with Mrs. Hopkins on Cape Cod, where Helen learned to swim and Annie noted wryly that some of Mrs. Hopkins' neighbors, who had never paid any attention to her when she was a charity pupil at the Perkins Institution, now greeted her as an old friend.

Annie's eyes were bad, and she made a trip to Boston to have them treated, leaving Helen with Mrs. Hopkins. Since she was matron of the cottage where Laura Bridgman lived, Mrs. Hopkins knew the manual alphabet, and while Annie was away she got out some books of fairy stories that had belonged to her daughter and read them to Helen.

In the autumn, Annie and Helen returned to Tuscumbia. Annie remained there a year, but by the following spring, Annie's eyes had grown so much worse that she had to go back to Boston for another operation. She was away three and a half months—her longest separation from Helen until many years later, when Helen was in her forties and Annie in her fifties.

Helen's education had progressed to the point where that fall she started having regular lessons with Teacher, in geography, zoology, reading, and arithmetic. Mastering arithmetic was a towering achievement for a child who could neither see nor hear. Let anyone who doubts it try to do fractions without a pencil. Often Helen would come up with the answer while Teacher was still struggling with the problem on paper. Annie herself could not account for it, except for the fact that Helen had a most unusually retentive memory. Also, since she could not see or hear, she was not distracted by things happening around her.

Upon her return from Boston, Annie decided to take Helen back there that winter. Helen had reached the stage where she needed a good, solid groundwork in her education. And Annie was always painfully aware of the gaps in her own education.

Later, when Helen realized that Annie had eye trouble, she could not understand why she spent practically all of her leisure time with her nose in a book. Sometimes she would snatch the book out of her hands and drag her off for a walk. She thought Teacher was reading for pleasure. But Teacher was reading to keep ahead of her pupil.

Boston those days was called "The Athens of America." Almost every American author of distinction had lived and written there: Hawthorne; Longfellow; Thoreau, at "Walden," near Boston; and Ralph Waldo Emerson. James Russell Lowell, John Greenleaf Whittier, and Oliver Wendell Holmes were still writing when Helen was a child in Boston.

In Boston, Annie told herself as she tried to allay her misgivings about the publicity which followed Helen wherever she went, she herself might find inspiration and books that would help with her own education. And Helen would have the advantages of the braille library at Perkins.

Annie's worry about the attention Helen would attract proved well founded. That winter, and for several winters thereafter, Helen Keller was Boston's most publicized celebrity, and the demands upon her time and her strength would have exhausted her if Annie had not weeded them out. The weeding-out process was not simple. Boston society matrons, on the lookout for celebrities to grace their drawing rooms, deluged the child with invitations. Sometimes they would fail to invite Annie, overlooking the fact that, since they did not know the manual alphabet, they had no way of communicating with Helen.

The word "exploitation" was not so commonly used those days as it is now, but while Annie may never have used the word, she knew its meaning.

"What do they want with my little Helen?" she would ask herself. "Just something to attract attention to themselves. They want to exhibit her, as a freak. Well, they shan't—not if I can help it!"

So Annie would turn down the invitations, which did not make her popular with "the Brahmins," as the rich and socially prominent families in Boston were called.

An incident that winter contributed further to Annie's unpopularity. After a great deal of pressure, she granted an interview to a reporter. Innocently she told him that she was entirely responsible for Helen's education. It was true, and Mr. Anagnos had said so many times publicly.

But the abuse Annie took after that interview left a scar that never quite healed. People called her conceited, an ingrate, unappreciative of all that the Perkins Institution had done for her. Latent jealousy on the part of some of the teachers at the school came out into the open. An utterly miserable Annie Sullivan wrote a pathetic letter of apology to the Perkins trustees. And never again in her life did she grant a newspaper interview.

In the early spring, however, Helen Keller—largely through her own courage and determination—achieved something so startling, so far beyond anything her teacher had ever hoped or dreamed for her, that Annie Sullivan's troubles were pushed into the background, almost forgotten.

CHAPTER 10

Triumph and Despair

"I-AM-NOT-DUMB-NOW!"

The voice was guttural, like the growl of an animal, the words so muffled that there were only two human beings on earth who could have understood them. But those words, uttered so haltingly and with agonizing physical effort, were heard all around the world.

For they were spoken by the most famous child in the world, nine-year-old Helen Keller. It was the second time in recorded history that a child who was deaf, dumb, and blind had spoken audibly. And Helen Keller's feat was heralded wherever newspapers were read.

The scene took place in the office of Miss Sarah Fuller, principal of the Horace Mann School for the Deaf, in Boston. It was March 1890, toward the end of Helen's first winter in Boston. Annie had taken her to Miss Fuller doubtfully and only because of Helen's own insistence.

Long before Helen realized that other people used their eyes for seeing, she became aware that they talked with their mouths and throats. Before Teacher came to her, she would sometimes stand between her parents with her hands on their faces. She would feel their lips move, and she would move her lips, too, but they paid no attention to her. Perhaps she was dimly aware that they were communicating with each other. At any rate, they were playing some sort of game from which she was excluded, and it contributed to her frustration and her resentment.

From the time she felt the vibration of her dog barking and a baby pig squealing in her arms, Helen knew that sounds came from the throat. Placing her hand against Teacher's throat, she learned that Teacher sometimes spoke with her throat and mouth, not with her fingers. She wanted to learn to speak that way, too.

Feeling with her hand the vibrations in her own throat, she knew that she could make sounds. But the sounds she made were so unpleasant that Teacher discouraged her. To pacify her by giving her something else to do, Teacher taught her to read lips with her fingers, no small achievement for a person who cannot see. But reading lips with her fingers was slow and awkward, and Helen was not satisfied.

"Why can't I talk the way you do?" her flying fingers would ask. "Why can't I?"

It was a question over which Teacher sadly shook her head. She had no answer.

In the late winter, one of the teachers at the Perkins Institution came back from Europe with a report that a child in Norway, blind, deaf, and dumb, had learned to speak audibly. That settled it, so far as Helen was concerned.

"If a little girl in Norway can do it, I can do it, too," Helen's fingers spelled, so rapidly that they almost ran the words together into a blur.

She would give Annie no peace. But Annie had nothing to go on, save a report that a blind-deaf child in Norway had learned to speak. No one knew who had taught her or how. Annie did not even have her address, and it took a long time for letters to travel between Boston and Norway those days. Finally, in desperation, she took Helen to Miss Fuller.

The expressions on their faces must have been in marked contrast the day they walked into Miss Fuller's office—Annie, worried, dreading the heartbreak that awaited Helen if Miss Fuller could do nothing, and Helen, eager, expectant, confident. Miss Fuller was doubtful. She had never tried to teach a blind-deaf child to speak. The difficulties looked insurmountable.

"But we might try," she concluded, noting the expression on the child's face. She had Helen read her lips as she explained to her how to make the different letter sounds.

"We'll try the M sound," she said. "It's made this way, by pressing your lips together as you let the sound come out of your throat. Try it."

After several attempts Helen succeeded fairly well.

"Now let's try the T sound," Miss Fuller said, "You touch your front teeth with your tongue—this way."

At the end of an hour, Helen had managed to make six letter sounds: M, T, P, A, S, and I.

"Never before have I seen any child so eager to learn," Miss Fuller said. Still by no means confident that she would succeed, she agreed to give Helen more lessons.

The magnitude of her task can best be illustrated if you try to imagine how you would go about showing a deaf person, who cannot see the movements of your lips, your tongue, the muscles in your face, how to distinguish between the letter sounds. M, B, and P, for instance, are all made by pressing the lips together. T and D are both made by touching the front teeth with the tongue. To make R and L, the tongue has to be curled. And there are sounds that have to be made at the back of the palate, like K and the hard G. Had Helen been able to see, it would have been difficult enough. But Helen Keller had only her prying fingers to guide her.

There were eleven lessons before Helen, straining every nerve and muscle in her body, uttered that first sentence, "I am not dumb now!"

"From now on," Miss Fuller said, "what she'll need is practice. I've done all I can."

That meant a lifetime of work for Annie Sullivan on top of everything else she did for her pupil. Day after day during the first months, Helen's determined fingers would explore her mouth until it was sore, going away back into her throat until Annie became nauseated. Over and over and over again, those letter sounds and words—new words fighting to escape from Helen Keller's throat. Almost from the first she refused to talk with her fingers anymore, even though Annie had to translate almost everything she said.

In Helen's triumph there was also heartbreak for Annie. Before they permitted her to start making letter sounds and pronouncing words, Helen should have been taught how to produce sounds correctly from her throat. This tragic mistake was not discovered until Helen had been talking for several years, too late to change the habit she had formed. As the result, her voice would always be unnatural, without inflection, the words so indistinct that it was difficult for a stranger to understand her.

It was not Annie's fault, nor Miss Fuller's for that matter. Comparatively little was known about teaching the deaf to speak those days. But Annie never forgave herself. All through the years, almost up to the day of her death, she struggled to improve Helen's speech.

Imperfect though her speech was, however, it was a miracle that she could speak at all, and she became even more famous than she had been before. Ragnhild Kaata, the little girl in Norway who spoke before Helen did, was forgotten. But Helen Keller, the "wonder child," was known the world over.

In Maine, they named a ship after her. In London, Queen Victoria asked a visiting American about her. In Athens, the Queen of Greece wept when Mr. Anagnos read to her a letter he had received from Helen. Annie still had to sort carefully the floods of invitations Helen received in Boston, but there were compensations.

Helen and Annie met Oliver Wendell Holmes when he invited them to have tea with him alone one Sunday afternoon in his study. Edward Everett Hale, who wrote *The Man Without a Country*, said he and Helen were distantly related, and he always addressed her as "Little Cousin." Annie decided it was time Helen received some religious instruction, and she took her to Phillips Brooks, one of the most distinguished clergymen of his day, and sat by translating his words into her hand as he held Helen on his lap. Helen became so fond of him that when she was allowed to name her new baby brother, she called him Phillips Brooks.

Annie and Helen made other friends, not so well known outside of Boston, who gave them a great deal, both materially and in warm comforting friendship in times of trouble. One was a wealthy industrialist, John Spaulding, whose friends called him "King John." His generosity helped make it possible for Helen to complete her education, and a bequest in his will went into the first home they ever owned.

There were the Chamberlins, with whom Annie Sullivan spent many of the happiest days in her life. Joseph E. Chamberlin was literary critic on the *Boston Transcript*. He and his family, including several children, lived near the village of Wrentham, about twenty-five miles from Boston. Their big, rambling house overlooked King Philip's Pond, named after the Indian chief, who was said to have breathed his last beneath a huge oak near the Chamberlins' house. It was while visiting the Chamberlins that Helen had her first toboggan ride, learned to dive and swim under water, paddle a canoe, and ride a tandem bicycle with Annie on the front seat to steer it.

Helen's correspondence was heavy. Thank you notes, in her neat, square-hand script, traveled to many faraway places. People were always sending her things. She was an indefatigable letter writer anyway. A sample is a letter written to the poet, John Greenleaf Whittier, on his birthday, in December 1890:

> Dear Kind Poet:
>
> This is your birthday; that was the first thought which came into my mind when I awoke this morning; and it made me glad to think I could write you a letter and tell you how much your little friends love their sweet poet and his birthday. This evening they are going to entertain their friends with readings from your poems and music. I hope the swift-winged messengers of love will be there to carry some of the sweet melody to you in your little study by the Merrimac.
>
> At first I was very sorry when I found that the sun had hidden his shining face behind dull clouds, but afterwards I thought why he did it, and I was happy. The sun knows that you like to see the world covered with beautiful white snow, and so he kept back all his brightness and let the little crystals form in the sky. When they are ready, they will softly fall and tenderly cover every object. Then the sun will appear in all his radiance and fill the world with light.
>
> If I were with you today, I would give you eighty-three kisses, one for each year you have lived. Eighty-three years seems very long to me. Does it seem long to you? I wonder how many years there will be in eternity. I am afraid I cannot think of so much time.
>
> I received the letter you wrote me last summer, and I thank you for it. Teacher is well and sends her kind remembrance to you.
>
> The happy Christmas time is almost here! I can hardly wait for the fun to begin! I hope your Christmas Day will be a very happy one, and that the New Year will be full of brightness and joy for you and everyone.
>
> From your little friend,
Helen Keller

The Quaker poet replied:

My Dear Young Friend:

    I was very glad to have such a pleasant letter on my birthday. I had two or three hundred others, and thine was one of the most welcome of all. I must tell thee how the day passed at Oak Knoll. Of course the sun did not shine, but we had great open wood fires in the rooms, which were all very sweet with roses and other flowers, which were sent to me from distant friends, and fruits of all kinds from California and other places. Some relatives and dear old friends were with me through the day. I do not wonder thee thinks eighty-three years a long time, but to me it seems but a very little while since I was a boy no older than thee, playing on the old farm at Haverhill. I thank thee for all thy good wishes and wish thee as many. Give my best regards to Miss Sullivan, and with a great deal of love I am

                Thy old friend,
                John G. Whittier

Helen's urge to express herself on paper was not limited to letter writing. She also wrote poems and stories, and before she was ten years old had contributed to *St. Nicholas Magazine*, a children's publication which was popular those days. People were often amazed at the facility with which she expressed herself.

The Kellers were spending Indian summer in the autumn of 1891 at their hunting lodge in the mountains when Helen wrote *The Frost King*. She was inspired by Teacher's description, spelled into her hand, of the beautiful colors Jack Frost had painted with his giant brush.

The Frost King was a fairy story, containing some descriptions of the frozen north and the king's wondrous ice palace of such exquisite imagery that even Teacher was surprised when she read it as Helen had punched it out in braille. She read it to the family that night at dinner.

"Did you read that in some book?" Captain Keller asked.

"Oh, no," Helen replied earnestly. "I wrote it out of my own head. It's for Mr. Anagnos, for his birthday."

The next day she copied it, in her neat script, took it to the post office and mailed it.

Some months later, the Perkins Institution published the story, along with comments by Mr. Anagnos that made anything he had previously written about Helen seem pale and tepid. He compared the child to Wordsworth, Keats, and Aristotle.

Shortly after the story was published, a letter came to the Perkins Institution accusing Helen of plagiarism. Before Helen was born, Margaret T. Canby had written a story called *The Frost Fairies*, published in a children's book entitled *Birdie and His Fairy Friends*.

Miss Canby's story and Helen's story were so alike that there could be no doubt that the child, consciously or unconsciously, had committed plagiarism. Some passages were repeated word for word, and the whole idea of the story was the same.

Mr. Anagnos, very much perturbed, started an investigation. At first nobody could figure out what had happened. Neither Annie, members of the Keller family, nor any of the teachers at the Perkins school had ever heard of Miss Canby's book. Finally it was discovered that Mrs. Hopkins had had a copy of the book among some children's books that had belonged to her daughter. She had read the story to Helen the summer when Annie went to Boston to have her eyes treated, leaving Helen with Mrs. Hopkins on Cape Cod.

The question was: Did Helen knowingly steal Miss Canby's story and try to pass it off as her own? Or had it remained dormant in the back of her extraordinarily retentive memory to come out eventually as an expression of her own imagination? And if it was plagiarism, was her teacher guilty, too? Most people thought so.

There followed what amounted to a formal trial for Helen, with four adults, two blind and two sighted, sitting as judges with

Mr. Anagnos. Annie was barred from the room. For two endless hours they questioned and cross-questioned the child while in her broken, halting speech she tried to convince them of her innocence. Without Teacher's familiar fingers in her hand, she could not at times understand what they were saying. There was no one who could use the manual alphabet so well as Teacher could.

Finally, the verdict was rendered, and an exhausted, tearful Helen walked out of the room into the arms of her teacher. Two of the judges voted against Helen, two for her. Mr. Anagnos cast his vote for her. Later, however, he recanted and publicly said he thought Helen and her teacher were both guilty.

Some people were kind. Miss Canby said publicly, "I do not see how anyone can be so unkind as to call it plagiarism. It is a wonderful feat of memory." And she wrote Helen a comforting letter, begging her not to worry about it.

To Annie, Dr. Bell wrote:

"We all do what Helen did. Our most original compositions are composed exclusively of expressions derived from others. We do the very same thing. Our forms of expression are copies in our earlier years, from the expressions of others which we have heard in childhood."

And Mark Twain, when he heard about it some years later, said that what they had done to Helen was the worst thing that had been done to a child since the British burned Joan of Arc at the stake.

CHAPTER 11

New Plans

THE INCIDENT of *The Frost King* left scars on Annie Sullivan and Helen Keller that would never quite disappear.

For months, whenever Helen would make an unusually bright remark, Annie, in spite of herself, would think, "I wonder where she picked that up."

Helen, when she was a young woman trying to earn her living as a professional writer, would tear a sheet of paper out of her typewriter, saying to herself, "I must have read that sentence somewhere."

Tormented by a sense of guilt—a feeling that she herself should somehow have prevented it—Annie undertook the difficult task of restoring Helen's confidence in herself. They left the Perkins Institution, never to return except for brief, casual visits, and went back to Alabama. All the sparkle had gone out of the child's personality, and she was so pale and listless that word went around that she was seriously ill. Her teacher had pushed her too hard, people said. At that time her teacher was not pushing her at all. Lessons were temporarily abandoned.

Then a request came for Helen to write the story of her life for

The Youth's Companion, a children's magazine with a very large circulation. And Annie made her do it.

"It's the only way to pull her out of it," Annie told herself over and over. "The child has talent, a great deal of talent. We can't let that thing wreck her whole life."

It must have taken every last ounce of moral courage they possessed for Helen to write that story, under Annie's watchful eye. Finally it was finished and sent off to the magazine. The editors liked it and published it, and there were no repercussions.

They were both at loose ends. To return to Boston was impossible, not only because of *The Frost King* incident, but for financial reasons. Captain Keller had never made much money with his newspaper; he farmed as a gentleman farmer, not commercially, and he had expensive tastes—fine horses, well-bred hunting dogs, a shooting lodge. He had long since ceased to pay Annie's salary, and he never did pay it again. Unless they were financed by some of their wealthy friends, travel for Annie and Helen was impossible.

Annie also felt that the time had come when Helen needed more advanced teaching than she could give her. That Helen spoke and wrote as well as she did was entirely due to the hours Annie spent reading. She read always the classics, the world's great literature—only the best was good enough for Helen. And through her reading she acquired a taste for beautiful English and a mastery of it that she passed on to her pupil. As for Helen, she had already learned to speak and write a little French, having learned it by thumbing through a braille French-English dictionary she found in the Perkins library!

Several months after they returned to Alabama, Dr. Bell came to their rescue. He gave them a trip to Niagara Falls, invited them to be his guests at the second inauguration of Grover Cleveland, and in the summer of 1893 took them out to the World's Fair in Chicago. The trips did them good, and Helen became her old buoyant, happy self, except occasionally while she was writing letters.

Following the Chicago trip, they went to stay with their friend, William Wade, a magazine publisher, who lived in Hulton, Pennsylvania. Annie explained to him her problem about Helen's studies, and he called in one of his friends, the Rev. John D. Irons, a Presbyterian clergyman, who had studied Latin and Greek extensively. With him, Helen started Latin, with Annie spelling the words into her hand. Annie had never had any Latin, but she did not need to know the language. All she had to do was spell the words.

"I shall get an education along with Helen," she told Mr. Wade. "And I can certainly use it!"

The following summer, in 1894, Dr. Bell arranged for Annie to address a meeting of the American Association to Promote the Teaching of Speech to the Deaf, at Chautauqua, New York. Undoubtedly he did it to help Annie win back confidence in herself. But it did not quite work. At the last moment Annie was overcome by shyness, and Dr. Bell had to read her speech for her. Some of her honest, forthright remarks will give an indication as to how she felt about her pupil at the time:

"Much has been said and written about Helen Keller. Too much, I think, has appeared in type. One can scarcely take up a newspaper or a magazine without finding more or less exaggerated accounts of her so-called 'marvelous accomplishments,' which I believe consist only in her being able to speak and write the language of her country with greater ease and fluency than the average seeing and hearing child of her age.

"It is easier for the credulous to say, 'She is a miracle, and her teacher is another miracle,' and for the unbelievers to declare, 'Such things cannot be; we are being imposed upon,' than it is to make a conscientious study of the principles involved in her education.

"I shall have cause for gratification if I succeed in convincing you that Helen Keller is neither a 'phenomenal child,' 'an intellectual prodigy,' nor an 'extraordinary genius,' but simply a very bright and lovely child, unmarred by self-consciousness or any taint of evil."

She then went on to explain how she had taught Helen and how she believed it was possible to teach any deaf child ease and fluency of expression simply by keeping a constant stream of normal, adult conversation flowing into his or her mind, subconscious or conscious. She might as well have saved her breath. Helen continued to be the "wonder child," and highly colored accounts of her accomplishments continued to roll off the presses.

At the Chautauqua meeting, Annie met John D. Wright and Dr. Thomas Humason, who were opening a school that fall in New York City to teach oral language to the deaf. They had heard Helen speak and hoped that, with the new methods, her voice might be made more normal.

That autumn, at the age of fourteen, Helen, with Annie always at her side, entered the Wright-Humason School. Then the tragic mistake that Miss Fuller and Annie had made was revealed. Very little could be done about Helen's voice. It was too late. She had acquired a firmly fixed habit of producing sound from her throat incorrectly. Nothing could change it.

Through the generosity of their friend "King John" Spaulding in Boston, Helen and Annie remained two years at the Wright-Humason School, Helen pursuing studies roughly equivalent to junior high school courses nowadays. Those were the most glamorous years of their lives.

They met everybody—the rich, the powerful, the famous. In the homes of their friends, the wealthy Laurence Hutton, Mary Mapes Dodge, and Richard Watson Gilder, editor of the *Century Magazine*; they met such giants in the financial world as John D. Rockefeller and Colonel H.H. Rogers, another Standard Oil millionaire, such literary celebrities as William Dean Howells, Charles Dudley Warner, Hamilton Wright Mabie, John LaFarge, Henry VanDyke, Kate Douglas Wiggins, and Mark Twain—especially Mark Twain, who would remain one of their closest friends until his death. There were others—Woodrow Wilson, then a professor at Princeton University; and some very famous theater people, Henry Irving and Joseph Jefferson, still remembered by old-timers who may never have seen him, but who heard of his performance as Rip van Winkle; and the first lady of the theater those days, Ellen Terry.

When they met Miss Terry, she kissed Annie and said, "I do not know whether I am glad to see you or not, for I feel so ashamed of myself when I think of how much you have done for the little girl."

It was all colorful, brilliant, and breathtaking. But Annie had some bad moments. She was so desperately afraid that something about her wretched background might slip out. In later years she would realize that this was a foolish snobbery. But Annie was still not thirty years old at that time, and the specter of Tewksbury was always with her.

She never talked about it to anyone. Into Helen's palms she spelled charming stories about her beautiful mother, her little sister Mary, her brother Jimmie, and her "delightful" father and his stories about the fairies and the little folk in Ireland. Her fears, lest the story of her childhood reach the ears of their new friends in New York, proved groundless. Mr. Anagnos and the teachers at Perkins, even though there was no longer the friendly feeling between them that there had been, kept her secret well.

During her second year at the Wright-Humason School, the question of Helen's future again came up. Helen, at the age of eleven, had announced that someday she was going to Harvard. Obviously she could not go to Harvard. But there is a women's college, Radcliffe, whose students attend classes with the Harvard men and whose diplomas are signed by the president of Harvard.

At the time when Helen made her announcement, Annie did not take her seriously. She thought she would outgrow it. The idea of a deaf-blind person going through college was too incredible. But Helen did not outgrow it. She was as determined about going to Harvard as she had been about learning to speak orally.

If Helen was going to Radcliffe or any other college, she would have to pass college entrance examinations. Worried and uncertain, Annie talked the problem over with the Huttons, Mark Twain, and some of her other New York friends.

Always there was the financial problem. About that time Annie had a battle royale with Captain Keller, who had decided that the way to recoup his lost fortunes was to take Helen out on the road and exhibit her! In his anger because Annie resisted him, he wanted to take Helen away from her. But fortunately Mrs. Keller stepped in. Helen remained with Annie, and she was not taken out on the road to be exhibited as a freak! Shortly thereafter, Captain Keller died.

Mrs. Hutton, whom Helen called "Aunt Eleanor," Colonel Rogers, Mark Twain, and some of their other friends decided that something must be done to make the future for Helen and her teacher more secure. Their friend, "King John" Spaulding had died. He had left them some money, but their friends thought it should be invested, not spent. Among themselves, with Dr. Bell joining in, they raised enough money to see Helen through college and to provide, they hoped, some security for her and Annie afterward.

The next question for Annie to ponder was how to go about preparing Helen for her college entrance examinations. They would be tough—the same examinations the boys had to pass to get into Harvard. Helen could be tutored, or she could go to a preparatory school. If she went to school, she would be competing for the first time with children who could see and hear. The children at the Wright-Humason School were not blind, but they were deaf. Against the advice of Mrs. Hutton and some of her other friends, Annie decided it should be a school.

"When she gets to college," she told them, "she will have to compete with students who can see and hear. I think we'd better try it out now and see if she can do it successfully before she goes to college. I think she can do it."

On the advice of Elizabeth Cary Agassiz, president emeritus of Radcliffe, Annie chose the Cambridge School for Young Ladies, which was essentially a preparatory school for girls planning to enter Radcliffe. It was located in Cambridge, near the college.

The head of the school was Arthur Gilman, and from the beginning he and Annie did not exactly see eye to eye. For some reason which she could not explain even to herself, Annie did not quite trust him. From the moment Helen entered the school, it received a great deal of publicity, and Annie knew from experience what publicity could do to people.

Annie had another worry—her eyes. They were never anywhere near normal, and she was having to have them treated more and more often. Helen, at this stage, knew there was something wrong with Teacher's eyes, but she had no idea how bad they were. Annie knew Helen would have a great deal of homework, and it would mean many hours of reading for her weak eyes, since not many of the textbooks she would need were printed in braille. Helen had now advanced beyond the point at which education for the blind, those days, ceased.

At first all went well. After she had been there a few months, Mr. Gilman wrote an article for the *Century Magazine*, in which he paid Annie this generous tribute:

"I could do little for Miss Keller was it not that Miss Sullivan continues her loving superintendence and follows her with the ministrations she has so willingly rendered all these years."

During her first year at the school, Helen's progress exceeded Annie's fondest hopes. They lived in a cottage nearby with some of the other girls, and that was good for Helen, although she had to spend twice as much time on her homework as they did. Annie went to classes with her and spelled into her hand what the teacher was saying. Mr. Gilman and one of the other teachers learned the manual alphabet. Helen, by this time, had learned to use a typewriter, and she did her written homework on that.

At the end of her first year, it was decided that Helen might as well take some of her college entrance examinations in subjects in which she was prepared. The examinations were held in late June, shortly after Helen's seventeenth birthday.

Annie could not be with her, but Mr. Gilman spelled the questions into her hand, and Helen wrote the answers on her typewriter. They had to have a room by themselves so that her typing would not distract the other students. Helen passed them all with flying colors and with honors in German and English.

In the autumn of Helen's second year at the school, the difficulties began. The course at the school normally lasted five years, but Helen had done so well that some of her teachers felt that she could finish in three years—two more years. With this Mr. Gilman did not agree, and he insisted on lightening Helen's schedule, over Annie's objections. He said Helen was working too hard, but Annie, who knew her better than anyone else did, knew she was not.

There was some trouble with her work, too. Some badly needed textbooks which had been especially printed for her in braille arrived late. Helen had started to take Greek, for which she needed a special cylinder for her typewriter. It also arrived late, and she had to learn how to manipulate it. She also had to learn how to construct geometrical figures with wires, on a cushion. But still she and Teacher plodded on.

Finally one day in November Helen had a cold, and Annie kept her in bed. Then trouble really began. Mr. Gilman ordered geometry and astronomy taken out of Helen's program. And without Annie's knowledge, he wrote Mrs. Keller that she was treating Helen cruelly and endangering her health. To Annie, Mrs. Keller wrote:

"I always think of Helen as partly your child, and whilst in this I think of her, I think of you, and utter ruin to the life you have striven so patiently to develop and round out."

Things went on fairly smoothly for about a month, Annie swallowing her hurt and her indignation. But in early December she found out that Mr. Gilman had started a movement to take Helen away from her.

Annie's first thought was to take Helen, and her younger sister, Mildred, who was also in her care, back to their mother, in Alabama. But Mr. Gilman would not permit it, and he showed Annie a telegram from Mrs. Keller authorizing him to take complete charge of Helen. He also brought up Annie's battle with Captain Keller, who had tried to take Helen away from her.

Mr. Gilman tried to take Helen and Mildred to his home, but, terrified at being separated from Teacher, they refused. They remained in the cottage where they had been living, but Annie was shut out.

Annie Sullivan used to say later that never in her life was she so close to suicide as she was that winter afternoon when she rode on a trolley car across the Charles River into Boston. But she managed to pull herself together, went to spend the night with friends, and sent desperate telegrams to Mrs. Keller, Dr. Bell, Mr. Chamberlin in Wrentham, and to Mrs. Hutton.

Upon receipt of her telegram, Mrs. Keller took the next train north. Dr. Bell sent to Boston his secretary, John Hitz, a lovable old man who was deeply fond of Annie and Helen. And Mrs. Hutton wrote Mr. Gilman a letter in which she stated that the money that had been raised for Helen's education was for both Helen and her teacher, and that if it was not spent that way, it would have to be returned!

Mrs. Keller, once on the scene, realized that she had been misled. She took Mildred back to Alabama with her, and Annie and Helen went to stay with the Chamberlins in Wrentham.

Nobody ever tried to take Helen Keller away from Annie Sullivan again.

CHAPTER 12

Happy Days

ANNIE AND Helen lived with the Chamberlins for eight months, through the rest of the winter and the following summer. Those were the first completely happy days Annie Sullivan had ever known.

The Chamberlins had a big house, and they were hospitable. Most of the guests were writers and editors, friendly and unpretentious, with none of the stuffiness or snobbishness Annie had encountered in the Boston Brahmins or in the Kellers' friends in Alabama. For the first time in years she was relaxed. Although she still carefully guarded her Tewksbury secret, she must have sensed that it would not matter to these people.

Annie loved good conversation, and the conversation at the Chamberlin dinner table was lively and interesting. She was herself a good conversationalist. Some of the Chamberlins learned the manual alphabet so that they could talk to Helen, and more than once she was told that Teacher was a very fascinating person.

At Red Farm, the Chamberlin home, there were outdoor sports; in the winter, tobogganing. They would load the toboggan on the crest of a steep bank overlooking King Philip's Pond, which would be frozen solid from shore to shore. Someone would give it a shove, and off it would go right through the air, down and through a snowdrift and skimming all the way across the pond on the ice. In the summer, there was gardening, long hikes through the woods, picnics, and swimming. Annie learned to swim and dive at Red Farm and to paddle stern in a canoe while Helen paddled bow. Helen learned to dive and to swim under water, with a rope tied around her waist so that she could find her way out.

Annie loved animals. Helen had a series of dogs while she was growing up, and Annie was as fond of them as she was. One of them, a huge mastiff, bit Annie. Captain Keller, over Annie's tearful protest, shot the dog, and Annie was sent to the Pasteur Institute in New York for anti-rabies treatment. Annie insisted that the dog was not mad, only confused and frightened. It was a new dog, not yet accustomed to its surroundings. She was probably right. At any rate she showed no sign of developing rabies.

There were dogs at Red Farm, and there were horses to be driven and ridden. Annie had learned to ride in Alabama; Captain Keller owned saddle horses as well as carriage horses. Helen had a pony, named Black Beauty after the horse in the book, which children still read and love, and she and Teacher would go off on long rides through the woods. Sometimes, when she was restless and unhappy, as she was after *The Frost King* incident, Annie would take wild rides by herself, recklessly jumping the horse over streams and gullies and fences.

Once during the Wrentham days (Annie and Helen rented a cottage at one of the nearby lakes and spent several summers there after they left Red Farm) someone gave Annie a horse of her own, a beautiful animal which she loved as though it were human. With a book tucked into the pocket of her plum-colored riding habit, Annie would go off by herself, and sometimes she would be found sitting up against a tree, reading for pleasure—which she was not supposed to do—the horse grazing contentedly nearby.

During this period, Annie was able for the first time to indulge her taste for pretty clothes. The income from the fund established by their friends in New York made it possible. Annie, still in her very early thirties, was small and slender. Even her scarred eyes could not completely mar the beauty of her face, the lovely wistful curve of her mouth. She knew how to select good clothes and wear them. Annie Sullivan had at last fulfilled her childhood dream of looking like the women in *Godey's Lady's Book*.

Helen celebrated her seventeenth birthday while they were staying with the Chamberlins. She had grown tall, and she moved with a kind of grace, Teacher lightly touching her elbow now and then to guide her. Her light brown hair curled in soft waves about her face, and one had to look at her intently before the realization dawned that she was blind. Her blue eyes always stared straight ahead.

Sometimes in letters to her mother or her sister, Helen would describe the new dresses she and Teacher had acquired. For instance:

"We've just had four lovely dresses made by a French dressmaker. I have two, of which one has a black silk skirt, with a black lace net over it, and a waist of white poplin, with turquoise velvet and chiffon and cream lace over a satin yoke. The other is woolen and of a very pretty green. The waist is trimmed with pink and green brocaded velvet and white lace, I think, and has double reefers on the front, tucked and trimmed with velvet, and also a row of tiny white buttons. Teacher, too, has a silk dress. The skirt is black, while the waist is mostly yellow, trimmed with delicate lavender chiffon and black velvet bows and lace. Her other dress is purple, trimmed with purple velvet, and the waist has a collar of cream lace. So you may imagine that we look quite like peacocks only we have no trains."

For Annie and Helen, however, life at Red Farm was not all good conversation, play, and dressing up in fine clothes. In February, after they had recovered from the shattering experience at the Gilman school, a young man named Merton S. Keith was engaged to tutor Helen for her college entrance examinations. During the rest of the winter, he came out once a week by train from Boston, twenty-five miles away. In the autumn, after a summer holiday, Annie and Helen moved into an apartment in Cambridge, and he came every day, five days a week.

Those weekly tutoring sessions at Red Farm were long, three hours and a half at a stretch. All three of the participants would be exhausted at the end. It was slow, laborious work, for Mr. Keith did not know the manual alphabet, and Teacher had to spell everything he said into Helen's hand.

The great difficulty—and it was a great difficulty—was with algebra and geometry. Mr. Keith found Helen's preparation in history and languages, including English, excellent, but in mathematics it was practically non-existent. The fault was partly Annie's, partly Helen's. Neither of them liked math. In fact they detested it and could see no value in it. But Helen had to pass college entrance examinations in math to get into Radcliffe. So Teacher had tried to devise means of making her pupil understand a subject which she herself did not understand. For problems in plane geometry, she worked out a system with wires and pins on a cushion. But Helen got little out of it.

All that winter at Red Farm and the following winter in Boston, Mr. Keith toiled with Helen, trying to get into her head an understanding of algebra and geometry through Teacher's tireless fingers pounding in her hand. There were almost no textbooks to help her, and those that were available were not of much use. There are several kinds of braille, and some were printed in one kind and some in another.

In vain did patient, plodding Mr. Keith try to arouse in Helen and Teacher an appreciation of what he regarded as the beauty of pure logic in mathematics. But his persistence won out in the end, to a degree where he felt that Helen was ready to take her college entrance examinations.

During the spring while she and Helen were at Red Farm, Annie's eyes began to bother her seriously. Helen's work with Mr. Keith entailed a great deal of study, and too few textbooks in braille were available. Helen was studying advanced Latin and Greek, which meant that Annie had to spend hours poring over Latin and Greek dictionaries looking up words for her. Nothing could have been worse for her eyes.

They finally became so bad that she went to New York to consult a specialist, who told her that if she did not have another operation, she would lose her sight completely. But Annie did not think she could afford to have an operation because of the time that would be involved, as well as the money. Eventually Mrs. Hutton sent her to a doctor in Boston who treated her eyes. They still gave her a good deal of pain and fits of nausea, but she could see better. And so she went on with her work.

On two hot days at the end of June 1898, Helen took her final entrance examinations for Radcliffe College. Again there was the problem of finding someone to read the questions to her. Annie was barred from the room, of course. Mr. Keith thought this was unfair, but lest there ever be any question as to Helen's having taken them and passed them fairly, she and Annie accepted the ruling without question.

It was finally decided that someone should punch the questions out for Helen in braille, so that she could read them, and that this person should be someone who did not know her or had ever had any connection with her whatever. Eugene Vining, a new teacher at the Perkins Institution, who was a complete stranger to Helen, was selected for the job. He and Helen went to work in a small room, Helen reading the questions in braille and typing the answers.

They got along very well until they came to algebra. Helen had studied algebra in English Braille, but Mr. Vining used another kind, American Braille. This was not discovered until just before the examinations. Mr. Vining tried to explain the difference in the notations to her, but they were by no means clear, and Helen went to her examinations with a sinking heart while Teacher worried.

Somehow she got through with them and passed. In one subject, advanced Latin, she received honors. In theory, she was now ready to enter Radcliffe any time she wanted to do so.

But new difficulties arose. To get into Radcliffe, in addition to passing her entrance examinations, she had to be accepted by the Academic Board, made up of members of the faculty.

Months went by while she and Annie waited, at Wrentham during the summer and back in Boston in the winter, where Helen took more advanced work with Mr. Keith, which she did not really need.

There was a conference with Miss Agnes Irwin, dean of Radcliffe, who tried to persuade Helen to give up the idea of taking her degree. She suggested that Helen take a few special courses in English and creative writing. But these would not lead to a diploma signed by the president of Harvard.

To Annie it did not seem so important that Helen get her diploma as it did to Helen. And some of their friends and backers thought it was foolish for her to try. No blind-deaf person had ever gone to college before, let alone trying for a diploma. Teacher pointed out some of the difficulties to her.

"You'll be competing," she said, "with some of the brightest young women in the country. They've got to be good to get into Radcliffe. And they will not be blind or deaf. You did very well at Mr. Gilman's school the first year. But Radcliffe will be more difficult. You must understand that no allowance will be made for you because of your handicap."

"Of course I understand," Helen told her. "But I think I can do it. At least I can try."

Word got around the country that Radcliffe did not want Helen Keller. It made some people angry. And two universities tried to make amends. Cornell and the University of Chicago both invited her to come to them. But Helen turned them down. She had made up her mind that she was going to Radcliffe and would receive a diploma signed by the president of Harvard University, and nobody could make her change it.

Finally she sat down at her typewriter and wrote a letter to the chairman of the Academic Board of Radcliffe College:

> Dear Sir:
>
> As an aid to me in determining my plans for study the coming year, I apply to you for information as to the possibility of my taking the regular course in Radcliffe College.
>
> Since receiving my certificate of admission to Radcliffe last July, I have been studying with a private tutor Horace, Aeschylus, French, German, Rhetoric, English History, English Literature and Criticism, and English Composition.
>
> In college I should wish to continue most if not all of these subjects. The conditions under which I work require the presence of Miss Sullivan, who has been my teacher and companion for thirteen years, as an interpreter of oral speech and as a reader of examination papers. In college she, or possibly in some subjects someone else, would of necessity be with me in the lecture room and at recitations. I should do all my written work on a typewriter, and if a professor could not understand my speech, I could write out my answers to his questions and hand them to him after the recitation.
>
> Is it possible for the College to accommodate itself to these unprecedented conditions, so as to enable me to pursue my studies at Radcliffe? I realize that the obstacles in the way of my receiving a college education are very great—to others they may seem insurmountable; but, dear Sir, a true soldier does not acknowledge defeat before the battle.

Her letter was dated May 5, 1900. More than a month later, she still had not heard from the Academic Board. In a letter to Mrs. Hutton, Helen commented on the offers from Cornell and the University of Chicago.

"But if I went to any other college," she wrote, "I am afraid it would be thought that I did not pass my examinations for Radcliffe satisfactorily."

She was finally accepted, and that fall, aged twenty, she entered Radcliffe College.

There was a lot of publicity about it, but Annie, probably from force of habit, did not mention it to Helen. A couple of days after college opened, Helen Keller was elected vice president of the freshman class. She was very much surprised.

"I didn't think most of the girls would even know I was alive!" she told Annie.

CHAPTER 13

Radcliffe

FOR HELEN Keller, the day she became a student at Radcliffe College was one of the proudest and happiest days of her life. Whatever misgivings Annie Sullivan may have had were shoved into the background as she watched the radiant expression on Helen's face.

They moved into a small house in Cambridge, with an Irish maid, Bridget Crimmins, to keep house for them. Annie grew very fond of Bridget, partly for Bridget's own sake and partly because she reminded her of Maggie Carroll, who had read the lives of the saints to her when she was a child at Tewksbury.

Right at the start it became apparent that the load on Annie's eyes was going to be heavier than it had ever been before. There were practically no college textbooks printed in braille. At great expense, Colonel Rogers, their millionaire friend, and Mr. Wade, the magazine publisher at whose home they had stayed in Pennsylvania, had some printed especially for Helen. But the process was slow, and she and Annie usually did not know far enough ahead what they would need for them to be printed in time to be of much use.

More scar tissue had formed on Annie's eyes. Her vision was

so limited that she had to hold the book almost up to the tip of her nose and move her head from side to side as she read. But there was neither money nor time for an operation, she insisted, and her worried friends could do nothing with her. When college opened, the eyes had had some rest. Annie and Helen had spent the summer in a cottage by a lake in Wrentham. So Annie went doggedly about her task.

Helen started out taking French, German, history, English composition, and English literature. French and German caused Annie her greatest difficulty, especially German printed in strange Gothic type. There were few foreign language dictionaries printed in braille. Later in her college course, Helen read Homer's *Iliad*, which is not even in classical Greek, with which she was fairly familiar, but in archaic Greek. The difference between archaic Greek and classical Greek would correspond roughly to the difference between Chaucer and Shakespeare!

A strange fact was that, after all the painful hours she spent looking up words for Helen in foreign language dictionaries—Greek, Latin, French, German—Annie never learned a foreign language herself. She had already had to learn the German and Greek alphabets. For endless hours, for eight years, while Helen was preparing for college and in college, Annie spelled strange foreign words into Helen's palm. But none of them ever stuck to her fingers.

Helen's other subjects, especially English literature, were a delight to Annie. But the burden on her eyes was heavy. For instance, in the Elizabethan period in English literature only the plays of Shakespeare and Spencer's *Faerie Queen* were obtainable in braille.

As Helen advanced toward her junior and senior years, some of the subjects she took must have been heavy going for Annie—medieval Latin, for instance, and a course in philosophy under the distinguished Professor Josiah Royce. But Helen also took a course in Shakespeare under Professor George L. Kittredge, probably the most celebrated Shakespearean scholar of his day. And Shakespeare, to Annie, was a greatly loved old friend, whom she had first come to know during her school days at the Perkins Institution for the Blind.

Tired as she must have been many times—times when her fingers moved mechanically, letter by letter, while her weary mind did not take in what they were spelling—a good deal of the learning Helen was acquiring must have rubbed off on Annie. In later life, her speech and the letters she wrote indicated that she was indeed a very well-educated person.

Her days were long and crowded with work. Until near the end of Helen's sophomore year, when Annie's eyes became so bad that a part-time substitute had to be found, she attended all Helen's classes with her, spelling continuously into her hand. In classes where there were recitations, this was not too difficult. She only had to make sure that Helen understood the questions. And sometimes, when the professor could not understand Helen's guttural, muffled speech, Annie would interpret for her. Only one of Helen's instructors, William Allan Neilson, who later became president of Smith College, learned the manual alphabet so that he could communicate with her.

Classes in which the professor lectured for thirty or forty minutes were more difficult for both Helen and Annie. All the other students took notes. Helen had to carry in her memory what he was saying as Annie's flying fingers spelled it into her hand.

Some of the professors were difficult to follow. They would speak rapidly sometimes, in a monotone and indistinctly. Beyond any doubt, Annie was more proficient in the use of the manual alphabet than anyone else in the world. And she had been spelling words into Helen's hand for so many years that she seldom had to finish an ordinary word. Helen would catch on after she had spelled a couple of letters. But keeping up with those professors taxed even Annie's skill, especially when they used strange, unfamiliar words. And she would be left behind. Annie never was very good at spelling.

After classes, they faced a mountain of homework. Books, books, books, and more books. Other Radcliffe girls, although the courses were tough, had time for play and occasional dating. But such things were denied Helen Keller. Homework for her meant hours and hours of concentrated attention to Annie's fingers moving in her hand. Night after night, hours after the other girls had finished their homework, had had a little recreation, and were in bed, Helen and Annie toiled on.

Helen was doing remarkably well in her college work. People marveled at her. She was like an airplane, sailing serenely, smoothly, effortlessly through the sky. And Annie was the hardworking, throbbing motor, unnoticed as when you watch an aircraft high overhead. Should the motor fail, however, the plane would fall crashing to the earth.

Summer vacations provided a wonderful relief to both Helen and Annie. One summer they had Helen's mother, her sister, and her young brother with them in a cottage by a lake in Wrentham. Annie loved the water, and swimming became one of her favorite sports. Like many inexperienced swimmers, she was inclined to overestimate her prowess.

One day she and Helen and Helen's brother Phillips were swimming when Phillips suddenly grabbed Helen's hand and spelled, "I don't see Teacher!"

Terrified, Helen sent Phillips for her mother. Mrs. Keller came rushing down to the dock, and within minutes some men who had been working nearby put out a rowboat looking for Teacher. They found her desperately trying to reach an island far out in the lake, exhausted and beginning to flounder. Seconds more, and they would have been too late. The swim she had attempted would have been a long one for even an expert. She had had a narrow escape, but the next day she was out swimming again!

One summer they spent at Halifax, Nova Scotia, where they did a great deal of sailing, which Helen thoroughly enjoyed. And there was a delightful vacation with Dr. and Mrs. Bell at their summer home on Cape Breton Island, Nova Scotia, where Helen helped Dr. Bell fly kites in an experiment he was conducting to discover the laws that would govern the motion of airships.

Annie, in later years, often said that the summer she and Helen spent with Dr. Bell was the happiest one she had ever had. The distinguished scientist was able to give her more confidence in herself than anyone else ever did. After she had recovered from her embarrassment at their first meeting, when he asked her what method she used in teaching Helen, and she could not answer him because she did not even know what he meant, she was always comfortable with him.

"I never really felt at ease with anyone until I met him," she once said. "I was extremely conscious of my crudeness, and because I felt this inferiority, I carried a chip on my shoulder which somebody was forever trying to snap off. Dr. Bell had a happy way of making people feel pleased with themselves."

She and Helen were about to take on a big job in addition to Helen's college work when a crisis developed with Annie's eyes. Helen had known for some time how bad those eyes were. She became so worried about them that she was almost ready to leave college.

Sometimes, Annie's fingers would spell into her hand: "I don't think you got that last paragraph. I'd better read it to you again."

And Helen would lie, saying, "Oh, yes, I did. I understood it perfectly."

But she had not. And her work suffered as a result. Finally, at Helen's insistence, Annie consulted a famous, and high-priced, eye doctor.

When she admitted that she had been reading to Helen five or six hours a day, he said, "That is sheer madness, Miss Sullivan! You must rest your eyes completely if Miss Keller is to finish her college course."

Fortunately, one of their young friends, Lenore Kinney, had learned the manual alphabet, and Annie reluctantly turned over to her some of the reading.

The new, big undertaking developed out of a course in English composition Helen was taking under Professor Charles Townsend Copeland, affectionately known to hundreds of Harvard and Radcliffe students as "Copey." In the beginning, he was not very well satisfied with Helen's themes. As much as possible she was trying to write themes exactly like those written by the other students, which meant that she was writing about a world with which, because of her blindness and deafness, she was unfamiliar.

One day he had her come to his office for a conference. "Why don't you write about things you know about?" he asked as Teacher spelled his words into Helen's hand. "Write about the world as it seems to you, the world you live in. Your childhood, for instance, that should make good reading."

So Helen started writing the story of her life, in themes, for Professor Copeland. He was so pleased with them that he showed them around to some of his friends, and one day Annie and Helen were awed by a visit from the editor of *The Ladies' Home Journal*. He had seen Helen's themes, and the magazine would like to publish them. They would need some editing and expanding, of course. The price he offered was so generous that it left Annie and Helen dazed.

Without realizing what they were getting themselves into, they set to work on their new task. But difficulties arose. The editing and expanding, which the magazine editor had mentioned so casually, involved a great deal more work than they had anticipated. And Helen's college work must not be neglected.

Unfortunately, *The Ladies' Home Journal* started publishing the story before work on the manuscript was completed. Annie and Helen were all in a state of panic when one day Lenore Kinney brought John Macy, a brilliant young Harvard instructor, to the house. He took in the situation at a glance, quickly learned the manual alphabet and went to work with Helen on the manuscript.

The Ladies' Home Journal had not finished printing the story when a publishing house, Doubleday, came along with an offer to bring it out in book form.

Most of the work on the book was done by John Macy, who also helped Helen with her college work when he could find the time. Included in the book, in addition to Helen's story as it appeared in the magazine, were a large number of her letters, written from the time she was a child until she was ready to enter college.

Also included were many of the letters Annie wrote to Mrs. Hopkins during the early days of Helen's education. Those letters really constitute the most important part of the book for educators, for they are the only day-by-day record of how Annie led little Helen out of her dark and silent world and set about the task of making her a normal, happy human being. Since most of the letters were later destroyed, those in the book are all that are available today. And on them is still based much of the teaching of the deaf-blind.

John Macy added a brief biography of Annie Sullivan, in which Tewksbury was not mentioned, and an account of Helen's education up to the time she entered college. The book came out on March 21, 1903, toward the end of Helen's junior year in college. Before it was published, her friend in Pennsylvania, Mr. Wade, had the entire manuscript put into braille, so that Helen could read it and make any changes she wanted.

The book was an immediate success, although there were some adverse comments from critics who could not understand why a person who was blind and deaf could have any conception of colors and sounds, as Helen indicated she had. In the years since it was published, under the title *The Story of My Life*, the book has gone into many editions and has been translated into almost every language known to man. It is still widely circulated and read. Helen Keller has written many books, some of which were highly successful, but none of them ever attained the circulation of *The Story of My Life.*

Once during Helen's college years, an attempt was made to divert her from her course. A well-meaning busybody, whose name has long since been forgotten, thought up the idea of having Annie and Helen head up a school for the deaf-blind in the United States.

At first the idea appealed to them. Annie Sullivan always felt a strong urge to help children who were afflicted as Helen was. And, as the whole world knows, Helen Keller has devoted her life to helping the blind and the deaf. Annie and Helen, however, felt that the project should wait until Helen had finished college.

The originator of the idea thought otherwise, and she went around to all those who had contributed money for Helen's education and tried to interest them in the plan. The school was to be called the Helen Keller Home. Some of them were not favorably impressed.

Dr. Bell was opposed, he said, because running a special school for deaf-blind children would cut Annie and Helen off from contact with seeing and hearing people. He suggested that an association for the deaf-blind be formed, with Annie to train teachers to instruct deaf-blind children in their homes, as she had taught Helen.

Finally a conference was called in New York, with Helen and Annie in attendance. When they were asked about the plan, they repeated their previous statement—that Helen should finish college first.

When Mark Twain, who was representing Colonel Rogers, heard that, he said "I don't know what the Lord's wishes are in this matter, but I do know that Colonel Rogers would not be willing to finance any of His undertakings on the recommendation of Mrs. —."

That settled it, and Annie and Helen returned happily to Radcliffe.

Ninety-six earnest young women in caps and gowns were graduated from Radcliffe College on a day in June 1904. One of them, a tall girl with light brown hair, received a great deal of attention. She was Helen Adams Keller, the first deaf-blind person to be graduated from college. All eyes followed her as she walked up to receive her diploma, signed by the president of Harvard University.

Nobody paid much attention to a little woman, not in cap and gown, but wearing a black dress, who sat beside her among the graduates, her fingers moving in Helen's hand.

Helen was graduated *cum laude*—with honor. The little woman in black was proud of her, but not quite satisfied. She had wanted it to be *summa cum laude*—with highest honor. And she thought it might have been had she done her job better.

CHAPTER 14

Enter Romance

ON THE day Helen Keller was graduated from Radcliffe, she and Annie, after the commencement exercises were over, took a trolley car out to their new home in Wrentham—the first home they ever owned.

During Helen's senior year, she and Annie sold some stock which their friend "King John" Spaulding had left them and bought an abandoned farm beside a lake.

The land, long neglected, had gone back into woods. The old farmhouse, large and structurally sound, was cut up into a lot of cluttery little rooms, as farmhouses were at the time when it was built. But Annie could see possibilities in it. So, carpenters, plumbers, electricians, and painters went to work on it.

The carpenters knocked out some partitions, put in more and larger windows. They made a study for Helen out of two pantries and a dairy. Across the front, on the second floor, they built a long balcony, where she could get some fresh air and exercise when the weather was bad.

Workmen cleaned up the woods and laid paths, along which they strung wires from tree to tree to guide Helen so that she could go for walks by herself. Landscape gardeners took over the grounds. There were some fine old trees near the house, and the lawn sloped gently down to the lake. Shrubs were planted, and a flower garden was started for Annie, who had learned a good deal about raising flowers from Helen's mother, in Alabama.

When they finished, they had made a beautiful home for Annie and Helen—a home which Annie felt provided a suitable background for Helen. It was a larger house than they really needed. Annie would learn later how much it cost to keep it up. They had undoubtedly spent more money on it than they would have spent if they had built a new, smaller house. But it belonged to them, free of debt, even though they would later feel the loss of income from the stocks they had sold.

From the beginning, the big white house was filled with guests. Helen's mother, sister, and brother came for the summer. So did Mrs. Hopkins, who had befriended Annie during her school days. As she looked about at all the splendor, Mrs. Hopkins could think of only one thing to say: "Oh, my! Oh, my!"

Another guest who came for long visits was John Hitz, the gentle old Swiss man who was Dr. Bell's secretary. Annie and Helen both loved him dearly. He and Helen would take long walks together—Helen, so tall, slender, and erect; Mr. Hitz, with his flowing white beard, quaint clothes, and bulging pockets, spelling German into her hand.

There were other guests, who came for shorter visits or only to dine—the Chamberlins and their friends, young members of the Harvard faculty Helen and Annie had come to know. Annie Sullivan had become a famous cook, having learned from Mrs. Keller's cook in Alabama how to prepare a number of delicious southern dishes. The house was filled with laughter and gay, witty conversation. And Annie, entertaining her guests, cooking special dishes for them and working in her flower garden, was completely happy. Her eyes, relieved from their heavy burden, no longer bothered her so much as they had while Helen was in college. She was able even to read for pleasure a little.

Other visitors came, uninvited. Groups of tourists, who wanted to see where and how Helen Keller lived. They brought picnic lunches, littered the lawn sometimes, and trampled on the flower beds. But Annie put up with them with what grace she could muster. They were the price of fame, and Helen Keller, graduated *cum laude* from Radcliffe College, was one of the wonders of the world.

As might be expected, fantastic stories were circulated about her home. One Swedish newspaper carried a story that the money for the house and grounds had been raised by national subscription and given to Helen along with an annual pension of two thousand dollars for the rest of her life. A French newspaper stated that "Boston, the most intellectual city, the Athens of America," had presented Helen with the house, "in homage to the young girl who had won a victory without parallel of the spirit over matter, of the immortal soul over the senses."

One of the guests who came most often was John Macy, the young Harvard instructor who had helped Helen with her book. For John Macy had fallen in love with Annie Sullivan.

For a year, Annie kept him dangling. She was filled with misgivings. First, there was Helen, who needed her constant care and attention—or so Annie was convinced. John would have to share her with Helen. She felt it would not be fair to him, and she could not believe that a marriage under such conditions could be made to work.

There was also the question of age. Annie was now thirty-nine. She was losing her figure, beginning to grow heavy. She still had beautiful clothes and knew how to wear them. But John was only twenty-eight, nearer Helen's age. In fact, during their courtship a story got into one of the Boston papers that it was Helen he was courting, not Annie.

Helen became involved in the arguments. One night she said to Annie, "If you love John and let him go, I shall feel like a hideous accident."

Finally Annie said, "Yes," but even after that she changed her mind so many times that John suggested that they have printed on the wedding invitations, "Subject to change without notice."

Annie and John were married on May 2, 1905, in the living room of the home in Wrentham. It was a small wedding. Members of John's family were there, Mrs. Keller, Mrs. Hopkins, Mr. Hitz, Lenore Kinney, who had read to Helen at Radcliffe when Annie's eyes gave out, and Lenore's husband, Philip Smith. They assembled at noon for lunch, which Annie had helped to prepare. She had baked the wedding cake herself.

At two o'clock they moved into the living room, where Annie and John took their places before a large window filled with flowers and ferns. There was no best man. Helen stood beside Annie, and, next to Helen, Lenore Kinney, spelling the words of the service into her hand. Helen's distant cousin, the distinguished author and clergyman, Dr. Edward Everett Hale, officiated.

It was Annie's wedding, but everybody was watching Helen and thinking about her. Even as a bride, Annie played a secondary role to her famous pupil. The following day, Dr. Hale wrote Helen a letter, in which he said:

"The tie between you and our dear Annie is as close as any tie can possibly be. I dare say plenty of people have told you that there is nothing like it in history or literature. You do not care anything about that. You know just how much she loves you and how much you love her. Now bear in mind that love is not measured in pints or pecks. It is infinite in all its relations. And never permit yourself for an instant to think that Annie loves you less than she ever did, or that the tie to her husband can tempt her to love you less. She will love you more."

Later in his letter, Dr. Hale suggested that Helen might not need that advice. And he was right. She never resented John Macy, but welcomed him into the family as a dearly loved brother. Nor did John Macy resent Helen. They remained friends as long as he lived.

After the marriage, life in the Wrentham household went on for a time as it had before—gay, carefree, with guests in and out, a gracious way of living, which Annie Sullivan, as a little girl at Tewksbury, had dimly imagined the women in *Godey's Lady's Book* enjoyed.

Some decision had to be made about Helen's future, however. It had always been her intention to support herself after she finished college. Otherwise, she thought, there would have been no use in her going to college. At one time she thought of doing settlement work.

Not long after Helen finished college, she received a letter from Andrew Carnegie, the steel magnate, offering her a pension of five thousand dollars a year for life. But Helen wrote him a polite letter turning it down.

"I intend to earn my living," she proudly announced.

To Annie and to John Macy, it was perfectly apparent that the way for Helen to support herself was by writing.

CHAPTER 15

Wanderers

THERE WERE a few happy, carefree years at Wrentham—four or five in all—before it became apparent that Helen Keller was not going to be able to earn her living as a professional writer.

The situation was complicated by the fact that through her earnings, she must also support her teacher. So long as she remained constantly at Helen's side, Annie had no way of earning money independently from Helen. In the past she had received some tempting offers, but these were no longer forthcoming. And anyway, to leave Helen was unthinkable.

By 1912, eight years after Helen finished college, she and Annie were having a hard time making ends meet. Before her marriage, Annie, who was as innocent about business affairs as a baby, had made a disastrous investment in a coal mine that never amounted to anything. This, with the loss of income from the stocks they had sold to build their home, had reduced their financial backlog almost to the vanishing point. They had nothing except the diminishing royalties from Helen's books. The house at Wrentham was expensive to keep up, and the demands on Helen to help the needy blind were heavy. They had reached the point where they had to look to John for help, and the income he received from his books and articles, brilliant and scholarly though they were, was not large.

Annie was not well. She worried constantly over their financial situation, the cost of keeping up their home, their dependence on John. And always she carried a heavy load of work, trying to keep up with Helen's mail, working to improve her speech. The housework had become a burden to her.

At the time there appeared to be some possibility of doing something about Helen's speech. Three years earlier, in 1910, she had met Charles White, of the Boston Conservatory of Music. Mr. White believed that the monotonous, guttural tones she produced could be changed into something more normal, and he started giving her voice lessons, without pay. For three years he worked with her. In the end there was some slight improvement, but Helen Keller's voice would always remain flat and dull, without inflection, and her words so muffled that it was difficult for strangers to understand her.

Those voice lessons were extremely important to Helen, for in the back of her mind she had an idea. Since she could not earn her living as a writer, she could think of only one possible way of supporting herself and Teacher. This would be by paid lectures if her speech improved as much as she hoped it would. If it did not—and as it turned out, she was disappointed—the only way she could lecture would be with Teacher at her side to interpret for her. For a long time, she did not mention her idea to Annie.

In September 1912, matters in the household at Wrentham reached a crisis. Annie was taken to a hospital for a major operation. She was critically ill, and the outcome was uncertain. John, who had taken a job as a secretary to the mayor of Schenectady, New York, resigned and returned home to be with her. And Helen, frantic with worry and desperately lonely, was sent to Washington to stay with Lenore Kinney and her husband.

In three weeks Annie was back home, her condition somewhat

improved, but the doctors told her she would have to take a long rest and be careful for at least a year.

By this time, with hospital and doctors' bills to be paid, the situation was so bad that something had to be done about it—and quickly. Helen told Annie about her plan.

Helen had received an offer to make a paid lecture in Montclair, New Jersey. She had received such offers many times before, but she and Annie had always rejected them as impossible. Annie had been out of the hospital for less than four months when she and Helen went to Montclair for Helen's first paid lecture.

It was a most trying experience for both of them. Helen spoke for a few minutes about what it was like to be blind and deaf and made a plea for help for others handicapped as she was. Annie interpreted for her, sentence by sentence, and then gave a talk of her own, describing Helen's accomplishments and how she had achieved them. Helen left the stage in tears, thinking she had made a miserable failure, and Annie felt like weeping herself as she tried to comfort her.

To their astonishment, however, they were called back to the stage for several curtain calls. The audience loved them! Newspaper accounts of their performance were friendly and complimentary. The result was that Helen accepted several offers to lecture for pay the following spring.

Traveling was not easy for either Helen or Annie. Annie's eyes suffered horribly as she pored over the fine print in railroad time tables, and half the time she would get them mixed up. Handling money was difficult for her, and more than once she gave enormous tips because she had not distinguished a five-dollar bill from a one-dollar bill. Guiding Helen around the streets in strange cities was torture. She would hesitate for a long time on curbs, looking in both directions, and even then vehicles would sometimes come bearing down on them from nowhere.

Helen, in a different hotel every night, was completely lost. To move about freely and with confidence, as she did in her own home, she had to know exactly where everything was. In a strange hotel room, she had to find her way about, running into furniture, stumbling over things. If someone carelessly moved any of her belongings—her braille slate, for instance—it could take her hours to find it. When Annie was not with her, she could only sit, helpless and completely alone.

But the lectures were highly successful, and somehow the two of them managed until one dreadful April night in Bath, Maine. Annie had a bad cold, which kept getting worse, and after the lecture that night she could barely drag herself and Helen back to their hotel. The cold had developed into a severe case of influenza, and during the night her temperature skyrocketed, and she became delirious.

Helen could do nothing except sit by her bed, gripping her hand, from which she got no response. Even if she could have found the telephone—and she did not dare leave Annie's side—she would have been unable to make herself understood. For her to find her way through a maze of hotel corridors and down to the desk clerk in the lobby was impossible.

Finally, in the morning, Annie roused herself enough to reach the telephone and call for help. Several days later two weary, frightened women made their way back to Wrentham. Never again did they try to go on a trip alone. And Helen swallowed her pride and wrote to Andrew Carnegie, accepting his proffered pension.

A few weeks later, in May 1914, John Macy sailed for Europe. It was the beginning of a rift between Annie and John that would widen and become permanent. All three of them—Annie, John, and Helen—would always remain reticent about the break. Both Annie and John insisted that Helen was in no way involved, and years later, long after the rift had become permanent, Annie, who was ill, begged Helen to turn to John for help if she did not recover. There was never a divorce, and he sometimes came to see them long after they had left Wrentham.

Money was needed, and so in the autumn of 1913, only a few months after that bad night in Bath, Maine, Annie and Helen accepted an offer from the Pond Lecture Bureau and again took to the road. But this time they were not alone. Helen's mother went with them on this and several succeeding trips, to Annie's enormous relief.

From the beginning, the lectures were tremendously successful. In Washington, Helen was introduced to the audience by Dr. Bell and in New Haven, Connecticut, by former President William Howard Taft, who was then teaching at Yale University. On that trip, Annie and Helen met Thomas A. Edison, Henry Ford, and the great tenor, Enrico Caruso. The audiences were large and enthusiastic, and the lecture bureau was delighted. In January 1914, Annie, Helen, and Mrs. Keller set out on another trip, all the way across the United States and up into Canada.

They had their program for the audiences well worked out by this time. Helen would talk for fifteen or twenty minutes, Annie translating what she said, sentence by sentence. At the end of fifteen or twenty minutes, the audience would begin to grow tired and restless because of the strain of trying to follow Helen. Then Annie would take over. This meant that Annie would fill a greater part of the program than Helen did, but people who would never have bought tickets to see and hear Annie alone listened with interest.

Annie talked about Helen, of course. Over and over, night after night, she assured them that Helen Keller was no genius, that she had worked hard for everything she had achieved. People didn't want to hear that, and they didn't believe her. Helen Keller, to them, was the "wonder child" grown up. It was impossible for them to think of her any other way.

Annie also talked about her theories of education. She thought it was a mistake to try to fit every child into a mold and to try to force him to learn things for which he had no aptitude or interest.

"But freedom," she would say, "does not mean that he should be allowed to grow like a weed or a barbarian. Nothing worthwhile is ever got without effort. I am thoroughly convinced that the child must not have forced upon him things he is not interested in because he is not ready for them. I am equally certain that learning must not be merely haphazard play. He must not nibble the sweets and leave out the substance.

"There must be coherence and an effective process of stimulating his pleasure in a given subject until he has gained the mental discipline necessary to pursue it further. Joyous freedom must be wedded to accuracy and clear understanding, through which come self-discipline and self-control. The teacher must not let him scatter his efforts, his will and his curiosity by studying in a careless, inattentive manner. The true function of the teacher is to keep him interested."

One of the most celebrated teachers of that period was the Italian Madame Maria Montessori, regarded as a pioneer both in modern education and for her work with "defective" children. She and Annie were on the platform together at a meeting of educators in San Francisco in the summer of 1915.

"I have been called a pioneer," Madame Montessori said, "but there"—pointing dramatically at Annie—"is your pioneer!"

Back and forth, up and down the country they traveled all through the late winter and spring of 1914—Annie, Helen, and Mrs. Keller. Some of their trips were badly planned. They would find themselves riding all night in a day coach, arriving in some town at dawn, with nobody to meet them. One strange hotel after another, some of them uncomfortable and dirty. Tiresome banquets, with the same poorly cooked chicken, carrots and peas, lettuce dressed with vinegar and little oil, tasteless brick ice cream, the dishes that were supposed to be hot more than half cold, the ice cream melting as much as it could with all the gelatin it contained. Always there were reporters, many of them with stupid, prying questions, and photographers with flashlights. In those days, photographers did not use bulbs as they do now. They exploded black powder in a little metal trough, with a deafening bang and a lot of smoke.

Helen worried about Annie's health. In a letter she wrote:

"I really wonder how Teacher is able to go on. She is very, very tired, although she will NOT admit it. At times she trembles so much that we marvel when she gets through the lecture, and nothing happens."

They were in Buffalo in May when Annie did not see a short flight of stairs, fell, and broke her arm at the elbow. Her vision had become so poor that she needed to be guided almost as much as Helen did. She also had high blood pressure and frequent colds that left her with a cough.

From Buffalo, Mrs. Keller accompanied them back to Wrentham and left them there, two lonely women in a big house that seemed unbearably empty. For company they had only Thora, Helen's Great Dane. Annie, with her fondness for dogs, treated Thora as though she were a human being.

Late that summer, Polly Thomson entered their lives, one of the rarest pieces of good fortune they would ever know. Because of the money they made on the lecture tours, their financial situation had eased somewhat, and they looked around for a secretary. Mrs. Keller, no longer young, could not go on traveling with them forever. She made her home with Helen's sister, Mildred, who was married and living in Montgomery, Alabama.

Polly's home was in Scotland, and she had come over to visit some relatives near Boston, when somebody brought her to see Annie and Helen. Polly was in her twenties and had taken a secretarial course in Scotland. She was sturdy and practical, with a sense of humor and a Scottish burr that won Annie's heart immediately. She had heard of Helen Keller, but knew little about her and had never had any association with the blind or the deaf. But she took the job and in a thoroughly businesslike manner set about learning the manual alphabet and straightening out Annie's and Helen's checkbooks, which had not been balanced in years. Her "visit" to the United States was to last for more than forty years. For she stayed on with Helen and traveled all over the world with her after Teacher died, until her own death in 1960.

Polly came to Annie and Helen a few months after the outbreak of World War I in Europe. Annie thought there might not be any more demand for the lectures because of the war, but the Pond Lecture Bureau thought otherwise, and the trips continued, with Polly's keen brown eyes guiding Annie and Helen through traffic, reading time tables, watching over their money, and doing a thousand and one things to make them comfortable and happy.

"How did we ever get along without her?" Annie used to ask Helen.

The lectures were successful, both financially and in the continuous ovations they brought to Helen. But by late 1915, Annie and Helen had become so interested and so involved in public issues that they could no longer bring themselves to go traveling about the country talking about education and the needs of the blind.

Helen was heart and soul in the women's suffrage movement. Annie did not go along with her on that. But they were both passionately concerned with efforts to stop the war. Helen, with Annie at her side, made two speeches in New York that labeled her as a pacifist. The audiences were large and enthusiastic. But the newspapers ripped her to pieces.

The following summer, 1916, Annie and Helen went out for a few weeks on the Chautauqua circuit, talking against war. The trip was a miserable, humiliating failure. By the summer of 1916, the American people were beginning to wake up to the danger of the war spreading from Europe over here.

Annie returned to Wrentham obviously a sick woman. The

cough that had never really left her had become much worse. It racked her whole body. And she had sharp pains in her side.

The doctor at Wrentham told her to go immediately to Lake Placid, New York. He may not have known that Annie's mother and her brother Jimmie had died of tuberculosis, since Annie still maintained secrecy about her childhood. But Annie knew.

CHAPTER 16
Winter in the Sun

ANNIE AND Polly Thomson took a night train to Lake Placid on November 20, 1916. Helen and her mother, who had come up from Alabama to look after her, saw them off. The following morning Helen wrote to her teacher:

"I don't know how I stood the pain of having you go last night. As we walked to the car, I felt suddenly overwhelmed with loneliness and nameless dread. It seemed as if some grim destiny would take you from me forever."

It may not have been a very wise letter to write to Annie at that moment, but it came from the heart.

The doctors at Lake Placid diagnosed the case as the doctor at Wrentham had expected. They took x-rays of Annie's chest and told her she had tuberculosis.

The area surrounding Lake Placid in the Adirondacks was at the time, next to Switzerland, probably the world's leading center for the treatment of tuberculosis. There were hospitals everywhere, filled with tuberculosis patients.

The prescribed treatment put the patient to bed for months, and in the daytime the bed would be wheeled out onto a terrace, even in the biting winter cold. The cure was supposed to result from prolonged inactivity, nourishing food, sunshine, and fresh air. There were no drugs available for treatment of the disease such as those used in recent years with some success, and the regimen imposed on patients was long and dull.

Annie was fifty years old when she went to Lake Placid. Although she could drive herself to lengths almost beyond human endurance for Helen, it was next to impossible for her to accept discipline from others—not even from doctors who were trying to save her life. She hated the cold, the other patients bored her, and she was as unmanageable as she had been during her first years at the Perkins school. And she was utterly miserable. In her letters, Polly told Helen, and Helen tried her best to cheer Annie up.

"I am grieved," she wrote, "to hear from Polly that you find it so depressing at Lake Placid. I don't wonder that you do, with such a trying combination of bad weather, medical bugbears, 'elderly, stodgy people,' and loneliness, and the worn-out feeling you speak of. But wait a little, and the splendid, silent sun shall pour its sweet balm upon you. Then perhaps the still, small voice in your heart will whisper a message of peace that you can hear amid the silent glory of the snow-robed mountains."

Helen had gone with her mother to Montgomery, Alabama, to spend the winter with her sister, Mildred.

"And there is a chance," she added, "of you spending Christmas here. We shall look for you and look awfully hard."

But nothing that the doctors or Polly could say and not even the prospects of being permitted to spend Christmas with Helen in Alabama had much effect. Annie Sullivan had always been a rebel, except where Helen was concerned. She could not resign herself to a winter in bed on a balcony surrounded by icy, snow-capped mountains.

One Sunday a small advertisement in the *New York Times* caught her attention. It contained a tiny picture of a beach in Puerto Rico, with palms in the background. It described the climate in Puerto Rico as "soft as June." In Puerto Rico there would be flowers, beauty, and romance.

When Polly came to see her during visiting hours she announced, "Polly, we are going to Puerto Rico."

There was a special cruise ship leaving for Puerto Rico every Saturday from New York. But Annie did not wait for it. She and Polly sailed on another ship the following Wednesday.

"It was an eleven days' sail," she wrote Helen from San Juan, "out of the snow, the piercing winds, and the leaden skies of the Adirondacks and into the sunshine of the southern seas. It seemed incredible, Helen! I had to pinch myself to see if I was awake or dreaming. There, beyond that narrow stretch of rippling, sun-warmed ocean, was Puerto Rico, like a great ship, afloat in violet waters!"

Thus began the longest period of separation between Helen Keller and Annie Sullivan as long as they both lived. It lasted four months, from late November 1916 until early April 1917, shortly after the United States entered World War I.

As always, with Annie and Helen, there were financial problems. They had made money on their lecture trips, but they had spent most of it. Helen later wrote that without Andrew Carnegie's five thousand dollar pension, the winter for Annie in Puerto Rico would have been impossible. That was the only time she ever hinted that there might have been a shortage of funds, either in her letters to Annie or in a book she wrote about her years later.

All that winter, Annie in her letters begged Helen to bring her mother and join her in Puerto Rico. Helen gave as her reason for not going her belief that Annie needed to be away from her, for a complete rest. She never mentioned money.

If Annie Sullivan had a dollar in her purse, she could not help spending it. She was like that all her life. But if Helen felt any dismay when Annie wrote her that she had had a chauffeur bring their car to Puerto Rico, she gave no sign of it. She was only happy that Annie had the car so that she could get out and take trips about the island. The only thing that mattered to her was that Annie get well. Since she was living with her family in Montgomery, she was undoubtedly able to keep her own expenses down.

She did write Annie that, after she was well, they might live more simply than they had in the past.

"I do think," she wrote, "that when you are better, we must start our life over again, reducing it to the simplest terms possible. (Of course the simple life does not exclude a few modern conveniences, or machinery that turns drudgery into joyous activity.) We can travel more as we like without lecturing, and we can see more of our friends. We can bring about this change anywhere—in Wrentham, or Puerto Rico, or the Sandwich Islands. All we need is courage to do the sensible thing. Don't you dare tell me it's too late!"

For fifteen dollars a month, Annie and Polly rented a four-room cottage, which in their letters they referred to as "the shack," high in the hills away from San Juan. It was set in a grove of orange and grapefruit trees, with a pineapple patch in front of it. It had no glass windows; houses in Puerto Rico have only shutters, to be closed when the hurricanes come. If it had any doors, they were wide open, for Annie wrote Helen a humorous account of oxen marching solemnly into her room and gazing at her "with deep pools of quiet in their eyes" while the little Puerto Rican dog she had adopted barked furiously.

All the winter there was a continuous stream of letters back and forth between Annie and Helen. Helen wrote on her typewriter. Although Annie's vision continued slowly and steadily to deteriorate, she was still able to read. But Annie had not used braille for thirty years. She had always detested it and was never very good at it. She had even forgotten the braille alphabet, and Helen had to send her a copy.

Her letters to Helen that winter were a labor of love, for, as she said, punching out braille for her was "like trying to punch a hole in the universe with a toe." But slowly and laboriously, with a stiletto that always felt awkward in her hand, she picked out long, beautifully composed letters to Helen. Not since the days when she wrote weekly letters to Mrs. Hopkins, during the first months after she had become Helen's teacher, had Annie Sullivan written so many letters. She could have used abbreviations, sloppy shortcuts, but she never did. Every sentence was rounded out, complete, and many of the descriptions of her beloved Puerto Rico were vivid and beautiful.

"The island is a dream of loveliness," she wrote, "a perfect riot of color, blooming trees and shrubs, roses, clematis, tree-like lilies, poinsettias, and many beautiful flowers I never saw before. But best of all, the climate is glorious, warm not hot. I mean it is not cruelly hot. There is always a delightful breeze from the ocean. The houses are painted all colors of the rainbow."

She and Polly, neither of whom spoke Spanish, had great fun making themselves understood by the Puerto Ricans, she said, "No matter what we say, they always answer, 'Si.' That means yes. They look bewildered when we shake our heads. The sign language is our chief means of communication."

In another letter she reminded Helen that John Bunyan had gone to jail rather than attend the parish church.

"And I'll be martyred somehow," she added, "before I'll return to the Adirondacks.

"I'm glad I didn't inherit the New England conscience. If I did, I should be worrying about the state of sin I am now enjoying in Puerto Rico. One can't help being happy here, Helen—happy and idle and aimless and pagan—all the sins we are warned against. I go to bed every night soaked with sunshine and orange blossoms and fall to sleep to the soporific sound of oxen munching banana leaves.

"We sit on the porch every evening and watch the sunset melt from one vivid color to another—rose asphodel (Do you know what color that is? I thought it was blue, but I have learned that it is golden yellow) to violet, then deep purple. Polly and I hold our breath as the stars come out in the sky—they hang low in the heavens like lamps of many colors—and myriads of fireflies come out on the grass and twinkle in the dark trees."

Having predicted, soon after her arrival in Puerto Rico, that it would be some time before she would be good for much, Annie seldom mentioned her health. But Polly kept Helen informed. Teacher was better, but she was still a long way from being well. Helen must have shown some concern, for Annie wrote her:

"Helen, you must not worry about the future. I am not going to die yet—I know that I am going to get well. I don't feel ill a bit. In fact, if it weren't for that horrid laboratory report, I shouldn't know there was anything wrong with me."

But in another letter, she wrote:

"You are never out of my thoughts. They keep me awake at night, and daylight brings no satisfactory answers to them. When I married John I thought I had solved the greatest of them. He promised me that, in case of my death, which in the natural course would come before his, he would be a brother to you, look after your happiness and take charge of your affairs. For years my mind was at rest on this—to you and me—most important of matters. But ever since he left us, I have worried.

"He seemed, and still seems, the only one to take care of you when I go. Perhaps, dear, it would be best all round to let him do what he can to make things a little easier for you when I am gone. He understands your business better than anyone else. And would it not be better in every way to let the suffering, the unhappiness that has come to all three of us die with me?"

Important events in world history were taking place that winter as the United States moved closer and closer to war with Germany. But Annie was almost as remote from them as though she were at the South Pole. She never saw any newspapers except when she and Polly went to San Juan, and then they would be several days old. She did not even have a calendar; all her letters to Helen were undated. She and Helen were still just as strongly opposed to the war and to our entrance into it as they had ever been. But while Helen fumed and fretted in Montgomery, Alabama, Annie contentedly soaked up sunshine and beauty in Puerto Rico. Nothing, except Helen's welfare and future, seemed to matter to her very much. Never before in her life—not even during the happy years at Wrentham—had she been so completely relaxed and carefree.

Annie had announced when she went to Puerto Rico that she would remain there until April. And when April finally came, she and Polly, with their chauffeur and car, sailed for New York where Helen and her mother met them. A few days earlier, the United States had declared war on Germany.

They went first to Wrentham, to dismantle their home and put it up for sale. Much as they loved it, the big house had long been a financial burden. Now, with prices going up on account of the war, they could hold onto it no longer. A big department store bought it and turned it into a rest home for girls.

The wrench of giving up their home took its toll on Annie. She was far from well when they rented a cottage by a lake in Vermont. By autumn she was feeling much better. So she decided to go back to Lake Placid for a check-up.

A very much embarrassed doctor told her, "This is one of those things that is supposed never to happen. Your charts got mixed up with the charts belonging to someone else. I am very happy to tell you, though, that you do not have tuberculosis. You have never had tuberculosis."

The joy which Helen and Polly experienced over the good news was not fully shared by Annie. She was constantly bothered by her failing eyesight, which made her move awkwardly and with a good deal of effort. She still tired quickly and felt far from well.

With the United States at war and with everything in a turmoil, it was impossible for Annie and Helen to think seriously of settling down in some remote place—Puerto Rico, the Sandwich Islands, or even California. Helen still hoped that she might use whatever influence she had to help end the war. So they went to New York.

They stayed temporarily in a small, inconspicuous hotel, looking about for a place to live. The headwaiter in the dining room told them he knew of a house for sale in Forest Hills, a suburb of New York. So they went out to look at it.

It was a small, ugly house in a poor neighborhood. But the price was within their means, so they bought it and set to work improving it as much as they could. There was a lot of "gingerbread" on it, and this they had removed. Ugly stained glass windows were replaced. The attic was converted into a study for Helen. And in the small, cramped garden, a row of evergreens was planted, so that Helen could walk back and forth behind them to get exercise.

Teacher could no longer see well enough to take her for long walks through the streets, and Polly, loaded down with secretarial work and household chores, could rarely find the time.

CHAPTER 17

Hollywood Adventure

AS ANNIE and Helen settled themselves, with Polly and a beautiful fawn-colored Great Dane, Sieglinde, in their new home in Forest Hills, their financial problems were still with them.

Andrew Carnegie's five thousand dollar annual pension could have supported them comfortably those days if they had spent it carefully and had no extra expenses. But they had extra expenses, some of them essential, most of them due to their inability to refuse pleas for help and to Annie's incurable urge to spend money when she had it, without thought of the future.

Polly Thomson was essential. She was supposed to receive a salary, and when Annie and Helen had the money, she did. When they did not, she worked without pay. When they could afford it, they had a maid, and Polly devoted herself to being a secretary and trying to keep their finances in order. When they could not afford a maid, Polly cooked and scrubbed and washed for them.

In her role as housekeeper when they needed one, Polly was even more essential than she was as a secretary. Annie's vision was so bad that she could no longer do much about the house. Helen had long ago learned to wash dishes and make beds, but naturally she could not cook or scrub or wash clothes. Seemingly, there was nothing Polly Thomson could not do.

Even with their reduced scale of living in the ugly little house in Forest Hills, Helen's pension could not cover everything. And since whatever they earned would depend on her, she desperately tried to think of a way to earn some money.

Her worry was deeper than that imposed by their present situation. It was a matter that had troubled her for some time, especially during those long, lonely months in Alabama while Teacher was in Puerto Rico. She knew that if she herself should die, Mr. Carnegie's pension would die with her. And then what would become of Teacher, getting old, in poor health, gradually going blind—and penniless? Helen's one ambition in life at that point was to find a way of earning enough money so that she could lay some away for Teacher.

Lecturing, as they had done it in the past, seemed to be out of the question. The United States was at war; people were deeply engrossed in a gigantic effort to win that war. Nobody was interested in hearing what Helen Keller had to say about the blind, or in anything else she had to say, for that matter. Least of all was the American public interested in what she had to say about the subject nearest to her heart, to find some way to end the war.

Briefly, Annie and Helen considered the possibility of going overseas to work with blind soldiers in the military hospitals. But the idea was hardly worth considering at all. They were both so handicapped that they would have been a burden to the military authorities, rather than a help. And Helen's reputation as a pacifist would very likely have made her unacceptable, anyway.

They were still working away, getting their new home in order, while Helen worried, when seemingly a kind of providence dropped a plum into Helen's lap. The plum was an offer to make a motion picture of Helen Keller's life.

It started with a visit early in 1918 from Dr. Francis Trevelyn Miller, who was writing a history of the world. He had had an inspiration, he said. A motion picture based on the life of Helen Keller and her long, heroic struggle through darkness and silence to achieve all that she had done might bring people to their senses, might inspire them to look for a way to peace instead of continuing the bloody struggle in the trenches. Naturally, Annie and Helen were very much interested.

Dr. Miller's idea was that money to finance the film might be raised by voluntary contributions from the public. But this idea was rejected by Annie. It would be impossible, she said, to raise the money that way.

They were about to abandon the idea when a widely known multimillionaire financier—whose name, at his own request, was never revealed—offered to finance the project. In high spirits, Annie and Helen and Polly, naively convinced that they were about to become rich, set out for Hollywood. The money advanced by the financier was a very large sum and for the next few months they lived like queens.

The undertaking ran into snags from the start. Before they left New York, Miss Elizabeth Marbury, one of the most famous theatrical agents in her day, predicted ominously that a commercially successful motion picture could not be made out of Helen Keller's life.

"After the scene at the pump and Helen's release, what do you have?" she demanded. "Nothing. No love interest. No drama. Nothing. Whatever happened—and what happened, I'll grant you, is magnificent and wonderful—happened inside Helen's head. You can't dramatize that. If you want a successful movie, you'll have to make up the rest of the story. It will have to be fiction."

This suggestion made Annie and Helen furious. If a motion picture was to be made, they insisted, it must be absolutely truthful. No fiction. No distortion of facts.

In Hollywood, the red carpet was rolled out for them literally. They were taken everywhere, met all the movie celebrities, including Mary Pickford, Douglas Fairbanks, and Charlie Chaplin.

They lived sumptuously, in a wonderful setting. One of the first things they did was to take up horseback riding—all three of them, with a groom for Helen. That entailed the purchase of expensive riding clothes. But they had plenty of money for once in their lives, no financial worries. Of course they might have laid some money aside for future use. But they did not. After all, they were going to be rich!

A child was engaged to take Helen's part in the early scenes, and young actresses were hired for the roles of the youthful Annie Sullivan and Helen Keller during her college days. The director was George Platt, highly regarded for his successful stage production of Maeterlinck's *Blue Bird*.

Production ran into trouble almost immediately because there were three different ideas as to what the picture should be. Annie and Dr. Miller insisted that it be a true historical record. Mr. Platt wanted it to be an artistic triumph. The financier, apparently thinking of Helen's financial interest, did not care what they did with it so long as it was a big commercial success. And nobody had complete authority.

The early scenes came off, as expected, with no difficulty. Everyone around the studio was thrilled. The scenes were beautiful and very moving. The scene where Helen spoke her first words, "I am not dumb now," was tremendously affecting.

But when they started getting into Helen's adult life, they ran into trouble, as Miss Marbury had predicted they would. They tried to develop a subplot, with love interest in it, but that did not work. Mr. Platt, apparently under the influence of Maeterlinck, worked out some elaborate symbolic scenes.

In one of them, Knowledge, represented by a beautiful maiden, wrestled with a monster, Ignorance, at the entrance to the café of Father Time for the soul of the infant Helen Keller. Then Helen, grown into womanhood and played by herself, appeared as the Mother of Sorrows before a large group of Hollywood extras representing suffering humanity. One scene had Helen galloping off somewhere on a white horse, blowing a trumpet and leading the world to deliverance. Helen named the picture. She called it *Deliverance*.

In the midst of all the difficulties, Helen surprised everybody by proving to be a really good actress, in spite of the weird things she was asked to do. Annie worked out a system of taps by which directions could be relayed to Helen as she or Polly pounded them out on the floor. Tough Hollywood movie people had tears in their eyes as they watched her. Nobody believed the picture could possibly be a failure. It was going to be a smash hit. It had to be!

At the studio, the film was still being cut and put together when Annie and Helen and Polly left Hollywood. They had to leave because they had run out of money and could not ask for more. In fact, they had to borrow money to get home. But they were not downhearted or worried. Riches lay ahead of them. They were sure of that.

They arrived home on the day after Christmas 1918, to a little house that looked not only ugly to them, after the luxury in which they had been living, but neglected and dirty. They had no more money, so Polly cleaned it up. And they settled down to wait.

The picture was supposed to be released in February, but it was not. Instead, there was a small private showing to which Annie and Helen and Polly were invited. Everyone agreed that the childhood scenes were perfect. But the scenes in which Helen herself appeared needed "strengthening" was the tactful word they used. More pictures were made, in New York, and again Annie and Helen and Polly settled down to wait.

They were still waiting in July, when Helen wrote her mother that the latest news was that the picture would open in a Broadway theater in October.

"That means," she added, "that we shall not receive our payments until then. We have been frightfully hard up, Mother. But we shall manage all right. Our credit is good, and people understand. Everyone believes in the success of the picture."

While they were waiting, Annie and Helen made a trip to Baltimore to visit the blinded soldiers in a military hospital called Evergreen. It was their first experience meeting young men newly blinded in battle, and it was hard on both of them, especially Annie, who could hear and who had some eyesight left. Blind men were everywhere, some of them mere boys, trying to accept the fact that they would have to spend the rest of their lives in darkness.

"Gee, Miss Keller," one of them said to Helen, Annie spelling out his words in her hand. "I read about you in school, but I never thought I'd be blind myself!"

The stupid things that some visitors said about the soldiers in their hearing—they seemed to think they were deaf as well as blind—infuriated Annie. Such remarks as "I'd rather my son was dead than blind," or, "What will he do when he goes home from here?"

Talking with the soldiers, Helen did not try to paint a rosy picture of the future. It was going to be difficult, she told them, no matter how they looked at it. They would have bad days, when they would feel terribly lonely, cut off from everyone. For such days, there would be only one cure—work. All of them were being taught to do things with their hands, weaving, making baskets, binding books, typing.

"And I can tell you from experience," she would add, "that each triumph brings its compensations."

Years later, during World War II, Helen and Polly would spend months again visiting blind soldiers in military hospitals, both here and abroad. Helen's speech was imperfect, but they understood her, and the inspiration she gave them, the doctors and nurses said, was beyond price.

In July, while they were still waiting for the opening of *Deliverance*, a friend drove Annie and Helen to Weston to see John Macy, who was ill.

"He seemed like a feeble old man," Helen wrote her mother.

"Something went wrong with his back, and that, with the heat, knocked him out, as he expressed it. He said he would come to New York as soon as he got back some strength."

Before returning to New York, they drove out to Wrentham. It must have been hard on Annie, although she apparently kept her feelings under control for Helen's sake. For Helen broke down.

"I thought," she wrote her mother, "I could visit the old Wrentham place with some equanimity, but alas! As we came away, I just sobbed aloud, greatly to my own mortification."

Annie and Helen returned to New York to find all the actors out on strike and the theaters dark. It was the beginning of Actors' Equity, the union to which all actors on the so-called legitimate stage now belong. They struck in the summer of 1919 to gain recognition for their newly formed union. Everybody was involved, from the most famous celebrities in show business down to the girls in the chorus lines.

Annie and Helen were naturally on the side of the striking actors, and Helen marched in the picket lines, along with the Barrymores, Ethel and John; Ed Wynne; Marie Dressler; and the distinguished baritone, John Charles Thomas.

With all the actors out on strike, the theater owners turned to movies. Motion picture actors were not involved in the strike. And one of the pictures they used was the Helen Keller movie, *Deliverance*. It opened on a wild, stormy night, August 18.

Box seats were sent to Annie, Helen, and Polly, but they did not go. Helen publicly stated the reason. The theater owners were using her motion picture as a strikebreaker! If they had gone anywhere that evening, they would have attended a gala performance which was put on by all the big Broadway stars to raise money for their strike fund. But the weather was bad; it was difficult for Polly to manage both Annie and Helen in large crowds, even under more favorable conditions, so they stayed home.

In spite of the weather, *Deliverance* opened to a packed house.

The opening night audience burst into cheers at some of the early scenes, especially the one in which Helen spoke her first words, "I am not dumb now."

When the newspapers came out the following day, the critics had given the picture what is known in show business as "rave" reviews. The *New York Times* called it a remarkable success, compelling. The *New York World* called it a masterpiece. One critic said it was far more absorbing than a love story. And ads inserted in the theater columns said:

"Strong men were moved to tears, children sat spellbound, women were torn with emotion, and all were awakened to a new realization of the possibilities of life."

When Polly read the reviews to Annie, who spelled them into Helen's hand, the three of them hugged each other in delight. *Deliverance* had come through. They would soon be rich. No more financial worries. Complete relaxation, with money for a finer house, a car and chauffeur, beautiful clothes, travel. Money to be put aside for Teacher. Money to buy presents for their friends and to give freely to people who needed it.

Deliverance lasted on Broadway a month, but there was never another packed house. Although Annie and Helen had no way of knowing it, the house that opening night must have been largely "papered," free tickets sent out to people whose influence might count. From then on, *Deliverance* played to steadily diminishing audiences, until finally it was taken off and sent out on the road.

It fared no better on the road. The critics may have liked it, as they obviously did. But the public did not. People went to the movies not to be inspired, but to be entertained. And there were plenty of more entertaining movies, with such stars as Norma Talmadge, Mabel Normand, Harold Lloyd, Elsie Ferguson, and the most famous "vamp" of all time, Theda Bara.

Financially, *Deliverance* was a complete and ignominious flop.

CHAPTER 18
Behind the Footlights

ANNIE AND Helen never received any money from their motion picture beyond the advance, which they spent in Hollywood. But *Deliverance* was not a total loss, for it opened a new way for Helen Keller to earn more money than she had ever earned in her life before.

As the weeks lengthened out into months after the Broadway opening, and no money was forthcoming, the plight of the three women in the little house in Forest Hills must have become more desperate than it had ever been before. Not only were they without any income, except for Mr. Carnegie's pension, but they were in debt. And always in the back of Helen's mind was the worry about Teacher's financial insecurity. More lecture tours seemed to be the only way out. But the lecture bureaus were not interested.

One day, when their finances were really at their lowest ebb, a young musician named George Lewis came to see them. Mr. Lewis, a war veteran recently discharged from the army, had written a song about Helen, which he called "Star of Happiness."

Young Mr. Lewis had not only a song, but an idea. He had seen *Deliverance*, had read the reviews after the Broadway opening, and thought Helen might do well on the stage. He knew more about vaudeville than he knew about any other branch of show business, and he suggested that she try to get a vaudeville contract.

Vaudeville those days was a very important part of the world of entertainment. There were two big chains, the Orpheum Circuit and Pantages. In nearly every city in the country, even in small cities, both had theaters, with the programs changing every week.

The programs were a kind of combination of the circus and the Chautauqua. There were animal acts, soft-shoe dancers, acrobats, Swiss bell ringers, and comedians. Some of the most successful radio and television comedians today—Jack Benny, for instance—got their start in vaudeville. People everywhere packed the vaudeville theaters. There were no night clubs to furnish entertainment back in the 1920s.

The Orpheum Circuit, the larger and more prosperous of the two chains, had recently introduced a new act. As headliners they were using opera stars, celebrated pianists and violinists, and noted speakers, and paying them salaries that compared favorably with those received by motion picture stars. Among the early headliners were the poet Carl Sandburg and Ernestine Schaumann-Heink, of the Metropolitan Opera and the concert stage, the most famous contralto of her day. Mr. Lewis thought Helen Keller could fill one of these spots.

Annie and Helen were shocked by the idea—Annie never did get over it—but in their need they told Mr. Lewis to go ahead and see what he could do.

Mr. Lewis knew two successful theatrical agents, Harry and Herman Weber, brothers. When he approached them with his idea, they were unimpressed.

"Vaudeville is entertainment," one of the brothers reminded him. "People go to laugh and have a good time. What's funny or entertaining about a woman who is blind and deaf? We could never sell an act like that."

But young Mr. Lewis was persistent. He made them read the reviews of *Deliverance*, containing some laudatory comments on Helen as an actress. And he finally persuaded them to go out to Forest Hills to see her.

They said later that what they expected to find was a gloomy household centered on a woman who could not see or hear. They got the surprise of their lives. Far from being pathetic, Helen Keller was a warm, gay, vital human being. She had poise and charm and a sense of humor that could not be obscured even by her imperfect speech. In a kind of daze, they found themselves offering to try to get her a vaudeville contract. After they left, they told themselves that she would either fill the theaters—or empty them. They were taking a chance, and they knew it. But the idea offered a challenge which they could not resist. Harry Weber became Helen's manager.

Before the Webers started trying to sell the act, they warned Annie and Helen that the audiences they would face in vaudeville were apt to be quite different from those they had encountered on lecture tours.

"They'll be made up of plain, ordinary people," Harry Weber told them. "They go to the show to have a good time. Sometimes they can be tough. If they like you, you'll be made. If they don't—well, we might as well bring down the curtain. I think they'll like you. If I didn't, I wouldn't try to sell your act. But I can't offer you any guarantee that they will."

His remarks did nothing to improve the morale of Annie and Helen, already jittery over the prospect of going into vaudeville. But they did appreciate his frankness. And they went along with him. They had no other place to go.

With Mr. Lewis, they worked out an act built around his song, "Star of Happiness." The Webers rejected it. It was too long, they said, and too elaborate.

"We've got to keep it simple," they insisted. "It can't run over twenty minutes."

When the Webers got through with it, the act was not unlike the performance Annie and Helen had given on the lecture platform, only it ran twenty minutes instead of an hour or an hour and a half. Also it had music—not Mr. Lewis' song, but Mendelssohn's "Spring Song," and a great deal of attention was given to the setting.

There were long, careful rehearsals until both Annie and Helen knew exactly what they were to do every minute while they were on stage. Helen had to know where and how she was to move. There could be no slip-ups.

The act was tried out on the night of February 16, 1920, in a small theater in Mount Vernon, a suburb of New York. The house was sold out. Many customers had to be turned away at the door.

When the curtain went up, what the audience saw was a stage set like a handsomely furnished drawing room. On the right, French windows opened out into a garden. On the left was a grand piano, on which had been placed a large, heavy vase filled with flowers. In the background were elegant velvet hangings.

Annie, wearing a beautiful new evening gown, came on stage first, a spotlight playing upon her. She walked down to the footlights, trying not to blink in the glare which hurt her eyes cruelly, and made a short speech about Helen. She told the audience who Helen Keller was—the Webers insisted that in some vaudeville audiences there might be patrons who had never heard of her, inconceivable though that might seem to Annie. She described Helen's handicaps and told them briefly how she had broken through the barrier that had cut her off from the rest of the world and how she had taught her. Then she retired to the rear of the stage while the orchestra played Mendelssohn's "Spring Song."

This was Helen's cue. Polly, standing with her behind the velvet curtains, gave her a nudge, and Helen parted the curtains and walked out onto the stage. Helen, tall, slender, and erect, was still an attractive woman at the age of forty. She, too, wore an elegant new evening gown. She looked like anything but a miserable, defeated middle-aged woman bereft of sight and hearing.

She stepped out on the stage right beside the grand piano. Resting her hand lightly upon it, she moved along until she came to the big vase. She was a little uncertain the first few times she did it before an audience, but later, to Harry Weber's delight, she became so sure of herself that she would keep time to the music a little as its rhythm reached her through the vibrations beneath her feet.

As Helen reached the vase, Annie stepped forward, and they advanced together to the footlights. Helen made a short speech about what a wonderful place this world could be if only people would work together and try to help one another. She and Annie had worked hard over her speech, and Helen hoped to be able to deliver it without having Annie translate it for her. But it was decided that this would be taking too big a chance. So Annie repeated it after her, sentence by sentence. When she had finished, the audience was invited to ask questions.

This was substantially the act as it was presented to vaudeville audiences for more than two years all over the United States and in part of Canada. From time to time, Annie and Helen changed their speeches a little. But the general outline and the setting remained the same.

The audience in Mount Vernon was warm, friendly, and enthusiastic. These people knew Helen Keller. She had lectured in Mount Vernon. But the big test was still to come. One week later, on a Monday afternoon, the show opened in the big Palace Theatre, on Broadway.

The Palace was the largest and most important vaudeville theater in the country. And a Monday afternoon audience, viewing a new show, was the toughest. Practically every actor and actress appearing in plays on Broadway would be there, along with the newspaper critics. If this audience rejected an act, it was doomed. Two more frightened women never appeared on the Palace stage than Annie and Helen that Monday afternoon.

The audience at their first performance at the Palace felt tense and uneasy. This audience did not need to be told who Helen Keller was. There were many present who had followed her career for years with interest and admiration. Many had heard her speak before, many had met her, and some were her personal friends. They wanted her to make a success in this new venture; they hoped she would, but they were doubtful. It was so different from anything she had ever done before. They listened with respect to Annie's little speech, but she was conscious of the uneasiness.

Helen, not yet sure of herself, shuffled a little, as most blind people do, as she moved along beside the grand piano. But once Annie had touched her arm, her confidence in herself began to come back. As they stood together behind the footlights, she became relaxed, calm, beautifully poised. There was a kind of radiance about her. As she started to speak, in her weird, guttural voice, a great surge of sympathy and admiration swept through the audience. Both Annie and Helen could feel it, and Helen finished her speech, Annie repeating each sentence after her, to great, crashing waves of applause. One of the critics wrote:

"Before she had been on the stage two minutes, Helen Keller had conquered again, and the Monday afternoon audience at the Palace, one of the most critical and cynical in the world, was hers."

Not only was the opening performance a tremendous success, but Helen Keller continued to "pack 'em in," as they say in show business, all the rest of that week and the next. The act was such a hit that it was held over for an extra week, something which did not happen very often at the Palace. After that, Helen, Annie, and Polly set out to tour the big Orpheum Circuit, her weekly salary running into four figures.

During the next two years, the act was rated as one of the biggest box office attractions in vaudeville. One tour lasted forty weeks and took them into practically every state in the Union. You could hardly name a city where they did not appear, and in many of them more than once. And always it was the same.

As Harry Weber put it: "Give her two minutes, and she'll have 'em eating out of her hand."

With Mr. Weber looking after them, there was no comparison between the comfort in which they traveled now with the discomfort they endured on the lecture trips. No more travel all night in day coaches, but drawing rooms and compartments on deluxe passenger trains. Always the best hotels, the best of everything. And instead of one-night stands, they would spend a week in each city, long enough so that Helen no longer had to sit alone, helpless, waiting for Annie or Polly to come to her, but after a couple of days could find her way about in her hotel room.

They had no sooner started on their first trip than yowls of protest rose from a part of the public, outraged that "dear little Helen Keller" was appearing in vaudeville with trained seals, trapeze performers, and Sophie Tucker, billed for years as "the last of the red hot mammas." It was all right and proper, that segment of the public thought, for her to lecture for a pittance in concert halls, churches, schools, and private homes. But to "make an exhibition of herself" in vaudeville—it was practically criminal.

For all of them Harry Weber had one answer: "Will you pay her what we do?"

The criticism did not bother Helen in the least. She loved vaudeville and everybody in it, including warm, generous Sophie Tucker, who took the trouble to show Polly how to apply stage makeup to the two stars. And even had the criticism hurt her, she would have gone on. For she was doing something she had wanted to do for years, laying aside some money for Annie. To do this she would have withstood any abuse, endured any insult.

It was a less happy experience for Annie. She was fifty-four years old when they had started their career in vaudeville. She was not well. In fact, she would never again be really well as long as she lived. Whenever she had to face the spotlight and the footlights, the stabs of pain in her eyes were almost beyond endurance. Gradually, inexorably, Annie was going blind.

She hated the sham, the cheapness, the petty jealousy among some of the performers backstage.

Sometimes discouraged young actors would come to her with their troubles. When they did, she would lecture them in her forthright manner:

"No matter what happens, keep on beginning and failing. Each time you fail, start all over again, and you will grow stronger, until you find that you have accomplished a purpose—not the one you began with perhaps, but one that you will be glad to remember."

Annie Sullivan knew what it meant to try and fail and try again.

CHAPTER 19

New Career

AS THE vaudeville tours continued, and the fund Helen Keller was building up for her teacher's security grew into a sizable amount, life became more and more of a burden to Annie.

She derived no satisfaction from the many compliments she received for her own performance. People told her that her voice was charming, and they would frequently say, "You always tell the story of Helen as if you were telling it for the first time."

How good Helen was may be judged from a letter a fellow vaudevillian, Carl Sandburg, wrote her on April 8, 1922, as her career in show business was drawing to a close:

> Dear Helen Keller:
> I saw and heard you last night at the Palace and enjoyed it a thousand ways. It was interesting to watch that audience minute by minute come along till they loved you big and far. For myself, the surprise was to find you something of a dancer, shifting in easy postures like a good-blooded race horse. I thrilled along with the audience to your saying you hear applause with your feet registering to vibration of the stage boards. Possibly the finest thing about your performance is that those who see and

hear you feel that zest for living. The zest you radiate is more important than any formula about how to live life.

But letters like that were few and far between. Her audience generally showed their admiration for Helen Keller by their applause and their interest by the questions they asked. Frivolous, sometimes stupid questions annoyed Annie greatly.

The question asked most often was: "Do you shut your eyes when you go to sleep?"

While Annie fumed inside, Helen would always act as though nobody had ever asked her that question before. She would look thoughtful, then smile and reply, "I've never stayed awake long enough to find out."

The vaudeville performances might not have been so irritating to Annie had she still possessed her own zest for living. But she was weary and far from well. She had always been susceptible to colds. They became more and more frequent, and she could not shake them off as she had been able to do when she was younger.

The pain in her eyes from the lights was almost beyond endurance. Eye doctors she consulted in various cities, trying to find some relief, told her she must stop at once. If she did not, they predicted, she would soon become totally blind. Cataracts had begun to form on her eyes.

Helen tried to persuade her to let Polly substitute for her, but Annie stubbornly refused. Helen was doing this for her. She must carry her share of the load. So she went doggedly on, tired, ill, in pain. No one could make her stop.

Finally in Toronto, late in 1921, she had to go to bed with a severe attack of influenza, and Polly took over temporarily. But as soon as she was able to stand up, Annie returned to the act, trying not to blink at the cruel, stabbing lights.

She gave her last performance one night in January 1922, in Des Moines, Iowa. A bad cold developed into bronchitis, and she lost her voice completely. From that night on, Polly took her place as long as the trips continued, telling in the third person how Annie Sullivan had led a little girl out of her dark and silent prison cell. Although Helen missed having Teacher at her side, she was relieved.

In the meantime, a large number of organizations devoted to aiding the blind had decided to get together and form a national coordinating agency to act as a clearinghouse for their efforts. In 1921, the American Foundation for the Blind came into existence, with M.C. Migel, of New York, as its president.

Looking about for someone to give prestige to the new organization and at the same time help to raise the money needed for its support, the Foundation naturally turned to the most famous blind person in the world, Helen Keller. She was an experienced speaker, and she had been demonstrating for years that she knew how to win the sympathy and admiration of audiences. For some unknown reason, Mr. Migel and his associates were unaware of what Helen Keller was doing at that time. Mr. Migel instructed his secretary to get in touch with her.

Annie and Helen and Polly were at home in Forest Hills between trips when one day the telephone rang. Polly answered it. She told Mr. Migel's secretary that of course Miss Keller would be very much interested in the Foundation and would like to help.

"But she can't do anything about it now," Polly added in her Scottish accent with a burr in it. "She is leaving tomorrow on a vaudeville tour."

The secretary was so shocked that she hung up without saying another word. Helen Keller in vaudeville! Unthinkable! For the time being, the Foundation abandoned its idea of using her as a shining symbol.

In the late spring of 1922, Annie, Helen, and Polly returned to Forest Hills to a house literally jammed with unanswered mail. They never had been able to catch up with it during the two years they were on the road, and now they must face it—thousands of letters. Letters all over the place, some of them a couple of years old, dusty, and smelling of mold. Something had to be done about them. Annie thought they should be answered.

While Polly did the housework (they could probably have hired a maid if Helen and Polly had been willing to dip into Teacher's security fund, but this they steadfastly refused to do), Teacher spent hour after painful hour going through those letters. Those that were important or urgent, Helen answered herself, but someone had to read them to her. Polly worked on them when she could find the time. But the great burden was on Annie.

Hundreds of letters were from children, many of whom had undoubtedly given up expecting a reply even if they remembered having written in the first place. They were the sort of letters children write to celebrities:

"I am fine. How are you? Are you surprised to get a letter from somebody you don't know? I am nine, going on ten. How old are you? Could you please send me your autograph? We have a Helen Keller club. Could you send us a picture of yourself? How did you happen to be blind and deaf?" And so on.

It hurt Annie not to answer them. She hated to disappoint a child. Friends urged her to throw them away and they did manage to destroy several bushels of them without her realizing it. But Annie read all she could, pausing frequently because her eyes could take no more punishment. Since it was impossible to answer all of them immediately, she stuffed them into filing cabinets, desk and bureau drawers, behind the books in bookcases. And in the meantime there was the current mail, always heavy, as it had been ever since Helen was a child.

For two years from 1922 until 1924, they toiled on, trying to keep up with the mail as it came in and at the same time to clean up the backlog. The only interruptions were brief summer vacations to get away from the heat, scattered vaudeville appearances, and speaking engagements. Helen was constantly in demand to address state commissions for the blind and advise them, always with Teacher's help, how to set up their programs and to plead before state legislatures for laws to prevent blindness in children from diseases like trachoma by providing proper medical care and to protect and aid the adult blind.

Finally, in 1924, the American Foundation for the Blind, having recovered from the shock over her appearing in vaudeville, again approached Helen and offered her a position with a steady income that would comfortably support the three women. Helen Keller, aged forty-four, entered upon a career she would follow for the rest of her life. Annie was fifty-eight years old.

The Foundation's immediate need was for money, and once more Annie, Helen, and Polly took to the road. Their purpose was to raise an endowment fund for the Foundation. Helen could have done nothing without Annie and Polly. And without Helen, there would have been no job, no income.

The drive had important support. President Coolidge became its honorary chairman; Henry van Dyke was its active chairman. Among the large contributors were Henry Ford and his son Edsel, John D. Rockefeller, Jr., Joseph Widener, George Eastman, and Felix Warburg.

But in their trips around the country, Annie and Helen aroused the interest of thousands of small contributors. Even school children gave their pennies. When they were not on the road, Annie helped Helen draft letters to possible contributors.

Helen's new career was to Annie's liking, although she herself did not enjoy asking people for money, even for someone else. The trips were not unlike the old lecture tours, only they were easier. They would stay two or three days in one locality, schedules were carefully arranged, and everything possible was done for their comfort. For a time, Annie seemed much more like her old self.

But her eyesight was slowly, inexorably failing, and by early 1927, at the insistence of her eye doctor and devoted friend, Dr. Conrad E. Berens, of New York, she had given up most of the traveling.

For some time Helen's publishers (Doubleday) had been trying to persuade her to bring her autobiography up to date with a new book. Soon after the New Year, 1927, Annie suggested that Helen take a year's leave of absence from the Foundation and write the book. Helen reluctantly agreed.

Before she started work on that book, however, a clergyman friend persuaded Helen to write a shorter book about her religion. She wrote it amid constant complications and interruptions.

In the spring, Polly left for Scotland on a well-earned vacation. Annie and Helen, with their Great Dane, Sieglinde, were alone in the house in Forest Hills. Helen did what she could to help with the housework, finding it a welcome relief from long hours at her typewriter. But Annie had to do the cooking. She managed largely by ear and touch. By listening intently, she could tell when the coffee began to percolate. She could tell when the toast was brown by the heat in it.

Their friends worried about the two of them alone in the house, and it was difficult to reach them. Helen, of course, could not hear the doorbell or the telephone, and half the time Annie did not bother to answer them. With Sieglinde in the house, Annie and Helen did not worry. Sieglinde was as big as a Shetland pony, and the sight of her and the sound of her thunderous bark would send strangers fleeing to the street in terror. Annie and Helen had raised her from puppyhood. With them and with visitors whom she knew, she was as gentle as a kitten. But to possible intruders, Sieglinde could be truly awesome.

Helen finished *My Religion* toward the end of the summer, before Polly's return, and Annie undertook to read the manuscript back to her. Before starting, she belatedly, and briefly, followed the instructions Dr. Berens had implored her to follow, giving her eyes a rest. He had provided her with some eyeglasses with powerful telescopic lenses. The lenses were so thick and so heavy that she could wear them only for short periods. She had not proceeded very far before even the telescopic lenses failed her. Annie could not read a word.

For a time she and Helen sat in stunned silence. Then Annie called Helen's publisher, F.N. Doubleday, for help. His response was quick and generous. He sent a young editorial assistant, Miss Nella Braddy, to the rescue. She read the manuscript to Annie, and Annie spelled it into Helen's hand.

Even before the work on *My Religion* was quite finished, Annie and Miss Braddy started gathering material together for the book the publishers had asked for, the book to bring Helen's autobiography up to date. It was a job before which any researcher would have quailed. They had to drag the material in bits and pieces out of filing cabinets so crammed that it was difficult to open the drawers.

Just as Annie had never kept any day-by-day record during the early stages of Helen's education, she had kept no record of the crowded years since her graduation from Radcliffe. There were no diaries, no scrapbooks, hardly any newspaper clippings. Even copies of the many articles Helen had written for various publications—some important, many small and obscure—were mostly lacking. There was a complete record of only one winter, the winter Annie spent in Puerto Rico. Helen had kept the letters she and Teacher exchanged that winter. Most of the book would have to be dug out of their memories—Annie's, Helen's, and Polly's.

Work on the book, which was called *Midstream*, began as soon as the manuscript of *My Religion* was sent off to the publishers. Nella Braddy was assigned to stay on with Annie and Helen until it was finished.

There were countless interruptions. While Helen was on leave of absence, she still owed some obligations to the Foundation. She and Annie were always available for advice and help.

Before the book was finished, Sieglinde died of old age, and Helen and Annie were so upset that no work was done for days.

And always there was the mail. Hundreds of letters pouring in as they had for years. Someone had to read them, sort them, and see to it that those that were important were answered. Polly returned in the autumn, took over the housework and answered letters whenever she could find the time. Nella Braddy learned the manual alphabet so that she, too, could communicate with Helen, thereby easing somewhat the load on Annie and Polly.

Hour after hour, day in and day out, Annie and Nella Braddy sat together, listening to the clicking of Helen's typewriter as she worked up in her attic study, while Polly busied herself with the housework and answered mail. Two people thrown together as they were either grow to dislike each other, or they become intimate friends. Annie and Nella Braddy became intimate friends.

Spending so many hours together as they did, it was natural that Annie should talk of the past. Nella Braddy was a sympathetic listener, and before the book was finished Annie had told her the whole story of her life, including the wretched childhood years at Tewksbury.

It was the first time Annie had ever told anyone about Tewksbury, unless, when she was much younger, she told it to Dr. Bell's gentle old secretary, Mr. Hitz. There is no record that she did, but once, probably during the early Wrentham days, she and Mr. Hitz made a trip to Feeding Hills, where she was born, and Annie tried to find out what had become of her sister Mary. Apparently she did not find out, although she and Mr. Hitz called on old Bridget Sullivan, widow of her father's brother. Annie did not reveal her identity, and only after she had gone did Bridget become vaguely suspicious.

Naturally Nella Braddy realized that there was a book in the story of Annie Sullivan's life. Amazingly, she finally persuaded Annie to let her write it. For years, Helen had wanted to write a biography of her teacher, but Annie always put her off, saying, "If you write about your life, you write about mine, too."

Once the decision was made to let Nella Braddy write the book, there was one thing Annie had to do. One afternoon in the autumn of 1930, she sent everybody out of the house in Forest

Hills, sat down alone with Helen and painfully spelled into her hand the whole story of Tewksbury, confessing that all the gay, enchanting tales she had told her about her own childhood were untrue.

Helen was fifty years old, Annie sixty-four. For forty-four years, Annie Sullivan had kept her secret from the one human being who was closer to her than anyone else on earth.

From 1929 on, Annie Sullivan made few public appearances, partly at the insistence of Dr. Berens and partly because it had become so difficult for her to move about in unfamiliar surroundings. She was clumsier than Helen Keller was.

That year, Dr. Berens removed a cataract from her right eye, and for a time she could see a little better. But she was as improvident with what was left of her eyesight as she had always been with money.

The printed word had become as important to her as it had been when she was a child at Tewksbury, where Tillie Delaney haltingly read aloud to her anything Annie could find. Helen, Polly, and Nella Braddy were forever finding her with her nose in a book and taking it away from her. Friends offered to read aloud to her, and sometimes they did, but it did not satisfy her. To enjoy a book completely, she had to read it herself.

She rebelled fiercely at her failing eyesight and her aging body. Annie Sullivan, who had so magnificently helped Helen Keller to overcome her handicaps, could not help herself.

At times she was unreasonable, bitterly resentful. After such outbursts she would apologize impulsively: "I have behaved like a naughty child and cried for the moon and disobeyed all my own injunctions to treat a handicap as an opportunity for courage."

Annie made one of her rare public appearances when in 1931, she received an honorary degree from Temple University, in Philadelphia. It was the only honorary degree she ever received, and it took Helen and the University a year to persuade her to accept it.

On December 17, 1930, she dictated to Polly a letter to Charles

E. Beury, president of the University, in which she declined to accept the degree and added:

"All the satisfaction that belongs to me—which I derive from the fact that I have discharged my duty toward my beloved pupil Helen Keller not unsuccessfully—I shall realize when she is honored."

Annie and Helen were to have received their honorary degrees together, and Helen, accompanied by Polly, went to Philadelphia to accept hers. A few hours later, Annie and Nella Braddy slipped quietly into Philadelphia and found seats far back in the audience.

After Helen had received her degree, the chairman of the assembly, to Annie's horror, proposed that a degree be conferred on Helen's teacher—"by force if necessary." He asked everyone who agreed with him to rise. Only Annie, embarrassed and miserable, remained seated.

A year later, only after the University authorities threatened to go to Forest Hills and confer the degree upon her there, Annie gave in and went to Philadelphia and accepted it. But she still thought she should not have done it.

While Annie felt guilty, Helen was happy. From the time she was a girl and realized that she got all the credit for her achievements, while Teacher got all the blame for her mistakes, Helen suffered over the injustice. She deeply resented any slight to her teacher, and there were many of them. There was little she could do to prevent them, however, since Annie invariably hung back when she tried to draw her forward and see that she got recognition.

Although she no longer went on tours for the Foundation with Helen and Polly and seldom appeared in public, Annie did a great deal of traveling in the early 1930s, all of it in Europe. There were three trips, in 1930, 1931, and 1932, and they were made partly at the urging of Dr. Berens, who thought the change and relaxation would be good for her.

The objective was always the same, to find some quiet, rural spot in England, France, or Scotland where they would settle down for a restful summer. But it could never be fully achieved. For Helen Keller had not been abroad before, and she was swamped with invitations, honors, and requests for speeches. She and Polly tried to spare Annie as much as possible, and they did manage to get in a few carefree weeks in a lovely cottage in Cornwall, in a village in Brittany, and in an old farmhouse in the Scottish Highlands.

By the end of the summer in 1932, Annie was so worn out and ill that Helen took a leave of absence from the Foundation, and they stayed on in Scotland through the winter. Doctors in Glasgow noted the fact that she was having some heart trouble. She would need a great deal of rest.

When they returned to Forest Hills in the spring of 1933, a solution was found to a problem that had worried Helen deeply. Her work for the Foundation required that she and Polly be away from home a great deal, always traveling and making speeches. Leaving Annie alone in the house in Forest Hills was sheer torment for Helen, even though Annie insisted that she was not alone. Three dogs had taken the place of Sieglinde—two terriers and another Great Dane.

Finally, when Helen was at her wit's end, a young man named Herbert Haas came to work for them. Annie liked him from the beginning. He was a cheerful young man, with a good sense of humor and a gift for telling stories. He could cook, take care of the house, look after the dogs, drive the car, and keep the household accounts straight. He knew how to fix typewriters and Helen's braille machine when it broke down. Not only did he quickly learn the manual alphabet, but he learned to write in braille, so he could copy articles Helen wanted to read. And most important of all, he could keep Annie amused by the hour with his droll conversation. Life in the house in Forest Hills was much better after Herbert Haas came.

Although she was far from well, and her eyesight was again

deteriorating in spite of all that Dr. Berens could do, Annie still had flashes of her old gaiety. She loved to entertain when Helen and Polly were at home, and guests who came were never made aware of Annie's failing health. Always there was good food, witty conversation, and two delightful hostesses. Only after they had left would their friends sometimes remember, with a kind of awe, that one of the hostesses was blind and deaf and the other practically blind!

Looking about for some new interest, Annie heard of a neglected blind and deaf baby girl in Kentucky. It took all the persuasive powers of Helen, Dr. Berens, and her other friends to keep Annie from adopting the baby and starting all over again with her, as she had with Helen. She was convinced that such a care and responsibility would somehow accomplish a miracle and bring back her old health and vigor. She finally gave in, but not without a struggle, and a home and another teacher were found for the baby girl.

By 1935, Annie's vision was again as bad as it had been before Dr. Berens removed the cataract from her right eye. To her, the obvious thing to do was to have another operation. But this time Dr. Berens shook his head. It would do no good, he said.

Weeping bitterly, Annie put her arms around his neck and pleaded with him to try just once more. He patiently and gently explained to her over and over again that it would not help her, but she refused to listen to him. Finally, he reluctantly performed the operation, and as he had predicted, it failed to help her. Annie Sullivan was as blind as she had been when she was a child at Tewksbury. Reading, which was the very bread of life to her, would never be possible again unless she read braille.

Helen Keller undertook to teach Annie to read braille, as Annie had taught it to her when she was a child. Annie had always disliked braille, and while she had learned again to write in braille the winter she was in Puerto Rico so that she could write to Helen, she had not read braille since the first successful operation on her eyes when she was fifteen years old. As hard as Helen tried, Annie was not a good pupil.

"It's not the big things in life that one misses through the loss of sight," she told a friend, "but such little things as being able to read. I have no patience, like Helen, for the braille system because I can't read fast enough.

"Helen is and always has been well balanced, in her blindness as well as in her deafness. But I'm making a futile fight of it, like a bucking bronco."

At times her rebellious spirit would flare up, as of old, and she would be angry and unmanageable. And again, to Helen, she would apologize: "I have wasted time grieving over my eyes. I am very, very sorry, but what is done is done. I have tasted the bitterest drop in my cup."

It was while she was in a hospital, recovering from an operation on her eye, that Annie Sullivan and Alexander Woollcott became friends. Alexander Woollcott those days was probably the most successful, respected—and feared—drama critic, columnist, and radio personality in New York. His merciless wit struck terror into the hearts of actors, playwrights, and producers.

But there was another side to Alexander Woollcott. He probably met Annie when he went to the hospital to see the movie producer, Samuel Goldwyn, who was a patient in the next room. He discovered that Annie had been sending all the big bouquets and plants she received to Mr. Goldwyn. Since she could not see them, they were of no use to her! So every day Alexander Woollcott would send Annie Sullivan a small, fragrant bouquet, something she could hold in her hand and sniff. Sometimes it would be a gardenia, sometimes a sprig of mignonette, sometimes some rose geranium leaves. And the little bouquets were accompanied by amusing notes.

Annie was shy and embarrassed the first time Alexander Woollcott came to see her after her return to the house in Forest

Hills. He made it very plain that he had come to see her, not Helen. And she could not understand why so successful and worldly a man should be interested in her.

But her shyness wore off after a time in her keen delight at his wit and his humor. He came again and again and presently began reading aloud to her. No one else had ever been so successful at reading aloud to Annie Sullivan. The visits continued for many months. For years, Alexander Woollcott kept on his desk a crystal elephant she had given him for being, as he expressed it, "a good boy."

In her restlessness and her rebellion against her blindness and her ill health, Annie often spoke longingly of Puerto Rico, where she had spent the winter when it was thought she had tuberculosis.

"If I could get back there, or to some similar place," she told Helen, "I believe I'd feel better. Puerto Rico did wonders for me that winter."

So in October 1935, Annie, Helen, Polly, and Herbert Haas went to Jamaica. While the others were enchanted with the palms, beautiful flowers and mountains, and gaily painted buildings, Annie was too tired to enjoy them, and she could not see them. They cut short their trip and returned to Forest Hills.

It was a busy winter for Helen, and she and Polly were away a great deal. Annie's interest in Helen's job and the work that was being done for the blind remained keen, and when Helen was at home, they talked a great deal about it. Annie regretted that more was not being done for the blind-deaf. But the training of a child who could neither see nor hear required service that was expensive and hard to obtain.

"What a blind-deaf person needs," Annie observed with a sigh, "is not a teacher but another self."

Annie Sullivan had been Helen Keller's "other self" for nearly fifty years.

Helen and Polly gave a birthday party for Annie on April 14, 1936, Annie's seventieth birthday. It was a festive occasion, and old friends heaped a great deal of praise upon Annie Sullivan. Some of it embarrassed her, and she did not take any of it very seriously, except Helen's toast:

"Here's to my teacher, whose birthday was Easter morning in my life."

That spring, Annie made one more effort to pull herself together. She thought a summer away from New York, somewhere in the mountains near a lake, would help her. Polly found a place in the Laurentian Mountains, near Quebec. But the trip was too much for Annie, and it was too cold. She spent most of the summer in bed.

They returned to New York in the early autumn, and after a brief stay in a hospital, where nothing could be done for her, back to the house in Forest Hills, which Annie would never leave again. Her tired heart was giving out.

For the rest of her life, Helen Keller would carry with her the memory of one lovely evening in October 1936. Annie was feeling better than usual and was able to sit up in a big armchair in her room. Herbert Haas had been to the rodeo in Madison Square Garden, and his amusing account of the show made Annie chuckle with delight as she spelled his words into Helen's hand.

Not long after that evening, Annie Sullivan dropped into a coma, from which she did not return. She slipped quietly out of this world on October 19, 1936.

Her funeral, in the Park Avenue Presbyterian Church, was attended by many famous persons. Dr. Harry Emerson Fosdick, pastor of the Rockefellers' church, on Riverside Drive, preached the sermon. Her body was cremated, and a few days later the urn containing her ashes was placed in the National Cathedral, in Washington, D.C., where rest the remains of Woodrow Wilson. It was the first time such an honor was accorded any teacher—or any woman. In the crypt beside the urn, space was reserved to receive someday the ashes of Helen Keller.

In March 1939, the *Atlantic Monthly* published an article by

Alexander Woollcott entitled "In Memoriam: Annie Sullivan." He concluded it with these words:

"At Annie Sullivan's funeral there could have been no one who was not quick with a sense of unimaginable parting which, after nearly fifty years, had just taken place. While I live, I shall remember those services. Not for the great of the land who turned out for that occasion, not for the flowers that filled the church with incomparable incense, nor for the wise and good things which Harry Emerson Fosdick said from the pulpit.

"No, what I shall remember longest was something I witnessed when the services were over, and the procession was filing down the aisle, Helen walking with Polly Thomson at her side. As they passed the pew where I was standing, I saw the tears streaming down Polly's cheeks. And something else I saw. It was a gesture from Helen—a quick flutter of her birdlike hands. She was trying to comfort Polly."

Helen Keller, 1909

THE STORY OF MY LIFE

by Helen Keller

CHAPTER 1

IT IS with a kind of fear that I begin to write the history of my life. I have, as it were, a superstitious hesitation in lifting the veil that clings about my childhood like a golden mist. The task of writing an autobiography is a difficult one. When I try to classify my earliest impressions, I find that fact and fancy look alike across the years that link the past with the present. The woman paints the child's experiences in her own fantasy. A few impressions stand out vividly from the first years of my life, but "the shadows of the prison-house are on the rest." Besides, many of the joys and sorrows of childhood have lost their poignancy, and many incidents of vital importance in my early education have been forgotten in the excitement of great discoveries. In order, therefore, not to be tedious I shall try to present in a series of sketches only the episodes that seem to me to be the most interesting and important.

I was born on June 27, 1880, in Tuscumbia, a little town of northern Alabama.

The family on my father's side is descended from Caspar Keller, a native of Switzerland, who settled in Maryland. One of my Swiss ancestors was the first teacher of the deaf in Zurich and wrote a book on the subject of their education—rather a singular coincidence; though it is true that there is no king who has not had a slave among his ancestors, and no slave who has not had a king among his.

My grandfather, Caspar Keller's son, "entered" large tracts of land in Alabama and finally settled there. I have been told that once a year he went from Tuscumbia to Philadelphia on horseback to purchase supplies for the plantation, and my aunt has in her possession many of the letters to his family, which give charming and vivid accounts of these trips.

My Grandmother Keller was a daughter of one of Lafayette's aides, Alexander Moore, and granddaughter of Alexander Spotswood, an early colonial governor of Virginia. She was also second cousin to Robert E. Lee.

My father, Arthur H. Keller, was a captain in the Confederate Army, and my mother, Kate Adams, was his second wife and many years younger. Her grandfather, Benjamin Adams, married Susanna E. Goodhue, and lived in Newbury, Massachusetts, for many years. Their son, Charles Adams, was born in Newburyport, Massachusetts, and moved to Helena, Arkansas. When the Civil War broke out, he fought on the side of the South and became a brigadier-general. He married Lucy Helen Everett, who belonged to the same family of Everetts as Edward Everett and Dr. Edward Everett Hale. After the war was over, the family moved to Memphis, Tennessee.

I lived, up to the time of the illness that deprived me of my sight and hearing, in a tiny house consisting of a large square room and a small one, in which the servant slept. It is a custom in the South to build a small house near the homestead as an annex to be used on occasion. Such a house my father built after the Civil War, and when he married my mother they went to live in it. It was completely covered with vines, climbing roses and honeysuckles. From the garden it looked like an arbor. The little porch was hidden from view by a screen of yellow roses and southern smilax. It was the favorite haunt of hummingbirds and bees.

CHAPTER 1

The Keller homestead, where the family lived, was a few steps from our little rose bower. It was called "Ivy Green" because the house and the surrounding trees and fences were covered with beautiful English ivy. Its old-fashioned garden was the paradise of my childhood.

Even in the days before my teacher came, I used to feel along the square, stiff boxwood hedges, and, guided by the sense of smell, would find the first violets and lilies. There, too, after a fit of temper, I went to find comfort and to hide my hot face in the cool leaves and grass. What joy it was to lose myself in that garden of flowers, to wander happily from spot to spot, until, coming suddenly upon a beautiful vine, I recognized it by its leaves and blossoms, and knew it was the vine which covered the tumbledown summer house at the farther end of the garden! Here, also, were trailing clematis, drooping jessamine, and some rare sweet flowers called butterfly lilies, because their fragile petals resemble butterflies' wings. But the roses—they were loveliest of all. Never have I found in the greenhouses of the North such heart-satisfying roses as the climbing roses of my southern home. They used to hang in long festoons from our porch, filling the whole air with their fragrance, untainted by any earthy smell; and in the early morning, washed in the dew, they felt so soft, so pure, I could not help wondering if they did not resemble the asphodels of God's garden.

The beginning of my life was simple and much like every other little life. I came, I saw, I conquered, as the first baby in the family always does. There was the usual amount of discussion as to a name for me. The first baby in the family was not to be lightly named, everyone was emphatic about that. My father suggested the name of Mildred Campbell, an ancestor whom he highly esteemed, and he declined to take any further part in the discussion. My mother solved the problem by giving it as her wish that I should be called after her mother, whose maiden name was Helen Everett. But in the excitement of carrying me to church, my father lost the name on the way, very naturally, since it was one in which he had declined to have a part. When the minister asked him for it, he just remembered that it had been decided to call me after my grandmother, and he gave her name as Helen Adams.

I am told that while I was still in long dresses, I showed many signs of an eager, self-asserting disposition. Everything that I saw other people do, I insisted upon imitating. At six months I could pipe out "How d'ye," and one day I attracted everyone's attention by saying "Tea, tea, tea" quite plainly. Even after my illness, I remembered one of the words I had learned in these early months. It was the word "water," and I continued to make some sound for that word after all other speech was lost. I ceased making the sound "wah-wah" only when I learned to spell the word.

They tell me I walked the day I was a year old. My mother had just taken me out of the bathtub and was holding me in her lap, when I was suddenly attracted by the flickering shadows of leaves that danced in the sunlight on the smooth floor. I slipped from my mother's lap and almost ran toward them. The impulse gone, I fell down and cried for her to take me up in her arms.

These happy days did not last long. One brief spring, musical with the song of robin and mockingbird, one summer rich in fruit and roses, one autumn of gold and crimson sped by and left their gifts at the feet of an eager, delighted child. Then, in the dreary month of February, came the illness which closed my eyes and ears and plunged me into the unconsciousness of a newborn baby. They called it acute congestion of the stomach and brain. The doctor thought I could not live. Early one morning, however, the fever left me as suddenly and mysteriously as it had come. There was great rejoicing in the family that morning, but no one, not even the doctor, knew that I should never see or hear again.

I fancy I still have confused recollections of that illness. I especially remember the tenderness with which my mother tried to soothe me in my waiting hours of fret and pain, and the agony and bewilderment with which I awoke after a tossing half

CHAPTER 1

sleep, and turned my eyes, so dry and hot, to the wall away from the once-loved light, which came to me dim and yet more dim each day. But, except for these fleeting memories, if, indeed, they be memories, it all seems very unreal, like a nightmare. Gradually I got used to the silence and darkness that surrounded me and forgot that it had ever been different, until she came—my teacher—who was to set my spirit free. But during the first nineteen months of my life, I had caught glimpses of broad, green fields, a luminous sky, trees and flowers which the darkness that followed could not wholly blot out. If we have once seen, "the day is ours, and what the day has shown."

CHAPTER 2

I CANNOT RECALL what happened during the first months after my illness. I only know that I sat in my mother's lap or clung to her dress as she went about her household duties. My hands felt every object and observed every motion, and in this way I learned to know many things. Soon I felt the need of some communication with others and began to make crude signs. A shake of the head meant "No" and a nod, "Yes," a pull meant "Come" and a push, "Go." Was it bread that I wanted? Then I would imitate the acts of cutting the slices and buttering them. If I wanted my mother to make ice cream for dinner, I made the sign for working the freezer and shivered, indicating cold. My mother, moreover, succeeded in making me understand a good deal. I always knew when she wished me to bring her something, and I would run upstairs or anywhere else she indicated. Indeed, I owe to her loving wisdom all that was bright and good in my long night.

I understood a good deal of what was going on about me. At five I learned to fold and put away the clean clothes when they were brought in from the laundry, and I distinguished my own from the rest. I knew by the way my mother and aunt dressed when they were going out, and I invariably begged to go with them. I was always sent for when there was company, and when the guests took their leave, I waved my hand to them, I think with a vague remembrance of the meaning of the gesture. One day some gentlemen called on my mother, and I felt the shutting of the front door and other sounds that indicated their arrival. On a sudden thought, I ran upstairs before anyone could stop me, to put on my idea of a company dress. Standing before the mirror, as I had seen others do, I anointed mine head with oil and covered my face thickly with powder. Then I pinned a veil over my head so that it covered my face and fell in folds down to my shoulders, and tied an enormous bustle round my small waist, so that it dangled behind, almost meeting the hem of my skirt. Thus attired I went down to help entertain the company.

I do not remember when I first realized that I was different from other people; but I knew it before my teacher came to me. I had noticed that my mother and my friends did not use signs as I did when they wanted anything done, but talked with their mouths. Sometimes I stood between two persons who were conversing and touched their lips. I could not understand, and was vexed. I moved my lips and gesticulated frantically without result. This made me so angry at times that I kicked and screamed until I was exhausted.

I think I knew when I was naughty, for I knew that it hurt Ella, my nurse, to kick her, and when my fit of temper was over I had a feeling akin to regret. But I cannot remember any instance in which this feeling prevented me from repeating the naughtiness when I failed to get what I wanted.

In those days a little colored girl, Martha Washington, the child of our cook, and Belle, an old setter, and a great hunter in her day, were my constant companions. Martha Washington understood my signs, and I seldom had any difficulty in making her do just as I wished. It pleased me to domineer over her, and she generally submitted to my tyranny rather than risk a hand-to-hand encounter. I was strong, active, indifferent to consequences. I knew my own mind well enough and always had my own way, even if I had to fight tooth and nail for it. We spent a great deal of time in the kitchen, kneading dough balls, helping make ice cream, grinding coffee, quarreling over the cake bowl, and feeding the hens and turkeys that swarmed about the kitchen steps. Many of them were so tame that they would eat from my hand and let me feel them. One big gobbler snatched a tomato from me one day and ran away with it. Inspired, perhaps, by Master Gobbler's success, we carried off to the woodpile a cake which the cook had just frosted, and ate every bit of it. I was quite ill afterward, and I wonder if retribution also overtook the turkey.

The guineafowl likes to hide her nest in out-of-the-way places, and it was one of my greatest delights to hunt for the eggs in the long grass. I could not tell Martha Washington when I wanted to go egg hunting, but I would double my hands and put them on the ground, which meant something round in the grass, and Martha always understood. When we were fortunate enough to find a nest, I never allowed her to carry the eggs home, making her understand by emphatic signs that she might fall and break them.

The sheds where the corn was stored, the stable where the horses were kept, and the yard where the cows were milked morning and evening were unfailing sources of interest to Martha and me. The milkers would let me keep my hands on the cows while they milked, and I often got well switched by the cow for my curiosity.

The making ready for Christmas was always a delight to me. Of course I did not know what it was all about, but I enjoyed the pleasant odors that filled the house and the tidbits that were given to Martha Washington and me to keep us quiet. We were sadly in the way, but that did not interfere with our pleasure in the least. They allowed us to grind the spices, pick over the raisins, and lick the stirring spoons. I hung my stocking because the others did; I cannot remember, however, that the ceremony interested me especially, nor did my curiosity cause me to wake before daylight to look for my gifts.

CHAPTER 2

Martha Washington had as great a love of mischief as I. Two little children were seated on the veranda steps one hot July afternoon. One was black as ebony, with little bunches of fuzzy hair tied with shoestrings sticking out all over her head like corkscrews. The other was white, with long golden curls. One child was six years old, the other two or three years older. The younger child was blind—that was I—and the other was Martha Washington. We were busy cutting out paper dolls; but we soon wearied of this amusement, and after cutting up our shoestrings and clipping all the leaves off the honeysuckle that were within reach, I turned my attention to Martha's corkscrews. She objected at first, but finally submitted. Thinking that turn and turn about is fair play, she seized the scissors and cut off one of my curls, and would have cut them all off but for my mother's timely interference.

Belle, our dog, my other companion, was old and lazy and liked to sleep by the open fire rather than to romp with me. I tried hard to teach her my sign language, but she was dull and inattentive. She sometimes started and quivered with excitement, then she became perfectly rigid, as dogs do when they point a bird. I did not then know why Belle acted in this way; but I knew she was not doing as I wished. This vexed me and the lesson always ended in a one-sided boxing match. Belle would get up, stretch herself lazily, give one or two contemptuous sniffs, go to the opposite side of the hearth and lie down again; and I, wearied and disappointed, went off in search of Martha.

Many incidents of those early years are fixed in my memory, isolated, but clear and distinct, making the sense of that silent, aimless, dayless life all the more intense.

One day I happened to spill water on my apron, and I spread it out to dry before the fire which was flickering on the sitting room hearth. The apron did not dry quickly enough to suit me, so I drew nearer and threw it right over the hot ashes. The fire leaped into life; the flames encircled me so that in a moment my clothes were blazing. I made a terrified noise that brought Viny, my old nurse, to the rescue. Throwing a blanket over me, she almost suffocated me, but she put out the fire. Except for my hands and hair, I was not badly burned.

About this time I found out the use of a key. One morning I locked my mother up in the pantry, where she was obliged to remain three hours, as the servants were in a detached part of the house. She kept pounding on the door, while I sat outside on the porch steps and laughed with glee as I felt the jar of the pounding. This most naughty prank of mine convinced my parents that I must be taught as soon as possible. After my teacher, Miss Sullivan, came to me, I sought an early opportunity to lock her in her room. I went upstairs with something which my mother made me understand I was to give to Miss Sullivan; but no sooner had I given it to her than I slammed the door too, locked it, and hid the key under the wardrobe in the hall. I could not be induced to tell where the key was. My father was obliged to get a ladder and take Miss Sullivan out through the window—much to my delight. Months after, I produced the key.

When I was about five years old, we moved from the little vine-covered house to a large new one. The family consisted of my father and mother, two older half-brothers, and, afterward, a little sister, Mildred. My earliest distinct recollection of my father is making my way through great drifts of newspapers to his side and finding him alone, holding a sheet of paper before his face. I was greatly puzzled to know what he was doing. I imitated this action, even wearing his spectacles, thinking they might help solve the mystery. But I did not find out the secret for several years. Then I learned what those papers were, and that my father edited one of them.

My father was most loving and indulgent, devoted to his home, seldom leaving us, except in the hunting season. He was a great hunter, I have been told, and a celebrated shot. Next to his family, he loved his dogs and gun. His hospitality was great, almost to a fault, and he seldom came home without bringing a guest. His special pride was the big garden where, it was said, he raised the finest watermelons and strawberries in the county; and to me he brought the first ripe grapes and the choicest berries. I remember his caressing touch as he led me from tree to tree, from vine to vine, and his eager delight in whatever pleased me.

He was a famous storyteller; after I had acquired language, he used to spell clumsily into my hand his cleverest anecdotes, and nothing pleased him more than to have me repeat them at an opportune moment.

I was in the North, enjoying the last beautiful days of the summer of 1896, when I heard the news of my father's death. He had had a short illness; there had been a brief time of acute suffering, then all was over. This was my first great sorrow—my first personal experience with death.

How shall I write of my mother? She is so near to me that it almost seems indelicate to speak of her.

For a long time, I regarded my little sister as an intruder. I knew that I had ceased to be my mother's only darling, and the thought filled me with jealousy. She sat in my mother's lap constantly, where I used to sit, and seemed to take up all her care and time. One day something happened which seemed to me to be adding insult to injury.

At that time I had a much-petted, much-abused doll, which I afterward named Nancy. She was, alas, the helpless victim of my outbursts of temper and of affection, so that she became much the worse for wear. I had dolls which talked, and cried, and opened and shut their eyes; yet I never loved one of them as I loved poor Nancy. She had a cradle, and I often spent an hour or more rocking her. I guarded both doll and cradle with the most jealous care; but once I discovered my little sister sleeping peacefully in the cradle. At this presumption on the part of one to whom as yet no tie of love bound me, I grew angry. I rushed upon the cradle and overturned it, and the baby might have been killed had my mother not caught her as she fell. Thus it is that when we walk in the valley of twofold solitude, we know little of the tender affections that grow out of endearing words and actions and companionship. But afterward, when I was restored to my human heritage, Mildred and I grew into each other's hearts, so that we were content to go hand-in-hand wherever caprice led us, although she could not understand my finger language, nor I her childish prattle.

CHAPTER 3

MEANWHILE THE desire to express myself grew. The few signs I used became less and less adequate, and my failures to make myself understood were invariably followed by outbursts of passion. I felt as if invisible hands were holding me, and I made frantic efforts to free myself. I struggled—not that struggling helped matters, but the spirit of resistance was strong within me; I generally broke down in tears and physical exhaustion. If my mother happened to be near, I crept into her arms, too miserable even to remember the cause of the tempest. After awhile, the need of some means of communication became so urgent that these outbursts occurred daily, sometimes hourly.

My parents were deeply grieved and perplexed. We lived a long way from any school for the blind or the deaf, and it seemed unlikely that anyone would come to such an out-of-the-way place as Tuscumbia to teach a child who was both deaf and blind. Indeed, my friends and relatives sometimes doubted whether I could be taught. My mother's only ray of hope came from Dickens' *American Notes*. She had read his account of Laura Bridgman, and remembered vaguely that she was deaf and blind, yet had been educated. But she also remembered with a hopeless pang that Dr. Howe, who had discovered the way to teach the deaf and blind, had been dead many years. His methods had probably died with him; and if they had not, how was a little girl in a far-off town in Alabama to receive the benefit of them?

When I was about six years old, my father heard of an eminent oculist in Baltimore, who had been successful in many cases that had seemed hopeless. My parents at once determined to take me to Baltimore to see if anything could be done for my eyes.

The journey, which I remember well, was very pleasant. I made friends with many people on the train. One lady gave me a box of shells. My father made holes in these so that I could string them, and for a long time they kept me happy and contented. The conductor, too, was kind. Often when he went his rounds, I clung to his coattails while he collected and punched the tickets. His punch, with which he let me play, was a delightful toy. Curled up in a corner of the seat, I amused myself for hours making funny little holes in bits of cardboard.

My aunt made me a big doll out of towels. It was the most comical shapeless thing, this improvised doll, with no nose, mouth, ears, or eyes—nothing that even the imagination of a child could convert into a face. Curiously enough, the absence of eyes struck me more than all the other defects put together. I pointed this out to everybody with provoking persistency, but no one seemed equal to the task of providing the doll with eyes. A bright idea, however, shot into my mind, and the problem was solved. I tumbled off the seat and searched under it until I found my aunt's cape, which was trimmed with large beads. I pulled two beads off and indicated to her that I wanted her to sew them on my doll. She raised my hand to her eyes in a questioning way, and I nodded energetically. The beads were sewn in the right place, and I could not contain myself for joy; but immediately I lost all interest in the doll. During the whole trip, I did not have one fit of temper; there were so many things to keep my mind and fingers busy.

When we arrived in Baltimore, Dr. Chisholm received us kindly, but he could do nothing. He said, however, that I could be educated, and advised my father to consult Dr. Alexander Graham Bell of Washington, who would be able to give him information about schools and teachers of deaf or blind children. Acting on the doctor's advice, we went immediately to Washington to see Dr. Bell, my father with a sad heart and many misgivings, I wholly unconscious of his anguish, finding pleasure in the excitement of moving from place to place. Child as I was, I at once felt the tenderness and sympathy which endeared Dr. Bell to so many hearts, as his wonderful achievements enlist their admiration. He held me on his knee while I examined his watch, and he made it strike for me. He understood my signs, and I knew it and loved him at once. But I did not dream that that interview would be the door through which I should pass from darkness into light, from isolation to friendship, companionship, knowledge, love.

Dr. Bell advised my father to write to Mr. Anagnos, director of the Perkins Institution in Boston, the scene of Dr. Howe's great labors for the blind, and ask him if he had a teacher competent to begin my education. This my father did at once, and in a few weeks there came a kind letter from Mr. Anagnos with the comforting assurance that a teacher had been found. This was in the summer of 1886. But Miss Sullivan did not arrive until the following March.

Thus I came up out of Egypt and stood before Sinai, and a power divine touched my spirit and gave it sight, so that I beheld many wonders. And from the sacred mountain I heard a voice which said, "Knowledge is love and light and vision."

CHAPTER 4

THE MOST important day I remember in all my life is the one on which my teacher, Anne Mansfield Sullivan, came to me. I am filled with wonder when I consider the immeasurable contrasts between the two lives which it connects. It was the third of March 1887, three months before I was seven years old.

On the afternoon of that eventful day, I stood on the porch, dumb, expectant. I guessed vaguely from my mother's signs and from the hurrying to and fro in the house that something unusual was about to happen, so I went to the door and waited on the steps. The afternoon sun penetrated the mass of honeysuckle that covered the porch, and fell on my upturned face. My fingers lingered almost unconsciously on the familiar leaves and blossoms which had just come forth to greet the sweet southern spring. I did not know what the future held of marvel or surprise for me. Anger and bitterness had preyed upon me continually for weeks and a deep languor had succeeded this passionate struggle.

Have you ever been at sea in a dense fog, when it seemed as if a tangible white darkness shut you in, and the great ship, tense and anxious, groped her way toward the shore with plummet and sounding line, and you waited with beating heart for something to happen? I was like that ship before my education began, only I was without compass or sounding line, and had no way of knowing how near the harbor was. "Light! Give me light!" was the wordless cry of my soul, and the light of love shone on me in that very hour.

I felt approaching footsteps; I stretched out my hand as I supposed, to my mother. Someone took it, and I was caught up and held close in the arms of her who had come to reveal all things to me and, more than all things else, to love me.

The morning after my teacher came, she led me into her room and gave me a doll. The little blind children at the Perkins Institution had sent it and Laura Bridgman had dressed it; but I did not know this until afterward. When I had played with it a little while, Miss Sullivan slowly spelled into my hand the word "d-o-l-l." I was at once interested in this finger play and tried to imitate it. When I finally succeeded in making the letters correctly, I was flushed with childish pleasure and pride. Running downstairs to my mother, I held up my hand and made the letters for doll. I did not know that I was spelling a word or even that words existed; I was simply making my fingers go in monkey-like imitation. In the days that followed, I learned to spell in this uncomprehending way a great many words, among them pin, hat, cup and a few verbs like sit, stand, and walk. But my teacher had been with me several weeks before I understood that everything has a name.

One day, while I was playing with my new doll, Miss Sullivan put my big rag doll into my lap also, spelled "d-o-l-l" and tried to make me understand that "d-o-l-l" applied to both. Earlier in the day we had had a tussle over the words "m-u-g" and "w-a-t-e-r." Miss Sullivan had tried to impress it upon me that "m-u-g" is mug and that "w-a-t-e-r" is water, but I persisted in confounding the two. In despair she had dropped the subject for the time, only to renew it at the first opportunity. I became impatient at her repeated attempts, and, seizing the new doll, I dashed it upon the floor. I was keenly delighted when I felt the fragments of the broken doll at my feet. Neither sorrow nor regret followed my passionate outburst. I had not loved the doll. In the still, dark world in which I lived there was no strong sentiment or tenderness. I felt my teacher sweep the fragments to one side of the hearth, and I had a sense of satisfaction that the cause of my discomfort was removed. She brought me my hat, and I knew I was going out into the warm sunshine. This thought, if a wordless sensation may be called a thought, made me hop and skip with pleasure.

We walked down the path to the well house, attracted by the fragrance of the honeysuckle with which it was covered. Someone was drawing water and my teacher placed my hand under the spout. As the cool stream gushed over one hand she spelled into the other the word water, first slowly, then rapidly. I stood still, my whole attention fixed upon the motions of her fingers. Suddenly I felt a misty consciousness as of something forgotten—a thrill of returning thought; and somehow the mystery of language was revealed to me. I knew then that "w-a-t-e-r" meant the wonderful cool something that was flowing over my hand. That living word awakened my soul, gave it light, hope, joy, set it free! There were barriers still, it is true, but barriers that could in time be swept away.

I left the well house eager to learn. Everything had a name, and each name gave birth to a new thought. As we returned to the house, every object which I touched seemed to quiver with life. That was because I saw everything with the strange, new sight that had come to me. On entering the door, I remembered the doll I had broken. I felt my way to the hearth and picked up the pieces. I tried vainly to put them together. Then my eyes filled with tears; for I realized what I had done, and for the first time I felt repentance and sorrow.

I learned a great many new words that day. I do not remember what they all were; but I do know that mother, father, sister, teacher were among them—words that were to make the world blossom for me, "like Aaron's rod, with flowers." It would have been difficult to find a happier child than I was as I lay in my crib at the close of that eventful day and lived over the joys it had brought me, and for the first time longed for a new day to come.

CHAPTER 5

I RECALL MANY incidents of the summer of 1887 that followed my soul's sudden awakening. I did nothing but explore with my hands and learn the name of every object that I touched; and the more I handled things and learned their names and uses, the more joyous and confident grew my sense of kinship with the rest of the world.

When the time of daisies and buttercups came, Miss Sullivan took me by the hand across the fields, where men were preparing the earth for the seed, to the banks of the Tennessee River, and there, sitting on the warm grass, I had my first lessons in the beneficence of nature. I learned how the sun and the rain make to grow out of the ground every tree that is pleasant to the sight and good for food, how birds build their nests and live and thrive from land to land, how the squirrel, the deer, the lion, and every other creature finds food and shelter. As my knowledge of things grew, I felt more and more the delight of the world I was in. Long before I learned to do a sum in arithmetic or describe the shape of the earth, Miss Sullivan had taught me to find beauty in the fragrant woods, in every blade of grass, and in the curves and dimples of my baby sister's hand. She linked my earliest thoughts with nature, and made me feel that "birds and flowers and I were happy peers."

But about this time I had an experience which taught me that nature is not always kind. One day my teacher and I were returning from a long ramble. The morning had been fine, but it was growing warm and sultry when at last we turned our faces homeward. Two or three times we stopped to rest under a tree by the wayside. Our last halt was under a wild cherry tree a short distance from the house. The shade was grateful, and the tree was so easy to climb that with my teacher's assistance I was able to scramble to a seat in the branches. It was so cool up in the tree that Miss Sullivan proposed that we have our luncheon there. I promised to keep still while she went to the house to fetch it.

Suddenly a change passed over the tree. All the sun's warmth left the air. I knew the sky was black, because all the heat, which meant light to me, had died out of the atmosphere. A strange odor came up from the earth. I knew it; it was the odor that always precedes a thunderstorm, and a nameless fear clutched at my heart. I felt absolutely alone, cut off from my friends and the firm earth. The immense, the unknown, enfolded me. I remained still and expectant; a chilling terror crept over me. I longed for my teacher's return; but above all things I wanted to get down from that tree.

There was a moment of sinister silence, then a multitudinous stirring of the leaves. A shiver ran through the tree, and the wind sent forth a blast that would have knocked me off had I not clung to the branch with might and main. The tree swayed and strained. The small twigs snapped and fell about me in showers. A wild impulse to jump seized me, but terror held me fast. I crouched down in the fork of the tree. The branches lashed about me. I felt the intermittent jarring that came now and then, as if something heavy had fallen and the shock had traveled up till it reached the limb I sat on. It worked my suspense up to the highest point, and just as I was thinking the tree and I should fall together, my teacher seized my hand and helped me down. I clung to her, trembling with joy to feel the earth under my feet once more. I had learned a new lesson—that nature "wages open war against her children, and under softest touch hides treacherous claws."

After this experience it was a long time before I climbed another tree. The mere thought filled me with terror. It was the sweet allurement of the mimosa tree in full bloom that finally overcame my fears. One beautiful spring morning when I was alone in the summer house, reading, I became aware of a wonderful subtle fragrance in the air. I started up and instinctively stretched out my hands. It seemed as if the spirit of spring had passed through the summer house. "What is it?" I asked, and the next minute I recognized the odor of the mimosa blossoms. I felt my way to the end of the garden, knowing that the mimosa tree was near the fence, at the turn of the path. Yes, there it was, all quivering in the warm sunshine, its blossom-laden branches almost touching the long grass. Was there ever anything so exquisitely beautiful in the world before! Its delicate blossoms shrank from the slightest earthly touch; it seemed as if a tree of paradise had been transplanted to earth. I made my way through a shower of petals to the great trunk and for one minute stood irresolute; then, putting my foot in the broad space between the forked branches, I pulled myself up into the tree. I had some difficulty in holding on, for the branches were very large and the bark hurt my hands. But I had a delicious sense that I was doing something unusual and wonderful so I kept on climbing higher and higher, until I reached a little seat which somebody had built there so long ago that it had grown part of the tree itself. I sat there for a long, long time, feeling like a fairy on a rosy cloud. After that I spent many happy hours in my tree of paradise, thinking fair thoughts and dreaming bright dreams.

CHAPTER 6

I HAD NOW the key to all language, and I was eager to learn to use it. Children who hear acquire language without any particular effort; the words that fall from others' lips they catch on the wing, as it were, delightedly, while the little deaf child must trap them by a slow and often painful process. But whatever the process, the result is wonderful. Gradually from naming an object, we advance step by step until we have traversed the vast distance between our first stammered syllable and the sweep of thought in a line of Shakespeare.

At first, when my teacher told me about a new thing I asked very few questions. My ideas were vague, and my vocabulary was inadequate; but as my knowledge of things grew, and I learned more and more words, my field of inquiry broadened, and I would return again and again to the same subject, eager for further information. Sometimes a new word revived an image that some earlier experience had engraved on my brain.

I remember the morning that I first asked the meaning of the word "love." This was before I knew many words. I had found a few early violets in the garden and brought them to my teacher. She tried to kiss me: but at that time I did not like to have anyone kiss me except my mother. Miss Sullivan put her arm gently round me and spelled into my hand, "I love Helen."

"What is love?" I asked.

She drew me closer to her and said, "It is here," pointing to my heart, whose beats I was conscious of for the first time. Her words puzzled me very much because I did not then understand anything unless I touched it.

I smelt the violets in her hand and asked, half in words, half in signs, a question which meant, "Is love the sweetness of flowers?"

"No," said my teacher.

Again I thought. The warm sun was shining on us.

"Is this not love?" I asked, pointing in the direction from which the heat came. "Is this not love?"

It seemed to me that there could be nothing more beautiful than the sun, whose warmth makes all things grow. But Miss Sullivan shook her head, and I was greatly puzzled and disappointed. I thought it strange that my teacher could not show me love.

A day or two afterward I was stringing beads of different sizes in symmetrical groups—two large beads, three small ones, and so on. I had made many mistakes, and Miss Sullivan had pointed them out again and again with gentle patience. Finally I noticed a very obvious error in the sequence and for an instant I concentrated my attention on the lesson and tried to think how I should have arranged the beads. Miss Sullivan touched my forehead and spelled with decided emphasis, "Think."

In a flash I knew that the word was the name of the process that was going on in my head. This was my first conscious perception of an abstract idea.

For a long time I was still—I was not thinking of the beads in my lap, but trying to find a meaning for "love" in the light of this new idea. The sun had been under a cloud all day, and there had been brief showers; but suddenly the sun broke forth in all its southern splendor.

Again I asked my teacher, "Is this not love?"

"Love is something like the clouds that were in the sky before the sun came out," she replied. Then in simpler words than these, which at that time I could not have understood, she explained: "You cannot touch the clouds, you know; but you feel the rain and know how glad the flowers and the thirsty earth are to have it after a hot day. You cannot touch love either; but you feel the sweetness that it pours into everything. Without love you would not be happy or want to play."

The beautiful truth burst upon my mind—I felt that there were invisible lines stretched between my spirit and the spirits of others.

From the beginning of my education, Miss Sullivan made it a practice to speak to me as she would speak to any hearing child; the only difference was that she spelled the sentences into my hand instead of speaking them. If I did not know the words and idioms necessary to express my thoughts, she supplied them, even suggesting conversation when I was unable to keep up my end of the dialogue.

This process was continued for several years; for the deaf child does not learn in a month, or even in two or three years, the numberless idioms and expressions used in the simplest daily intercourse. The little hearing child learns these from constant repetition and imitation. The conversation he hears in his home stimulates his mind and suggests topics and calls forth the spontaneous expression of his own thoughts. This natural exchange of ideas is denied to the deaf child. My teacher, realizing this, determined to supply the kinds of stimulus I lacked. This she did by repeating to me as far as possible, verbatim, what she heard, and by showing me how I could take part in the conversation. But it was a long time before I ventured to take the initiative, and still longer before I could find something appropriate to say at the right time.

The deaf and the blind find it very difficult to acquire the amenities of conversation. How much more this difficulty must be augmented in the case of those who are both deaf and blind! They cannot distinguish the tone of the voice or, without assistance, go up and down the gamut of tones that give significance to words; nor can they watch the expression of the speaker's face, and a look is often the very soul of what one says.

CHAPTER 7

THE NEXT important step in my education was learning to read.

As soon as I could spell a few words, my teacher gave me slips of cardboard on which were printed words in raised letters. I quickly learned that each printed word stood for an object, an act, or a quality. I had a frame in which I could arrange the words in little sentences; but before I ever put sentences in the frame, I used to make them in objects. I found the slips of paper which represented, for example, "doll," "is," "on," "bed" and placed each name on its object; then I put my doll on the bed with the words "is," "on," "bed" arranged beside the doll, thus making a sentence of the words, and at the same time carrying out the idea of the sentence with the things themselves.

One day, Miss Sullivan tells me, I pinned the word "girl" on my pinafore and stood in the wardrobe. On the shelf I arranged the words, "is," "in," "wardrobe." Nothing delighted me so much as this game. My teacher and I played it for hours at a time. Often everything in the room was arranged in object sentences.

From the printed slip it was but a step to the printed book. I took my *Reader for Beginners* and hunted for the words I knew;

when I found them my joy was like that of a game of hide-and-seek. Thus I began to read. Of the time when I began to read connected stories, I shall speak later.

For a long time, I had no regular lessons. Even when I studied most earnestly, it seemed more like play than work. Everything Miss Sullivan taught me, she illustrated by a beautiful story or a poem. Whenever anything delighted or interested me, she talked it over with me just as if she were a little girl herself. What many children think of with dread, as a painful plodding through grammar, hard sums, and harder definitions, is today one of my most precious memories.

I cannot explain the peculiar sympathy Miss Sullivan had with my pleasures and desires. Perhaps it was the result of long association with the blind. Added to this she had a wonderful faculty for description. She went quickly over uninteresting details, and never nagged me with questions to see if I remembered the day-before-yesterday's lesson. She introduced dry technicalities of science little by little, making every subject so real that I could not help remembering what she taught.

We read and studied out of doors, preferring the sunlit woods to the house. All my early lessons have in them the breath of the woods—the fine, resinous odor of pine needles, blended with the perfume of wild grapes. Seated in the gracious shade of a wild tulip tree, I learned to think that everything has a lesson and a suggestion. "The loveliness of things taught me all their use." Indeed, everything that could hum or buzz or sing or bloom had a part in my education—noisy-throated frogs, katydids, and crickets held in my hand until forgetting their embarrassment, they trilled their reedy note, little downy chickens and wildflowers, the dogwood blossoms, meadow violets, and budding fruit trees. I felt the bursting cotton balls and fingered their soft fiber and fuzzy seeds; I felt the low soughing of the wind through the cornstalks, the silky rustling of the long leaves, and the indignant snort of my pony, as we caught him in the pasture and put the bit in his mouth—ah me! How well I remember the spicy, clovery smell of his breath!

Sometimes I rose at dawn and stole into the garden while the heavy dew lay on the grass and flowers. Few know what joy it is to feel the roses pressing softly into the hand, or the beautiful motion of the lilies as they sway in the morning breeze. Sometimes I caught an insect in the flower I was plucking, and I felt the faint noise of a pair of wings rubbed together in a sudden terror, as the little creature became aware of a pressure from without.

Another favorite haunt of mine was the orchard, where the fruit ripened early in July. The large, downy peaches would reach themselves into my hand, and as the joyous breezes flew about the trees, the apples tumbled at my feet. Oh, the delight with which I gathered up the fruit in my pinafore, pressed my face against the smooth cheeks of the apples, still warm from the sun, and skipped back to the house!

Our favorite walk was to Keller's Landing, an old tumbledown lumber wharf on the Tennessee River, used during the Civil War to land soldiers. There we spent many happy hours and played at learning geography. I built dams of pebbles, made islands and lakes, and dug riverbeds, all for fun, and never dreamed that I was learning a lesson. I listened with increasing wonder to Miss Sullivan's descriptions of the great round world with its burning mountains, buried cities, moving rivers of ice, and many other things as strange. She made raised maps in clay, so that I could feel the mountain ridges and valleys, and follow with my fingers the devious course of rivers. I liked this, too; but the division of the earth into zones and poles confused and teased my mind.

The illustrative strings and the orange stick representing the poles seemed so real that even to this day the mere mention of the temperate zone suggests a series of twine circles; and I believe that if anyone should set about it he could convince me that white bears actually climb the North Pole.

Arithmetic seems to have been the only study I did not like. From the first I was not interested in the science of numbers. Miss Sullivan tried to teach me to count by stringing beads in groups, and by arranging kindergarten straws I learned to add and subtract. I never had patience to arrange more than five or six groups at a time. When I had accomplished this, my conscience was at rest for the day, and I went out quickly to find my playmates.

In this same leisurely manner, I studied zoology and botany.

Once a gentleman, whose name I have forgotten, sent me a collection of fossils—tiny mollusk shells beautifully marked, and bits of sandstone with the print of birds' claws, and a lovely fern in bas-relief. These were the keys which unlocked the treasures of the antediluvian world for me. With trembling fingers I listened to Miss Sullivan's descriptions of the terrible beasts, with uncouth, unpronounceable names, which once went tramping through the primeval forests, tearing down the branches of gigantic trees for food, and died in the dismal swamps of an unknown age. For a long time, these strange creatures haunted my dreams, and this gloomy period formed a somber background to the joyous. Now, filled with sunshine and roses and echoing with the gentle beat of my pony's hoof.

Another time a beautiful shell was given me, and with a child's surprise and delight, I learned how a tiny mollusk had built the lustrous coil for his dwelling place, and how on still nights, when there is no breeze stirring the waves, the nautilus sails on the blue waters of the Indian Ocean in his "ship of pearl." After I had learned a great many interesting things about the life and habits of the children of the sea—how in the midst of dashing waves the little polyps build the beautiful coral isles of the Pacific, and the foraminifera have made the chalk hills of many a land—my teacher read me *The Chambered Nautilus*, and showed me that the shell-building process of the mollusks is symbolical of the development of the mind. Just as the wonder-working mantle of the nautilus changes the material it absorbs from the water and makes it a part of itself, so the bits of knowledge one gathers undergo a similar change and become pearls of thought.

Again, it was the growth of a plant that furnished the text for a lesson. We bought a lily and set it in a sunny window. Very soon the green, pointed buds showed signs of opening. The slender, fingerlike leaves on the outside opened slowly, reluctant, I thought, to reveal the loveliness they hid; once having made a start, however, the opening process went on rapidly, but in order and systematically. There was always one bud larger and more beautiful than the rest, which pushed her outer covering back with more pomp, as if the beauty in soft, silky robes knew that she was the lily queen by right divine, while her more timid sisters doffed their green hoods shyly, until the whole plant was one nodding bough of loveliness and fragrance.

Once there were eleven tadpoles in a glass globe set in a window full of plants. I remember the eagerness with which I made discoveries about them. It was great fun to plunge my hand into the bowl and feel the tadpoles frisk about, and to let them slip and slide between my fingers. One day a more ambitious fellow leaped beyond the edge of the bowl and fell on the floor, where I found him to all appearance more dead than alive. The only sign of life was a slight wriggling of his tail. But no sooner had he returned to his element than he darted to the bottom, swimming round and round in joyous activity. He had made his leap, he had seen the great world, and was content to stay in his pretty glass house under the big fuchsia tree until he attained the dignity of froghood. Then he went to live in the leafy pool at the end of the garden, where he made the summer nights musical with his quaint love song.

Thus, I learned from life itself. At the beginning I was only a little mass of possibilities. It was my teacher who unfolded and developed them. When she came, everything about me breathed of love and joy and was full of meaning. She has never since let pass an opportunity to point out the beauty that is in everything, nor has she ceased trying in thought and action and example to make my life sweet and useful.

It was my teacher's genius, her quick sympathy, her loving tact which made the first years of my education so beautiful. It was because she seized the right moment to impart knowledge that made it so pleasant and acceptable to me. She realized that a child's mind is like a shallow brook which ripples and dances merrily over the stony course of its education and reflects here a flower, there a bush, yonder a fleecy cloud; and she attempted to guide my mind on its way, knowing that like a brook it should be fed by mountain streams and hidden springs, until it broadened out into a deep river, capable of reflecting in its placid surface, billowy hills, the luminous shadows of trees and the blue heavens, as well as the sweet face of a little flower.

Any teacher can take a child to the classroom, but not every teacher can make him learn. He will not work joyously unless he feels that liberty is his, whether he is busy or at rest; he must feel the flush of victory and the heart-sinking of disappointment before he takes with a will the tasks distasteful to him and resolves to dance his way bravely through a dull routine of textbooks.

My teacher is so near to me that I scarcely think of myself apart from her. How much of my delight in all beautiful things is innate, and how much is due to her influence, I can never tell. I feel that her being is inseparable from my own, and that the footsteps of my life are in hers. All the best of me belongs to her—there is not a talent, or an aspiration, or a joy in me that has not been awakened by her loving touch.

Helen Keller with Anne Sullivan in July 1888

CHAPTER 8

THE FIRST Christmas after Miss Sullivan came to Tuscumbia was a great event. Everyone in the family prepared surprises for me, but what pleased me most, Miss Sullivan and I prepared surprises for everybody else. The mystery that surrounded the gifts was my greatest delight and amusement. My friends did all they could to excite my curiosity by hints and half-spelled sentences which they pretended to break off in the nick of time. Miss Sullivan and I kept up a game of guessing which taught me more about the use of language than any set lessons could have done. Every evening, seated round a glowing wood fire, we played our guessing game, which grew more and more exciting as Christmas approached.

On Christmas Eve the Tuscumbia schoolchildren had their tree, to which they invited me. In the center of the schoolroom stood a beautiful tree ablaze and shimmering in the soft light, its branches loaded with strange, wonderful fruit. It was a moment of supreme happiness. I danced and capered round the tree in an ecstasy. When I learned that there was a gift for each child, I was delighted, and the kind people who had prepared the tree permitted me to hand the presents to the children. In the pleasure of doing this, I did not stop to look at my own gifts; but when I was ready for them, my impatience for the real Christmas to begin almost got beyond control. I knew the gifts I already had were not those of which friends had thrown out such tantalizing hints, and my teacher said the presents I was to have would be even nicer than these. I was persuaded, however, to content myself with the gifts from the tree and leave the others until morning.

That night, after I had hung my stocking, I lay awake a long time, pretending to be asleep and keeping alert to see what Santa Claus would do when he came. At last I fell asleep with a new doll and a white bear in my arms. Next morning it was I who waked the whole family with my first "Merry Christmas!" I found surprises, not in the stocking only, but on the table, on all the chairs, at the door, on the very windowsill; indeed, I could hardly walk without stumbling on a bit of Christmas wrapped up in tissue paper. But when my teacher presented me with a canary, my cup of happiness overflowed.

Little Tim was so tame that he would hop on my finger and eat candied cherries out of my hand. Miss Sullivan taught me to take all the care of my new pet. Every morning after breakfast, I prepared his bath, made his cage clean and sweet, filled his cups with fresh seed and water from the well house, and hung a spray of chickweed in his swing.

One morning I left the cage on the window seat while I went to fetch water for his bath. When I returned I felt a big cat brush past me as I opened the door. At first I did not realize what had happened; but when I put my hand in the cage and Tim's pretty wings did not meet my touch or his small pointed claws take hold of my finger, I knew that I should never see my sweet little singer again.

CHAPTER 9

THE NEXT important event in my life was my visit to Boston in May 1888. As if it were yesterday, I remember the preparations, the departure with my teacher and my mother, the journey, and finally the arrival in Boston. How different this journey was from the one I had made to Baltimore two years before! I was no longer a restless, excitable little creature, requiring the attention of everybody on the train to keep me amused. I sat quietly beside Miss Sullivan, taking in with eager interest all that she told me about what she saw out of the car window: the beautiful Tennessee River, the great cotton fields, the hills and woods, and the crowds of laughing people at the stations, who waved to the people on the train and brought delicious candy and popcorn balls through the car. On the seat opposite me sat my big rag doll, Nancy, in a new gingham dress and a beruffled sunbonnet, looking at me out of two bead eyes. Sometimes, when I was not absorbed in Miss Sullivan's descriptions, I remembered Nancy's existence and took her up in my arms, but I generally calmed my conscience by making myself believe that she was asleep.

As I shall not have occasion to refer to Nancy again, I wish to tell here a sad experience she had soon after our arrival in

Boston. She was covered with dirt—the remains of mud pies I had compelled her to eat, although she had never shown any special liking for them. The laundress at the Perkins Institution secretly carried her off to give her a bath. This was too much for poor Nancy. When I next saw her she was a formless heap of cotton, which I should not have recognized at all except for the two bead eyes which looked out at me reproachfully.

When the train at last pulled into the station at Boston it was as if a beautiful fairy tale had come true. The "once upon a time" was now; the "far away country" was here.

We had scarcely arrived at the Perkins Institution for the Blind when I began to make friends with the little blind children. It delighted me inexpressibly to find that they knew the manual alphabet. What joy to talk with other children in my own language! Until then I had been like a foreigner speaking through an interpreter. In the school where Laura Bridgman was taught, I was in my own country. It took me some time to appreciate the fact that my new friends were blind. I knew I could not see; but it did not seem possible that all the eager, loving children who gathered round me and joined heartily in my frolics were also blind. I remember the surprise and the pain I felt as I noticed that they placed their hands over mine when I talked to them and that they read books with their fingers. Although I had been told this before, and although I understood my own deprivations, yet I had thought vaguely that since they could hear, they must have a sort of "second sight," and I was not prepared to find one child and another and yet another deprived of the same precious gift. But they were so happy and contented that I lost all sense of pain in the pleasure of their companionship.

One day spent with the blind children made me feel thoroughly at home in my new environment, and I looked eagerly from one pleasant experience to another as the days flew swiftly by. I could not quite convince myself that there was much world left, for I regarded Boston as the beginning and the end of creation.

While we were in Boston, we visited Bunker Hill, and there I had my first lesson in history. The story of the brave men who had fought on the spot where we stood excited me greatly. I climbed the monument, counting the steps, and wondering as I went higher and yet higher if the soldiers had climbed this great stairway and shot at the enemy on the ground below.

The next day, we went to Plymouth by water. This was my first trip on the ocean and my first voyage in a steamboat. How full of life and motion it was! But the rumble of the machinery made me think it was thundering, and I began to cry, because I feared if it rained we should not be able to have our picnic out of doors. I was more interested, I think, in the great rock on which the Pilgrims landed than in anything else in Plymouth. I could touch it, and perhaps that made the coming of the Pilgrims and their toils and great deeds seem more real to me. I have often held in my hand a little model of the Plymouth Rock which a kind gentleman gave me at Pilgrim Hall, and I have fingered its curves, the split in the center and the embossed figures "1620," and turned over in my mind all that I knew about the wonderful story of the Pilgrims.

How my childish imagination glowed with the splendor of their enterprise! I idealized them as the bravest and most generous men that ever sought a home in a strange land. I thought they desired the freedom of their fellow men as well as their own. I was keenly surprised and disappointed years later to learn of their acts of persecution that make us tingle with shame, even while we glory in the courage and energy that gave us our "Country Beautiful."

Among the many friends I made in Boston were Mr. William Endicott and his daughter. Their kindness to me was the seed from which many pleasant memories have since grown. One day we visited their beautiful home at Beverly Farms. I remember with delight how I went through their rose garden, how their dogs, big Leo and little curly-haired Fritz with long ears, came to meet me, and how Nimrod, the swiftest of the horses, poked his nose into my hands for a pat and a lump of sugar. I also remember the beach, where for the first time I played in the sand. It was hard, smooth sand, very different from the loose, sharp sand, mingled with kelp and shells, at Brewster. Mr. Endicott told me about the great ships that came sailing by from Boston, bound for Europe. I saw him many times after that, and he was always a good friend to me; indeed, I was thinking of him when I called Boston "the City of Kind Hearts."

CHAPTER 10

JUST BEFORE the Perkins Institution closed for the summer, it was arranged that my teacher and I should spend our vacation at Brewster, on Cape Cod, with our dear friend, Mrs. Hopkins. I was delighted, for my mind was full of the prospective joys and of the wonderful stories I had heard about the sea.

My most vivid recollection of that summer is the ocean. I had always lived far inland and had never had so much as a whiff of salt air; but I had read in a big book called *Our World* a description of the ocean which filled me with wonder and an intense longing to touch the mighty sea and feel it roar. So my little heart leaped high with eager excitement when I knew that my wish was at last to be realized.

No sooner had I been helped into my bathing suit than I sprang out upon the warm sand and, without thought of fear, plunged into the cool water. I felt the great billows rock and sink. The buoyant motion of the water filled me with an exquisite, quivering joy. Suddenly my ecstasy gave place to terror; for my foot struck against a rock and the next instant there was a rush of water over my head. I thrust out my hands to grasp some support; I clutched at the water and at the seaweed which the waves tossed in my face. But all my frantic efforts were in vain. The waves seemed to be playing a game with me, and tossed me from one to another in their wild frolic. It was fearful! The good, firm earth had slipped from my feet, and everything seemed shut out from this strange, all-enveloping element—life, air, warmth, and love. At last, however, the sea, as if weary of its new toy, threw me back on the shore, and in another instant I was clasped in my teacher's arms. Oh, the comfort of the long, tender embrace! As soon as I had recovered from my panic sufficiently to say anything, I demanded: "Who put salt in the water?"

After I had recovered from my first experience in the water, I thought it great fun to sit on a big rock in my bathing suit and feel wave after wave dash against the rock, sending up a shower of spray which quite covered me. I felt the pebbles rattling as the waves threw their ponderous weight against the shore; the whole beach seemed racked by their terrific onset, and the air throbbed with their pulsations. The breakers would swoop back to gather themselves for a mightier leap, and I clung to the rock, tense, fascinated, as I felt the dash and roar of the rushing sea!

I could never stay long enough on the shore. The tang of the untainted, fresh and free sea air was like a cool, quieting thought, and the shells and pebbles and the seaweed with tiny living creatures attached to it never lost their fascination for me. One day Miss Sullivan attracted my attention to a strange object which she had captured basking in the shallow water. It was a great horseshoe crab—the first one I had ever seen. I felt of him and thought it very strange that he should carry his house on his back. It suddenly occurred to me that he might make a delightful pet; so I seized him by the tail with both hands and carried him home. This feat pleased me highly, as his body was very heavy, and it took all my strength to drag him half a mile. I would not leave Miss Sullivan in peace until she had put the crab in a trough near the well where I was confident he would be secure. But next morning I went to the trough, and lo, he had disappeared! Nobody knew where he had gone, or how he had escaped. My disappointment was bitter at the time; but little by little I came to realize that it was not kind or wise to force this poor dumb creature out of his element, and after a while I felt happy in the thought that perhaps he had returned to the sea.

CHAPTER 11

IN THE autumn I returned to my southern home with a heart full of joyous memories. As I recall that visit north, I am filled with wonder at the richness and variety of the experiences that cluster about it. It seems to have been the beginning of everything. The treasures of a new, beautiful world were laid at my feet, and I took in pleasure and information at every turn. I lived myself into all things. I was never still a moment; my life was as full of motion as those little insects that crowd a whole existence into one brief day. I met many people who talked with me by spelling into my hand, and thought in joyous sympathy leaped up to meet thought, and behold, a miracle had been wrought! The barren places between my mind and the minds of others blossomed like the rose.

I spent the autumn months with my family at our summer cottage, on a mountain about fourteen miles from Tuscumbia. It was called Fern Quarry, because near it there was a limestone quarry, long since abandoned. Three frolicsome little streams ran through it from springs in the rocks above, leaping here and tumbling there in laughing cascades wherever the rocks tried to bar their way. The opening was filled with ferns which completely covered the beds of limestone and in places hid the streams. The rest of the mountain was thickly wooded. Here were great oaks and splendid evergreens with trunks like mossy pillars, from the branches of which hung garlands of ivy and mistletoe, and persimmon trees, the odor of which pervaded every nook and corner of the wood—an illusive, fragrant something that made the heart glad. In places the wild muscadine and scuppernong vines stretched from tree to tree, making arbors which were always full of butterflies and buzzing insects. It was delightful to lose ourselves in the green hollows of that tangled wood in the late afternoon, and to smell the cool, delicious odors that came up from the earth at the close of day.

Our cottage was a sort of rough camp, beautifully situated on the top of the mountain among oaks and pines. The small rooms were arranged on each side of a long open hall. Round the house was a wide piazza, where the mountain winds blew, sweet with all wood scents. We lived on the piazza most of the time—there we worked, ate, and played. At the back door there was a great butternut tree, round which the steps had been built, and in front the trees stood so close that I could touch them and feel the wind shake their branches, or the leaves twirl downward in the autumn blast.

Many visitors came to Fern Quarry. In the evening, by the campfire, the men played cards and whiled away the hours in talk and sport. They told stories of their wonderful feats with fowl, fish, and quadruped—how many wild ducks and turkeys they had shot, what "savage trout" they had caught, and how they had bagged the craftiest foxes, outwitted the most clever 'possums and overtaken the fleetest deer, until I thought that surely the lion, the tiger, the bear, and the rest of the wild tribe would not be able to stand before these wily hunters. "Tomorrow to the chase!" was their goodnight shout as the circle of merry friends broke up for the night. The men slept in the hall outside our door, and I could feel the deep breathing of the dogs and the hunters as they lay on their improvised beds.

CHAPTER 11

At dawn I was awakened by the smell of coffee, the rattling of guns, and the heavy footsteps of the men as they strode about, promising themselves the greatest luck of the season. I could also feel the stamping of the horses, which they had ridden out from town and hitched under the trees, where they stood all night, neighing loudly, impatient to be off. At last the men mounted, and, as they say in the old songs, away went the steeds with bridles ringing and whips cracking and hounds racing ahead, and away went the champion hunters "with hark and whoop and wild halloo!"

Later in the morning, we made preparations for a barbecue. A fire was kindled at the bottom of a deep hole in the ground, big sticks were laid crosswise at the top, and meat was hung from them and turned on spits. People squatted around the fire, driving away the flies with long branches. The savory odor of the meat made me hungry long before the tables were set.

When the bustle and excitement of preparation was at its height, the hunting party made its appearance, struggling in by twos and threes, the men hot and weary, the horses covered with foam, and the jaded hounds panting and dejected—and not a single kill! Every man declared that he had seen at least one deer, and that the animal had come very close; but however hotly the dogs might pursue the game, however well the guns might be aimed, at the snap of the trigger there was not a deer in sight. They had been as fortunate as the little boy who said he came very near seeing a rabbit—he saw his tracks. The party soon forgot its disappointment, however, and we sat down, not to venison, but to a tamer feast of veal and roast pig.

One summer, I had my pony at Fern Quarry. I called him Black Beauty, as I had just read the book, and he resembled his namesake in every way, from his glossy black coat to the white star on his forehead. I spent many of my happiest hours on his back. Occasionally, when it was quite safe, my teacher would let go the leading rein, and the pony sauntered on or stopped at his sweet will to eat grass or nibble the leaves of the trees that grew beside the narrow trail.

On mornings when I did not care for the ride, my teacher and I would start after breakfast for a ramble in the woods, and allow ourselves to get lost amid the trees and vines, with no road to follow except the paths made by cows and horses. Frequently we came upon impassable thickets which forced us to take a roundabout way. We always returned to the cottage with armfuls of laurel, goldenrod, ferns, and gorgeous swamp flowers such as grow only in the South.

Sometimes I would go with Mildred and my little cousins to gather persimmons. I did not eat them; but I loved their fragrance and enjoyed hunting for them in the leaves and grass. We also went nutting, and I helped them open the chestnut burs and break the shells of hickory nuts and walnuts—the big, sweet walnuts!

At the foot of the mountain there was a railroad, and the children watched the trains whiz by. Sometimes a terrific whistle brought us to the steps, and Mildred told me in great excitement that a cow or a horse had strayed on the track. About a mile distant there was a trestle spanning a deep gorge. It was very difficult to walk over, the ties were wide apart and so narrow that one felt as if one were walking on knives. I had never crossed it until one day Mildred, Miss Sullivan, and I were lost in the woods, and wandered for hours without finding a path.

Suddenly, Mildred pointed with her little hand and exclaimed, "There's the trestle!" We would have taken any way rather than this; but it was late and growing dark, and the trestle was a shortcut home. I had to feel for the rails with my toe; but I was not afraid, and got on very well, until all at once there came a faint "puff, puff" from the distance.

"I see the train!" cried Mildred, and in another minute it would have been upon us had we not climbed down on the cross braces while it rushed over our heads. I felt the hot breath from the engine on my face, and the smoke and ashes almost choked us. As the train rumbled by, the trestle shook and swayed until I thought we should be dashed to the chasm below. With the utmost difficulty, we regained the track. Long after dark we reached home and found the cottage empty; the family were all out hunting for us.

Helen Keller, 1904

CHAPTER 12

AFTER MY first visit to Boston, I spent almost every winter in the North. Once I went on a visit to a New England village with its frozen lakes and vast snow fields. It was then that I had opportunities such as had never been mine, to enter into the treasures of the snow.

I recall my surprise on discovering that a mysterious hand had stripped the trees and bushes, leaving only here and there a wrinkled leaf. The birds had flown, and their empty nests in the bare trees were filled with snow. Winter was on hill and field. The earth seemed benumbed by his icy touch, and the very spirits of the trees had withdrawn to their roots, and there, curled up in the dark, lay fast asleep. All life seemed to have ebbed away, and even when the sun shone the day was

> Shrunk and cold,
> As if her veins were sapless and old,
> And she rose up decrepitly
> For a last dim look at earth and sea.
>
> The withered grass and the bushes were transformed into a forest of icicles.

Then came a day when the chill air portended a snowstorm. We rushed out-of-doors to feel the first few tiny flakes descending. Hour by hour the flakes dropped silently, softly from their airy height to the earth, and the country became more and more level. A snowy night closed upon the world, and in the morning one could scarcely recognize a feature of the landscape. All the roads were hidden, not a single landmark was visible, only a waste of snow with trees rising out of it.

In the evening a wind from the northeast sprang up, and the flakes rushed hither and thither in furious melee. Around the great fire we sat and told merry tales, and frolicked, and quite forgot that we were in the midst of a desolate solitude, shut in from all communication with the outside world. But during the night the fury of the wind increased to such a degree that it thrilled us with a vague terror. The rafters creaked and strained, and the branches of the trees surrounding the house rattled and beat against the windows, as the winds rioted up and down the country.

On the third day after the beginning of the storm, the snow ceased. The sun broke through the clouds and shone upon a vast, undulating white plain. High mounds, pyramids heaped in fantastic shapes, and impenetrable drifts lay scattered in every direction.

Narrow paths were shoveled through the drifts. I put on my cloak and hood and went out. The air stung my cheeks like fire. Half walking in the paths, half working our way through the lesser drifts, we succeeded in reaching a pine grove just outside a broad pasture. The trees stood motionless and white—like figures in a marble frieze. There was no odor of pine needles. The rays of the sun fell upon the trees, so that the twigs sparkled like diamonds and dropped in showers when we touched them. So dazzling was the light, it penetrated even the darkness that veiled my eyes.

As the days wore on, the drifts gradually shrunk, but before they were wholly gone another storm came, so that I scarcely felt the earth under my feet once all winter. At intervals the trees lost their icy covering, and the bulrushes and underbrush were bare; but the lake lay frozen and hard beneath the sun.

    Our favorite amusement during that winter was tobogganing. In places the shore of the lake rises abruptly from the water's edge. Down these steep slopes we used to coast. We would get on our toboggan, a boy would give us a shove, and off we went! Plunging through drifts, leaping hollows, swooping down upon the lake, we would shoot across its gleaming surface to the opposite bank. What joy! What exhilarating madness! For one wild, glad moment we snapped the chain that binds us to earth, and joining hands with the winds we felt ourselves divine!

CHAPTER 13

IT WAS in the spring of 1890 that I learned to speak. The impulse to utter audible sounds had always been strong within me. I used to make noises, keeping one hand on my throat while the other hand felt the movements of my lips. I was pleased with anything that made a noise and liked to feel the cat purr and the dog bark. I also liked to keep my hand on a singer's throat or on a piano when it was being played. Before I lost my sight and hearing, I was fast learning to talk, but after my illness it was found that I had ceased to speak because I could not hear. I used to sit in my mother's lap all day long and keep my hands on her face because it amused me to feel the motions of her lips; and I moved my lips, too, although I had forgotten what talking was. My friends say that I laughed and cried naturally, and for awhile I made many sounds and word elements, not because they were a means of communication, but because the need of exercising my vocal organs was imperative. There was, however, one word the meaning of which I still remembered, WATER. I pronounced it "wa-wa." Even this became less and less intelligible until the time when Miss Sullivan began to teach me. I stopped using it only after I had learned to spell the word with my fingers.

I had known for a long time that the people about me used a method of communication different from mine; and even before I knew that a deaf child could be taught to speak, I was conscious of dissatisfaction with the means of communication I already possessed. One who is entirely dependent upon the manual alphabet has always a sense of restraint, of narrowness. This feeling began to agitate me with a vexing, forward-reaching sense of a lack that should be filled. My thoughts would often rise and beat up like birds against the wind, and I persisted in using my lips and voice. Friends tried to discourage this tendency, fearing lest it would lead to disappointment. But I persisted, and an accident soon occurred which resulted in the breaking down of this great barrier—I heard the story of Ragnhild Kaata.

In 1890 Mrs. Lamson, who had been one of Laura Bridgman's teachers, and who had just returned from a visit to Norway and Sweden, came to see me, and told me of Ragnhild Kaata, a deaf and blind girl in Norway who had actually been taught to speak. Mrs. Lamson had scarcely finished telling me about this girl's success before I was on fire with eagerness. I resolved that I, too, would learn to speak. I would not rest satisfied until my teacher took me, for advice and assistance, to Miss Sarah Fuller, principal of the Horace Mann School. This lovely, sweet-natured lady offered to teach me herself, and we began the twenty-sixth of March 1890.

Miss Fuller's method was this: she passed my hand lightly over her face and let me feel the position of her tongue and lips when she made a sound. I was eager to imitate every motion and in an hour had learned six elements of speech: M, P, A, S, T, I. Miss Fuller gave me eleven lessons in all. I shall never forget the surprise and delight I felt when I uttered my first connected sentence, "It is warm." True, they were broken and stammering syllables; but they were human speech. My soul, conscious of new strength, came out of bondage, and was reaching through those broken symbols of speech to all knowledge and all faith.

No deaf child who has earnestly tried to speak the words which he has never heard—to come out of the prison of silence, where no tone of love, no song of bird, no strain of music ever pierces the stillness—can forget the thrill of surprise, the joy of discovery which came over him when he uttered his first word. Only such a one can appreciate the eagerness with which I talked to my toys, to stones, trees, birds, and dumb animals, or the delight I felt when at my call Mildred ran to me or my dogs obeyed my commands. It is an unspeakable boon to me to be able to speak in winged words that need no interpretation. As I talked, happy thoughts fluttered up out of my words that might perhaps have struggled in vain to escape my fingers.

But it must not be supposed that I could really talk in this short time. I had learned only the elements of speech. Miss Fuller and Miss Sullivan could understand me, but most people would not have understood one word in a hundred. Nor is it true that, after I had learned these elements, I did the rest of the work myself. But for Miss Sullivan's genius, untiring perseverance and devotion, I could not have progressed as far as I have toward natural speech. In the first place, I labored night and day before I could be understood even by my most intimate friends; in the second place, I needed Miss Sullivan's assistance constantly in my efforts to articulate each sound clearly and to combine all sounds in a thousand ways. Even now she calls my attention every day to mispronounced words.

All teachers of the deaf know what this means, and only they can at all appreciate the peculiar difficulties with which I had to contend. In reading my teacher's lips, I was wholly dependent on my fingers: I had to use the sense of touch in catching the vibrations of the throat, the movements of the mouth, and the expression of the face; and often this sense was at fault. In such cases I was forced to repeat the words or sentences, sometimes for hours, until I felt the proper ring in my own voice. My work was practice, practice, practice. Discouragement and weariness cast me down frequently; but the next moment the thought that I should soon be at home and show my loved ones what I had accomplished, spurred me on, and I eagerly looked forward to their pleasure in my achievement.

"My little sister will understand me now," was a thought stronger than all obstacles. I used to repeat ecstatically, "I am not dumb now." I could not be despondent while I anticipated the delight of talking to my mother and reading her responses from her lips. It astonished me to find how much easier it is to talk than to spell with the fingers, and I discarded the manual alphabet as a medium of communication on my part; but Miss Sullivan and a few friends still use it in speaking to me, for it is more convenient and more rapid than lip reading.

Just here, perhaps, I had better explain our use of the manual alphabet, which seems to puzzle people who do not know us. One who reads or talks to me spells with his hand, using the single-hand manual alphabet generally employed by the deaf. I place my hand on the hand of the speaker so lightly as not to impede its movements. The position of the hand is as easy to feel as it is to see. I do not feel each letter anymore than you see each letter separately when you read. Constant practice makes the fingers very flexible, and some of my friends spell rapidly—about as fast as an expert writes on a typewriter. The mere spelling is, of course, no more a conscious act than it is in writing.

When I had made speech my own, I could not wait to go home. At last the happiest of happy moments arrived. I had made my homeward journey, talking constantly to Miss Sullivan, not for the sake of talking, but determined to improve to the last minute. Almost before I knew it, the train stopped at the Tuscumbia station, and there on the platform stood the whole family. My eyes fill with tears now as I think how my mother pressed me close to her, speechless and trembling with delight, taking in every syllable that I spoke, while little Mildred seized my free hand and kissed it and danced, and my father expressed his pride and affection in a big silence. It was as if Isaiah's prophecy had been fulfilled in me, "The mountains and the hills shall break forth before you into singing, and all the trees of the field shall clap their hands!"

CHAPTER 14

THE WINTER of 1892 was darkened by the one cloud in my childhood's bright sky. Joy deserted my heart, and for a long, long time I lived in doubt, anxiety, and fear. Books lost their charm for me, and even now the thought of those dreadful days chills my heart. A little story called *The Frost King*, which I wrote and sent to Mr. Anagnos, of the Perkins Institution for the Blind, was at the root of the trouble. In order to make the matter clear, I must set forth the facts connected with this episode, which justice to my teacher and to myself compels me to relate.

I wrote the story when I was at home, the autumn after I had learned to speak. We had stayed up at Fern Quarry later than usual. While we were there, Miss Sullivan had described to me the beauties of the late foliage, and it seems that her descriptions revived the memory of a story, which must have been read to me, and which I must have unconsciously retained. I thought then that I was "making up a story," as children say, and I eagerly sat down to write it before the ideas should slip from me. My thoughts flowed easily; I felt a sense of joy in the composition. Words and images came tripping to my finger ends, and as I thought out sentence after sentence, I wrote them on my braille slate. Now, if words and images come to me without effort, it is a pretty sure sign that they are not the offspring of my own mind, but stray waifs that I regretfully dismiss. At that time I eagerly absorbed everything I read without a thought of authorship, and even now I cannot be quite sure of the boundary line between my ideas and those I find in books. I suppose that is because so many of my impressions come to me through the medium of others' eyes and ears.

When the story was finished, I read it to my teacher, and I recall now vividly the pleasure I felt in the more beautiful passages, and my annoyance at being interrupted to have the pronunciation of a word corrected. At dinner it was read to the assembled family, who were surprised that I could write so well. Someone asked me if I had read it in a book.

This question surprised me very much; for I had not the faintest recollection of having had it read to me. I spoke up and said, "Oh, no, it is my story, and I have written it for Mr. Anagnos."

Accordingly I copied the story and sent it to him for his birthday. It was suggested that I should change the title from "Autumn Leaves" to *The Frost King*, which I did. I carried the little story to the post office myself, feeling as if I were walking on air. I little dreamed how cruelly I should pay for that birthday gift.

Mr. Anagnos was delighted with *The Frost King,* and published it in one of the Perkins Institution reports. This was the pinnacle of my happiness, from which I was in a little while dashed to earth. I had been in Boston only a short time when it was discovered that a story similar to *The Frost King,* called *The Frost Fairies* by Miss Margaret T. Canby, had appeared before I was born in a book called *Birdie and His Fairy Friends.* The two stories were so much alike in thought and language that it was evident Miss Canby's story had been read to me, and that mine was—a plagiarism. It was difficult to make me understand this; but when

I did understand, I was astonished and grieved. No child ever drank deeper of the cup of bitterness than I did. I had disgraced myself; I had brought suspicion upon those I loved best. And yet how could it possibly have happened? I racked my brain until I was weary to recall anything about the frost that I had read before I wrote *The Frost King*; but I could remember nothing, except the common reference to Jack Frost, and a poem for children, "The Freaks of King Frost," and I knew I had not used that in my composition.

At first Mr. Anagnos, though deeply troubled, seemed to believe me. He was unusually tender and kind to me, and for a brief space the shadow lifted. To please him I tried not to be unhappy, and to make myself as pretty as possible for the celebration of Washington's birthday, which took place very soon after I received the sad news.

I was to be Ceres in a kind of masque given by the blind girls. How well I remember the graceful draperies that enfolded me, the bright autumn leaves that wreathed my head, and the fruit and grain at my feet and in my hands, and beneath all the piety of the masque the oppressive sense of coming ill that made my heart heavy.

The night before the celebration, one of the teachers of the Institution had asked me a question connected with *The Frost King,* and I was telling her that Miss Sullivan had talked to me about Jack Frost and his wonderful works. Something I said made her think she detected in my words a confession that I did remember Miss Canby's story of *The Frost Fairies,* and she laid her conclusions before Mr. Anagnos, although I had told her most emphatically that she was mistaken.

Mr. Anagnos, who loved me tenderly, thinking that he had been deceived, turned a deaf ear to the pleadings of love and innocence. He believed, or at least suspected, that Miss Sullivan and I had deliberately stolen the bright thoughts of another and imposed them on him to win his admiration. I was brought before a court of investigation composed of the teachers and officers of the Institution, and Miss Sullivan was asked to leave me. Then I was questioned and cross-questioned with what seemed to me a determination on the part of my judges to force me to acknowledge that I remembered having had *The Frost Fairies* read to me. I felt in every question the doubt and suspicion that was in their minds, and I felt, too, that a loved friend was looking at me reproachfully, although I could not have put all this into words. The blood pressed about my thumping heart, and I could scarcely speak, except in monosyllables. Even the consciousness that it was only a dreadful mistake did not lessen my suffering, and when at last I was allowed to leave the room, I was dazed and did not notice my teacher's caresses, or the tender words of my friends, who said I was a brave little girl and they were proud of me.

As I lay in my bed that night, I wept as I hope few children have wept. I felt so cold, I imagined I should die before morning, and the thought comforted me. I think if this sorrow had come to me when I was older, it would have broken my spirit beyond repairing. But the angel of forgetfulness has gathered up and carried away much of the misery and all the bitterness of those sad days.

Miss Sullivan had never heard of *The Frost Fairies* or of the book in which it was published. With the assistance of Dr. Alexander Graham Bell, she investigated the matter carefully, and at last it came out that Mrs. Sophia C. Hopkins had a copy of Miss Canby's *Birdie and His Fairy Friends* in 1888, the year that we spent the summer with her at Brewster. Mrs. Hopkins was unable to find her copy; but she has told me that at that time, while Miss Sullivan was away on a vacation, she tried to amuse me by reading from various books, and although she could not remember reading *The Frost Fairies* anymore than I, yet she felt sure that *Birdie and His Fairy Friends* was one of them. She explained the disappearance of the book by the fact that she had a short time before sold her house and disposed of many juvenile books, such as old schoolbooks and fairy tales, and that *Birdie and His Fairy Friends* was probably among them.

The stories had little or no meaning for me then; but the mere spelling of the strange words was sufficient to amuse a little child who could do almost nothing to amuse herself; and although I do not recall a single circumstance connected with the reading of the stories, yet I cannot help thinking that I made a great effort to remember the words, with the intention of having my teacher explain them when she returned. One thing is certain, the language was ineffaceably stamped upon my brain, though for a long time no one knew it, least of all myself.

When Miss Sullivan came back, I did not speak to her about *The Frost Fairies,* probably because she began at once to read *Little Lord Fauntleroy*, which filled my mind to the exclusion of everything else. But the fact remains that Miss Canby's story was read to me once, and that long after I had forgotten it, it came back to me so naturally that I never suspected that it was the child of another mind.

In my trouble I received many messages of love and sympathy. All the friends I loved best, except one, have remained my own to the present time.

Miss Canby herself wrote kindly, "Some day you will write a great story out of your own head, that will be a comfort and help to many." But this kind prophecy has never been fulfilled. I have never played with words again for the mere pleasure of the game. Indeed, I have ever since been tortured by the fear that what I write is not my own. For a long time, when I wrote a letter, even to my mother, I was seized with a sudden feeling of terror, and I would spell the sentences over and over, to make sure that I had not read them in a book. Had it not been for the persistent encouragement of Miss Sullivan, I think I should have given up trying to write altogether.

I have read *The Frost Fairies* since, also the letters I wrote in which I used other ideas of Miss Canby's. I find in one of them, a letter to Mr. Anagnos, dated September 29, 1891, words and sentiments exactly like those of the book. At the time I was writing *The Frost King,* and this letter, like many others, contains phrases which show that my mind was saturated with the story. I represent my teacher as saying to me of the golden autumn leaves, "Yes, they are beautiful enough to comfort us for the flight of summer"—an idea direct from Miss Canby's story.

This habit of assimilating what pleased me and giving it out again as my own appears in much of my early correspondence and my first attempts at writing. In a composition which I wrote about the old cities of Greece and Italy, I borrowed my glowing descriptions, with variations, from sources I have forgotten. I knew Mr. Anagnos's great love of antiquity and his enthusiastic appreciation of all beautiful sentiments about Italy and Greece. I therefore gathered from all the books I read every bit of poetry or of history that I thought would give him pleasure. Mr. Anagnos, in speaking of my composition on the cities, has said, "These ideas are poetic in their essence." But I do not understand how he ever thought a blind and deaf child of eleven could have invented them. Yet I cannot think that because I did not originate the ideas, my little composition is therefore quite devoid of interest. It shows me that I could express my appreciation of beautiful and poetic ideas in clear and animated language.

Those early compositions were mental gymnastics. I was learning, as all young and inexperienced persons learn, by assimilation and imitation, to put ideas into words. Everything I found in books that pleased me, I retained in my memory, consciously or unconsciously, and adapted it. The young writer, as Stevenson has said, instinctively tries to copy whatever seems most admirable, and he shifts his admiration with astonishing versatility. It is only after years of this sort of practice that even great men have learned to marshal the legion of words which come thronging through every byway of the mind.

I am afraid I have not yet completed this process. It is certain that I cannot always distinguish my own thoughts from those I read, because what I read becomes the very substance and texture of my mind. Consequently, in nearly all that I write, I produce something which very much resembles the crazy patchwork I used to make when I first learned to sew. This patchwork was made of all sorts of odds and ends—pretty bits of silk and velvet—but the coarse pieces that were not pleasant to touch always predominated. Likewise my compositions are made up of crude notions of my own, inlaid with the brighter thoughts and riper opinions of the authors I have read. It seems to me that the great difficulty of writing is to make the language of the educated mind express our confused ideas, half feelings, half thoughts, when we are little more than bundles of instinctive tendencies. Trying to write is very much like trying to put a Chinese puzzle together. We have a pattern in mind which we wish to work out in words; but the words will not fit the spaces, or, if they do, they will not match the design. But we keep on trying because we know that others have succeeded, and we are not willing to acknowledge defeat.

"There is no way to become original, except to be born so," says Stevenson, and although I may not be original, I hope sometime to outgrow my artificial, periwigged compositions. Then, perhaps, my own thoughts and experiences will come to the surface. Meanwhile I trust and hope and persevere, and try not to let the bitter memory of *The Frost King* trammel my efforts.

So this sad experience may have done me good and set me thinking on some of the problems of composition. My only regret is that it resulted in the loss of one of my dearest friends, Mr. Anagnos.

Since the publication of *The Story of My Life* in the *Ladies' Home Journal*, Mr. Anagnos has made a statement, in a letter to Mr. Macy, that at the time of *The Frost King* matter, he believed I was innocent. He says, the court of investigation before which

I was brought consisted of eight people: four blind, four seeing persons. Four of them, he says, thought I knew that Miss Canby's story had been read to me, and the others did not hold this view. Mr. Anagnos states that he cast his vote with those who were favorable to me.

But, however the case may have been, with whichever side he may have cast his vote, when I went into the room where Mr. Anagnos had so often held me on his knee and, forgetting his many cares, had shared in my frolics, and found there persons who seemed to doubt me, I felt that there was something hostile and menacing in the very atmosphere, and subsequent events have borne out this impression. For two years he seems to have held the belief that Miss Sullivan and I were innocent. Then he evidently retracted his favorable judgment, why I do not know. Nor did I know the details of the investigation. I never knew even the names of the members of the "court" who did not speak to me. I was too excited to notice anything, too frightened to ask questions. Indeed, I could scarcely think what I was saying, or what was being said to me.

I have given this account of *The Frost King* affair because it was important in my life and education; and, in order that there might be no misunderstanding, I have set forth all the facts as they appear to me, without a thought of defending myself or of laying blame on anyone.

CHAPTER 15

THE SUMMER and winter following the "Frost King" incident I spent with my family in Alabama. I recall with delight that homegoing. Everything had budded and blossomed. I was happy. *The Frost King* was forgotten.

When the ground was strewn with the crimson and golden leaves of autumn, and the musk-scented grapes that covered the arbor at the end of the garden were turning golden brown in the sunshine, I began to write a sketch of my life—a year after I had written *The Frost King*.

I was still excessively scrupulous about everything I wrote. The thought that what I wrote might not be absolutely my own tormented me. No one knew of these fears except my teacher. A strange sensitiveness prevented me from referring to *The Frost King*; and often when an idea flashed out in the course of conversation I would spell softly to her, "I am not sure it is mine." At other times, in the midst of a paragraph I was writing, I said to myself, "Suppose it should be found that all this was written by someone long ago!" An impish fear clutched my hand, so that I could not write anymore that day. And even now I sometimes feel the same uneasiness and disquietude. Miss Sullivan consoled and helped me in every way she could think of; but the terrible experience I had passed through left a lasting impression on my mind, the significance of which I am only just beginning to understand. It was with the hope of restoring my self-confidence that she persuaded me to write for the *Youth's Companion* a brief account of my life. I was then twelve years old. As I look back on my struggle to write that little story, it seems to me that I must have had a prophetic vision of the good that would come of the undertaking, or I should surely have failed.

I wrote timidly, fearfully, but resolutely, urged on by my teacher, who knew that if I persevered, I should find my mental foothold again and get a grip on my faculties. Up to the time of the "Frost King" episode, I had lived the unconscious life of a little child; now my thoughts were turned inward, and I beheld things invisible. Gradually I emerged from the penumbra of that experience with a mind made clearer by trial and with a truer knowledge of life.

The chief events of the year 1893 were my trip to Washington during the inauguration of President Cleveland, and visits to Niagara and the World's Fair. Under such circumstances my studies were constantly interrupted and often put aside for many weeks, so that it is impossible for me to give a connected account of them.

We went to Niagara in March 1893. It is difficult to describe my emotions when I stood on the point which overhangs the American Falls and felt the air vibrate and the earth tremble.

It seems strange to many people that I should be impressed by the wonders and beauties of Niagara. They are always asking: "What does this beauty or that music mean to you? You cannot see the waves rolling up the beach or hear their roar. What do they mean to you?" In the most evident sense they mean everything. I cannot fathom or define their meaning anymore than I can fathom or define love or religion or goodness.

During the summer of 1893, Miss Sullivan and I visited the

World's Fair with Dr. Alexander Graham Bell. I recall with unmixed delight those days when a thousand childish fancies became beautiful realities. Every day in imagination I made a trip around the world, and I saw many wonders from the uttermost parts of the earth—marvels of invention, treasuries of industry, and skill and all the activities of human life actually passed under my finger tips.

I liked to visit the Midway Plaisance. It seemed like the "Arabian Nights," it was crammed so full of novelty and interest. Here was the India of my books in the curious bazaar with its Shivas and elephant gods; there was the land of the pyramids concentrated in a model Cairo with its mosques and its long processions of camels; yonder were the lagoons of Venice, where we sailed every evening when the city and the fountains were illuminated. I also went on board a Viking ship which lay a short distance from the little craft. I had been on a man-of-war before, in Boston, and it interested me to see, on this Viking ship, how the seaman was once all in all—how he sailed and took storm and calm alike with undaunted heart, and gave chase to whosoever reechoed his cry, "We are of the sea!" and fought with brains and sinews, self-reliant, self-sufficient, instead of being thrust into the background by unintelligent machinery, as Jack is today. So it always is—"man only is interesting to man."

At a little distance from this ship there was a model of the *Santa Maria*, which I also examined. The captain showed me Columbus' cabin and the desk with an hourglass on it. This small instrument impressed me most because it made me think how weary the heroic navigator must have felt as he saw the sand dropping grain by grain while desperate men were plotting against his life.

Mr. Higinbotham, president of the World's Fair, kindly gave me permission to touch the exhibits, and with an eagerness as insatiable as that with which Pizarro seized the treasures of Peru, I took in the glories of the Fair with my fingers. It was a sort of tangible kaleidoscope, this white city of the West. Everything fascinated me, especially the French bronzes. They were so lifelike, I thought they were angel visions which the artist had caught and bound in earthly forms.

At the Cape of Good Hope exhibit, I learned much about the processes of mining diamonds. Whenever it was possible, I touched the machinery while it was in motion, so as to get a clearer idea how the stones were weighed, cut, and polished. I searched in the washings for a diamond and found it myself—the only true diamond, they said, that was ever found in the United States.

Dr. Bell went everywhere with us and in his own delightful way described to me the objects of greatest interest. In the electrical building, we examined the telephones, autophones, phonographs, and other inventions, and he made me understand how it is possible to send a message on wires that mock space and outrun time, and, like Prometheus, to draw fire from the sky. We also visited the anthropological department, and I was much interested in the relics of ancient Mexico, in the rude stone implements that are so often the only record of an age—the simple monuments of nature's unlettered children (so I thought as I fingered them) that seem bound to last while the memorials of kings and sages crumble in dust away—and in the Egyptian mummies, which I shrank from touching. From these relics I learned more about the progress of man than I have heard or read since.

All these experiences added a great many new terms to my vocabulary, and in the three weeks I spent at the Fair, I took a long leap from the little child's interest in fairy tales and toys to the appreciation of the real and the earnest in the workaday world.

CHAPTER 16

BEFORE OCTOBER 1893, I had studied various subjects by myself in a more or less desultory manner. I read the histories of Greece, Rome, and the United States. I had a French grammar book in raised print, and as I already knew some French, I often amused myself by composing in my head short exercises, using the new words as I came across them, and ignoring rules and other technicalities as much as possible. I even tried, without aid, to master the French pronunciation, as I found all the letters and sounds described in the book. Of course this was tasking slender powers for great ends; but it gave me something to do on a rainy day, and I acquired a sufficient knowledge of French to read with pleasure La Fontaine's *Fables*, *Le Medecin Malgre Lui*, and passages from *Athalie*.

I also gave considerable time to the improvement of my speech. I read aloud to Miss Sullivan and recited passages from my favorite poets, which I had committed to memory; she corrected my pronunciation and helped me to phrase and inflect. It was not, however, until October 1893, after I had recovered from the fatigue and excitement of my visit to the World's Fair, that I began to have lessons in special subjects at fixed hours.

Miss Sullivan and I were at that time in Hulton, Pennsylvania, visiting the family of Mr. William Wade. Mr. Irons, a neighbor of theirs, was a good Latin scholar; it was arranged that I should study under him. I remember him as a man of rare, sweet nature and of wide experience. He taught me Latin grammar principally; but he often helped me in arithmetic, which I found as troublesome as it was uninteresting. Mr. Irons also read with me Tennyson's *In Memoriam.* I had read many books before, but never from a critical point of view. I learned for the first time to know an author, to recognize his style as I recognize the clasp of a friend's hand.

At first I was rather unwilling to study Latin grammar. It seemed absurd to waste time analyzing every word I came across—noun, genitive, singular, feminine—when its meaning was quite plain. I thought I might just as well describe my pet in order to know it—order, vertebrate; division, quadruped; class, mammalia; genus, felinus; species, cat; individual, Tabby. But as I got deeper into the subject, I became more interested, and the beauty of the language delighted me. I often amused myself by reading Latin passages, picking up words I understood and trying to make sense. I have never ceased to enjoy this pastime.

There is nothing more beautiful, I think, than the evanescent fleeting images and sentiments presented by a language one is just becoming familiar with—ideas that flit across the mental sky, shaped and tinted by capricious fancy. Miss Sullivan sat beside me at my lessons, spelling into my hand whatever Mr. Irons said, and looking up new words for me. I was just beginning to read Caesar's *Gallic War* when I went to my home in Alabama.

CHAPTER 17

IN THE summer of 1894, I attended the meeting at Chautauqua of the American Association to Promote the Teaching of Speech to the Deaf. There it was arranged that I should go to the Wright-Humason School for the Deaf in New York City. I went there in October 1894, accompanied by Miss Sullivan. This school was chosen especially for the purpose of obtaining the highest advantages in vocal culture and training in lip reading. In addition to my work in these subjects, I studied, during the two years I was in the school, arithmetic, physical geography, French, and German.

Miss Reamy, my German teacher, could use the manual alphabet, and after I had acquired a small vocabulary, we talked together in German whenever we had a chance, and in a few months I could understand almost everything she said. Before the end of the first year I read *Wilhelm Tell* with the greatest delight. Indeed, I think I made more progress in German than in any of my other studies. I found French much more difficult. I studied it with Madame Olivier, a French lady who did not know the manual alphabet, and who was obliged to give her instruction orally. I could not read her lips easily; so my progress was much slower than in German. I managed, however, to read *Le Medecin Malgre Lui* again. It was very amusing, but I did not like it nearly so well as *Wilhelm Tell*.

My progress in lip reading and speech was not what my teachers and I had hoped and expected it would be. It was my ambition to speak like other people, and my teachers believed that this could be accomplished; but, although we worked hard and faithfully, yet we did not quite reach our goal. I suppose we aimed too high, and disappointment was therefore inevitable.
I still regarded arithmetic as a system of pitfalls. I hung about the dangerous frontier of "guess," avoiding with infinite trouble to myself and others the broad valley of reason. When I was not guessing, I was jumping at conclusions, and this fault, in addition to my dullness, aggravated my difficulties more than was right or necessary.

But although these disappointments caused me great depression at times, I pursued my other studies with unflagging interest, especially physical geography. It was a joy to learn the secrets of nature: how—in the picturesque language of the Old Testament—the winds are made to blow from the four corners of the heavens, how the vapors ascend from the ends of the earth, how rivers are cut out among the rocks, and mountains overturned by the roots, and in what ways man may overcome many forces mightier than himself. The two years in New York were happy ones, and I look back to them with genuine pleasure.

I remember especially the walks we all took together every day in Central Park, the only part of the city that was congenial to me. I never lost a jot of my delight in this great park. I loved to have it described every time I entered it; for it was beautiful in all its aspects, and these aspects were so many that it was beautiful in a different way each day of the nine months I spent in New York.

In the spring we made excursions to various places of interest. We sailed on the Hudson River and wandered about on its green banks, of which Bryant loved to sing. I liked the simple, wild grandeur of the palisades. Among the places I visited were West Point, Tarrytown, the home of Washington Irving, where I walked through "Sleepy Hollow."

The teachers at the Wright-Humason School were always planning how they might give the pupils every advantage that those who hear enjoy—how they might make much of few tendencies and passive memories in the cases of the little ones—and lead them out of the cramping circumstances in which their lives were set.

Before I left New York, these bright days were darkened by the greatest sorrow that I have ever borne, except the death of my father. Mr. John P. Spaulding, of Boston, died in February 1896. Only those who knew and loved him best can understand what his friendship meant to me. He, who made everyone happy in a beautiful, unobtrusive way, was most kind and tender to Miss Sullivan and me. So long as we felt his loving presence and knew that he took a watchful interest in our work, fraught with so many difficulties, we could not be discouraged. His going away left a vacancy in our lives that has never been filled.

CHAPTER 18

IN OCTOBER 1896, I entered the Cambridge School for Young Ladies, to be prepared for Radcliffe.

When I was a little girl, I visited Wellesley and surprised my friends by the announcement, "Some day I shall go to college—but I shall go to Harvard!" When asked why I would not go to Wellesley, I replied that there were only girls there. The thought of going to college took root in my heart and became an earnest desire, which impelled me to enter into competition for a degree with seeing and hearing girls, in the face of the strong opposition of many true and wise friends. When I left New York the idea had become a fixed purpose; and it was decided that I should go to Cambridge. This was the nearest approach I could get to Harvard and to the fulfillment of my childish declaration.

At the Cambridge School, the plan was to have Miss Sullivan attend the classes with me and interpret to me the instruction given.

Of course my instructors had had no experience in teaching any but normal pupils, and my only means of conversing with them was reading their lips. My studies for the first year were English history, English literature, German, Latin, arithmetic,

Latin composition and occasional themes. Until then I had never taken a course of study with the idea of preparing for college; but I had been well drilled in English by Miss Sullivan, and it soon became evident to my teachers that I needed no special instruction in this subject beyond a critical study of the books prescribed by the college. I had had, moreover, a good start in French, and received six months' instruction in Latin; but German was the subject with which I was most familiar.

In spite, however, of these advantages, there were serious drawbacks to my progress. Miss Sullivan could not spell out in my hand all that the books required, and it was very difficult to have textbooks embossed in time to be of use to me, although my friends in London and Philadelphia were willing to hasten the work. For a while, indeed, I had to copy my Latin in braille, so that I could recite with the other girls. My instructors soon became sufficiently familiar with my imperfect speech to answer my questions readily and correct mistakes. I could not make notes in class or write exercises; but I wrote all my compositions and translations at home on my typewriter.

Each day Miss Sullivan went to the classes with me and spelled into my hand with infinite patience all that the teachers said. In study hours she had to look up new words for me and read and reread notes and books I did not have in raised print. The tedium of that work is hard to conceive. Frau Grote, my German teacher, and Mr. Gilman, the principal, were the only teachers in the school who learned the finger alphabet to give me instruction. No one realized more fully than dear Frau Grote how slow and inadequate her spelling was. Nevertheless, in the goodness of her heart, she laboriously spelled out her instructions to me in special lessons twice a week, to give Miss Sullivan a little rest. But, though everybody was kind and ready to help us, there was only one hand that could turn drudgery into pleasure.

That year I finished arithmetic, reviewed my Latin grammar, and read three chapters of Caesar's *Gallic War*. In German I read, partly with my fingers and partly with Miss Sullivan's assistance, Schiller's *Lied von der Glocke* and *Der Taucher*, Heine's *Die Harzreise*, Freytag's *Aus dem Staat Friedrichs des Grossen*, Riehl's *Der Fluch Der Schonheit*, Lessing's *Minna von Barnhelm*, and Goethe's *Aus meinem Leben*. I took the greatest delight in these German books, especially Schiller's wonderful lyrics, the history of Frederick the Great's magnificent achievements, and the account of Goethe's life. I was sorry to finish *Die Harzreise*, so full of happy witticisms and charming descriptions of vine-clad hills, streams that sing and ripple in the sunshine, and wild regions, sacred to tradition and legend, the gray sisters of a long-vanished, imaginative age—descriptions such as can be given only by those to whom nature is "a feeling, a love, and an appetite."

Mr. Gilman instructed me part of the year in English literature. We read together, *As You Like It,* Burke's *Speech on Conciliation with America*, and Macaulay's *The Life of Samuel Johnson*. Mr. Gilman's broad views of history and literature and his clever explanations made my work easier and pleasanter than it could have been had I only read notes mechanically with the necessarily brief explanations given in the classes.

Burke's speech was more instructive than any other book on a political subject that I had ever read. My mind stirred with the stirring times, and the characters round which the life of two contending nations centered seemed to move right before me. I wondered more and more, while Burke's masterly speech rolled on in mighty surges of eloquence, how it was that King George and his ministers could have turned a deaf ear to his warning prophecy of our victory and their humiliation. Then I entered into the melancholy details of the relation in which the great statesman stood to his party and to the representatives of the people. I thought how strange it was that such precious seeds of truth and wisdom should have fallen among the tares of ignorance and corruption.

In a different way, Macaulay's *Life of Samuel Johnson* was

interesting. My heart went out to the lonely man who ate the bread of affliction in Grub Street, and yet, in the midst of toil and cruel suffering of body and soul, always had a kind word, and lent a helping hand to the poor and despised. I rejoiced over all his successes, I shut my eyes to his faults, and wondered, not that he had them, but that they had not crushed or dwarfed his soul. But in spite of Macaulay's brilliancy and his admirable faculty of making the commonplace seem fresh and picturesque, his positiveness wearied me at times, and his frequent sacrifices of truth to effect kept me in a questioning attitude very unlike the attitude of reverence in which I had listened to the Demosthenes of Great Britain.

At the Cambridge School, for the first time in my life, I enjoyed the companionship of seeing and hearing girls of my own age. I lived with several others in one of the pleasant houses connected with the school, the house where Mr. Howells used to live, and we all had the advantage of home life. I joined them in many of their games, even blind man's buff and frolics in the snow; I took long walks with them; we discussed our studies and read aloud the things that interested us. Some of the girls learned to speak to me, so that Miss Sullivan did not have to repeat their conversation.

At Christmas, my mother and little sister spent the holidays with me, and Mr. Gilman kindly offered to let Mildred study in his school. So Mildred stayed with me in Cambridge, and for six happy months we were hardly ever apart. It makes me most happy to remember the hours we spent helping each other in study and sharing our recreation together.

I took my preliminary examinations for Radcliffe from the 29th of June to the 3rd of July in 1897. The subjects I offered were elementary and advanced German, French, Latin, English, and Greek and Roman history, making nine hours in all. I passed in everything, and received "honors" in German and English.

Perhaps an explanation of the method that was in use when

I took my examinations will not be amiss here. The student was required to pass in sixteen hours—twelve hours being called elementary and four advanced. He had to pass five hours at a time to have them counted. The examination papers were given out at nine o'clock at Harvard and brought to Radcliffe by a special messenger. Each candidate was known, not by his name, but by a number. I was No. 233, but, as I had to use a typewriter, my identity could not be concealed.

It was thought advisable for me to have my examinations in a room by myself, because the noise of the typewriter might disturb the other girls. Mr. Gilman read all the papers to me by means of the manual alphabet. A man was placed on guard at the door to prevent interruption.

The first day I had German. Mr. Gilman sat beside me and read the paper through first, then sentence by sentence, while I repeated the words aloud, to make sure that I understood him perfectly. The papers were difficult, and I felt very anxious as I wrote out my answers on the typewriter. Mr. Gilman spelled to me what I had written, and I made such changes as I thought necessary, and he inserted them. I wish to say here that I have not had this advantage since in any of my examinations. At Radcliffe no one reads the papers to me after they are written, and I have no opportunity to correct errors unless I finish before the time is up. In that case I correct only such mistakes as I can recall in the few minutes allowed, and make notes of these corrections at the end of my paper. If I passed with higher credit in the preliminaries than in the finals, there are two reasons. In the finals, no one read my work over to me, and in the preliminaries I offered subjects with some of which I was in a measure familiar before my work in the Cambridge School; for at the beginning of the year I had passed examinations in English, History, French, and German, which Mr. Gilman gave me from previous Harvard papers.

Mr. Gilman sent my written work to the examiners with a certificate that I, candidate No. 233, had written the papers.

All the other preliminary examinations were conducted in the same manner. None of them was so difficult as the first. I remember that the day the Latin paper was brought to us, Professor Schilling came in and informed me I had passed satisfactorily in German. This encouraged me greatly, and I sped on to the end of the ordeal with a light heart and a steady hand.

Helen Keller, 1907

CHAPTER 19

WHEN I began my second year at the Gilman school, I was full of hope and determination to succeed. But during the first few weeks I was confronted with unforeseen difficulties. Mr. Gilman had agreed that that year I should study mathematics principally. I had physics, algebra, geometry, astronomy, Greek, and Latin. Unfortunately, many of the books I needed had not been embossed in time for me to begin with the classes, and I lacked important apparatus for some of my studies. The classes I was in were very large, and it was impossible for the teachers to give me special instruction. Miss Sullivan was obliged to read all the books to me, and interpret for the instructors, and for the first time in eleven years it seemed as if her dear hand would not be equal to the task.

It was necessary for me to write algebra and geometry in class and solve problems in physics, and this I could not do until we bought a braille writer, by means of which I could put down the steps and processes of my work. I could not follow with my eyes the geometrical figures drawn on the blackboard, and my only means of getting a clear idea of them was to make them on a cushion with straight and curved wires, which had bent and pointed ends. I had to carry in my mind, as Mr. Keith says in his report, the lettering of the figures, the hypothesis and conclusion, the construction and the process of the proof. In a word, every study had its obstacles. Sometimes I lost all courage and betrayed my feelings in a way I am ashamed to remember, especially as the signs of my trouble were afterward used against Miss Sullivan, the only person of all the kind friends I had there, who could make the crooked straight and the rough places smooth.

Little by little, however, my difficulties began to disappear. The embossed books and other apparatus arrived, and I threw myself into the work with renewed confidence. Algebra and geometry were the only studies that continued to defy my efforts to comprehend them. As I have said before, I had no aptitude for mathematics; the different points were not explained to me as fully as I wished. The geometrical diagrams were particularly vexing because I could not see the relation of the different parts to one another, even on the cushion. It was not until Mr. Keith taught me that I had a clear idea of mathematics.

I was beginning to overcome these difficulties when an event occurred which changed everything.

Just before the books came, Mr. Gilman had begun to remonstrate with Miss Sullivan on the ground that I was working too hard, and in spite of my earnest protestations, he reduced the number of my recitations. At the beginning we had agreed that I should, if necessary, take five years to prepare for college, but at the end of the first year the success of my examinations showed Miss Sullivan, Miss Harbaugh (Mr. Gilman's head teacher), and one other, that I could without too much effort complete my preparation in two years more. Mr. Gilman at first agreed to this; but when my tasks had become somewhat perplexing, he insisted that I was overworked, and that I should remain at his school three years longer. I did not like his plan, for I wished to enter college with my class.

On the seventeenth of November, I was not very well and did

not go to school. Although Miss Sullivan knew that my indisposition was not serious, yet Mr. Gilman, on hearing of it, declared that I was breaking down and made changes in my studies which would have rendered it impossible for me to take my final examinations with my class. In the end the difference of opinion between Mr. Gilman and Miss Sullivan resulted in my mother's withdrawing my sister Mildred and me from the Cambridge School.

After some delay it was arranged that I should continue my studies under a tutor, Mr. Merton S. Keith, of Cambridge. Miss Sullivan and I spent the rest of the winter with our friends, the Chamberlins in Wrentham, twenty-five miles from Boston.

From February to July 1898, Mr. Keith came out to Wrentham twice a week, and taught me algebra, geometry, Greek, and Latin. Miss Sullivan interpreted his instruction.

In October 1898, we returned to Boston. For eight months Mr. Keith gave me lessons five times a week, in periods of about an hour. He explained each time what I did not understand in the previous lesson, assigned new work, and took home with him the Greek exercises which I had written during the week on my typewriter, corrected them fully, and returned them to me.

In this way my preparation for college went on without interruption. I found it much easier and pleasanter to be taught by myself than to receive instruction in class. There was no hurry, no confusion. My tutor had plenty of time to explain what I did not understand, so I got on faster and did better work than I ever did in school. I still found more difficulty in mastering problems in mathematics than I did in any other of my studies. I wish algebra and geometry had been half as easy as the languages and literature. But even mathematics Mr. Keith made interesting; he succeeded in whittling problems small enough to get through my brain. He kept my mind alert and eager, and trained it to reason clearly, and to seek conclusions calmly and logically, instead of jumping wildly into space and arriving nowhere. He was always gentle and forbearing, no matter how dull I might be, and believe me, my stupidity would often have exhausted the patience of Job.

On the 29th and 30th of June 1899, I took my final examinations for Radcliffe College. The first day I had elementary Greek and advanced Latin, and the second day geometry, algebra, and advanced Greek.

The college authorities did not allow Miss Sullivan to read the examination papers to me; so Mr. Eugene C. Vining, one of the instructors at the Perkins Institution for the Blind, was employed to copy the papers for me in American Braille. Mr. Vining was a stranger to me, and could not communicate with me, except by writing braille. The proctor was also a stranger, and did not attempt to communicate with me in any way.

The braille worked well enough in the languages, but when it came to geometry and algebra, difficulties arose. I was sorely perplexed, and felt discouraged wasting much precious time, especially in algebra. It is true that I was familiar with all literary braille in common use in this country—English, American, and New York Point; but the various signs and symbols in geometry and algebra in the three systems are very different, and I had used only the English Braille in my algebra.

Two days before the examinations, Mr. Vining sent me a braille copy of one of the old Harvard papers in algebra. To my dismay, I found that it was in the American notation. I sat down immediately and wrote to Mr. Vining, asking him to explain the signs. I received another paper and a table of signs by return mail, and I set to work to learn the notation. But on the night before the algebra examination, while I was struggling over some very complicated examples, I could not tell the combinations of bracket, brace, and radical. Both Mr. Keith and I were distressed and full of forebodings for the morrow; but we went over to the college a little before the examination began, and had Mr. Vining explain more fully the American symbols.

In geometry my chief difficulty was that I had always been

accustomed to read the propositions in line print, or to have them spelled into my hand; and somehow, although the propositions were right before me, I found the braille confusing, and could not fix clearly in my mind what I was reading. But when I took up algebra, I had a harder time still. The signs, which I had so lately learned, and which I thought I knew, perplexed me. Besides, I could not see what I wrote on my typewriter. I had always done my work in braille or in my head. Mr. Keith had relied too much on my ability to solve problems mentally, and had not trained me to write examination papers. Consequently my work was painfully slow, and I had to read the examples over and over before I could form any idea of what I was required to do. Indeed, I am not sure now that I read all the signs correctly. I found it very hard to keep my wits about me.

But I do not blame anyone. The administrative board of Radcliffe did not realize how difficult they were making my examinations, nor did they understand the peculiar difficulties I had to surmount. But if they unintentionally placed obstacles in my way, I have the consolation of knowing that I overcame them all.

CHAPTER 20

THE STRUGGLE for admission to college was ended, and I could now enter Radcliffe whenever I pleased. Before I entered college, however, it was thought best that I should study another year under Mr. Keith. It was not, therefore, until the fall of 1900 that my dream of going to college was realized.

I remember my first day at Radcliffe. It was a day full of interest for me. I had looked forward to it for years. A potent force within me, stronger than the persuasion of my friends, stronger even than the pleadings of my heart, had impelled me to try my strength by the standards of those who see and hear. I knew that there were obstacles in the way; but I was eager to overcome them. I had taken to heart the words of the wise Roman who said, "To be banished from Rome is but to live outside of Rome." Debarred from the great highways of knowledge, I was compelled to make the journey across country by unfrequented roads—that was all; and I knew that in college there were many bypaths where I could touch hands with girls who were thinking, loving, and struggling like me.

I began my studies with eagerness. Before me I saw a new world opening in beauty and light, and I felt within me the capacity to know all things. In the wonderland of mind, I should be as free as another. Its people, scenery, manners, joys, tragedies should be living, tangible interpreters of the real world. The lecture halls seemed filled with the spirit of the great and the wise, and I thought the professors were the embodiment of wisdom. If I have since learned differently, I am not going to tell anybody.

But I soon discovered that college was not quite the romantic lyceum I had imagined. Many of the dreams that had delighted my young inexperience became beautifully less and "faded into the light of common day." Gradually I began to find that there were disadvantages in going to college.

The one I felt and still feel most is lack of time. I used to have time to think, to reflect, my mind and I. We would sit together in the evening and listen to the inner melodies of the spirit, which one hears only in leisure moments when the words of some loved poet touch a deep, sweet chord in the soul that until then had been silent. But in college there is no time to commune with one's thoughts. One goes to college to learn, it seems, not to think. When one enters the portals of learning, one leaves the dearest pleasures—solitude, books, and imagination—outside with the whispering pines. I suppose I ought to find some comfort in the thought that I am laying up treasures for future enjoyment, but I am improvident enough to prefer present joy to hoarding riches against a rainy day.

My studies the first year were French, German, history, English composition, and English literature. In the French course, I read some of the works of Corneille, Moliere, Racine, Alfred de Musset, and Sainte-Beuve, and in the German those of Goethe and Schiller. I reviewed rapidly the whole period of history from the fall of the Roman Empire to the eighteenth century, and in English literature studied critically Milton's poems and *Areopagitica*.

I am frequently asked how I overcome the peculiar conditions under which I work in college. In the classroom I am of course practically alone. The professor is as remote as if he were speaking through a telephone. The lectures are spelled into my hand as rapidly as possible, and much of the individuality of the lecturer is lost to me in the effort to keep in the race. The words rush through my hand like hounds in pursuit of a hare which they often miss. But in this respect I do not think I am much worse off than the girls who take notes. If the mind is occupied with the mechanical process of hearing and putting words on paper at pell-mell speed, I should not think one could pay much attention to the subject under consideration or the manner in which it is presented. I cannot make notes during the lectures, because my hands are busy listening. Usually I jot down what I can remember of them when I get home. I write the exercises, daily themes, criticisms and hour tests, the mid-year and final examinations, on my typewriter, so that the professors have no difficulty in finding out how little I know. When I began the study of Latin prosody, I devised and explained to my professor a system of signs indicating the different meters and quantities.

I use the Hammond typewriter. I have tried many machines, and I find the Hammond is the best adapted to the peculiar needs of my work. With this machine movable type shuttles can be used, and one can have several shuttles, each with a different set of characters—Greek, French, or mathematical, according to the kind of writing one wishes to do on the typewriter. Without it, I doubt if I could go to college.

Very few of the books required in the various courses are printed for the blind, and I am obliged to have them spelled into my hand. Consequently, I need more time to prepare my lessons than other girls. The manual part takes longer, and I have perplexities which they have not. There are days when the close attention I must give to details chafes my spirit, and the thought that I must spend hours reading a few chapters, while in the world without other girls are laughing and singing and dancing, makes me rebellious; but I soon recover my buoyancy and laugh the discontent out of my heart. For, after all, everyone who wishes to gain true knowledge must climb the Hill Difficulty alone, and since there is no royal road to the summit, I must zigzag it in my own way. I slip back many times, I fall, I stand still, I run against the edge of hidden obstacles, I lose my temper and find it again and keep it better, I trudge on, I gain a little, I feel encouraged, I get more eager and climb higher and begin to see the widening horizon. Every struggle is a victory. One more effort and I reach the luminous cloud, the blue depths of the sky, the uplands of my desire. I am not always alone, however, in these struggles. Mr. William Wade and Mr. E.E. Allen, principal of the Pennsylvania Institution for the Instruction of the Blind, get for me many of the books I need in raised print. Their thoughtfulness has been more of a help and encouragement to me than they can ever know.

Last year, my second year at Radcliffe, I studied English composition, the Bible as English composition, the governments of America and Europe, the Odes of Horace, and Latin comedy. The class in composition was the pleasantest. It was very lively. The lectures were always interesting, vivacious, witty; for the instructor, Mr. Charles Townsend Copeland, more than anyone else I have had until this year, brings before you literature in all its original freshness and power. For one short hour, you are permitted to drink in the eternal beauty of the old masters without needless interpretation or exposition. You revel in their fine thoughts. You enjoy with all your soul the sweet thunder of the Old Testament, forgetting the existence of Jahweh and Elohim; and you go home feeling that you have had "a glimpse of that perfection in which spirit and form dwell in immortal harmony; truth and beauty bearing a new growth on the ancient stem of time."

This year is the happiest because I am studying subjects that especially interest me: economics, Elizabethan literature, Shakespeare under Professor George L. Kittredge, and the history of philosophy under Professor Josiah Royce. Through philosophy one enters with sympathy of comprehension into the traditions of remote ages and other modes of thought, which erewhile seemed alien and without reason.

But college is not the universal Athens I thought it was. There one does not meet the great and the wise face to face; one does not even feel their living touch. They are there, it is true; but they seem mummified. We must extract them from the crannied wall of learning and dissect and analyze them before we can be sure that we have a Milton or an Isaiah, and not merely a clever imitation. Many scholars forget, it seems to me, that our enjoyment of the great works of literature depends more upon the depth of our sympathy than upon our understanding. The trouble is that very few of their laborious explanations stick in the memory. The mind drops them as a branch drops its overripe fruit. It is possible to know a flower, root and stem and all, and all the processes of growth, and yet to have no appreciation of the flower fresh bathed in heaven's dew. Again and again I ask impatiently, "Why concern myself with these explanations and hypotheses?" They fly hither and thither in my thought like blind birds beating the air with ineffectual wings. I do not mean to object to a thorough knowledge of the famous works we read. I object only to the interminable comments and bewildering criticisms that teach but one thing: there are as many opinions as there are men. But when a great scholar like Professor Kittredge interprets what the master said, it is "as if new sight were given the blind." He brings back Shakespeare, the poet.

There are, however, times when I long to sweep away half the things I am expected to learn; for the overtaxed mind cannot enjoy the treasure it has secured at the greatest cost. It is impossible, I think, to read in one day four or five different books in different languages and treating of widely different subjects, and not lose sight of the very ends for which one reads. When one reads hurriedly and nervously, having in mind written tests and examinations, one's brain becomes encumbered with a lot of choice bric-a-brac for which there seems to be little use. At the present time my mind is so full of heterogeneous matter that I almost despair of ever being able to put it in order. Whenever I enter the region that was the kingdom of my mind, I feel like the proverbial bull in the china shop. A thousand odds and ends of knowledge come crashing about my head like hailstones, and when I try to escape them, theme goblins and college nixies of all sorts pursue me, until I wish—oh, may I be forgiven the wicked wish!—that I might smash the idols I came to worship.

But the examinations are the chief bugbears of my college life. Although I have faced them many times and cast them down and made them bite the dust, yet they rise again and menace me with pale looks, until like Bob Acres I feel my courage oozing out at my finger ends. The days before these ordeals take place are spent in cramming your mind with mystic formula and indigestible dates—unpalatable diets, until you wish that books and science and you were buried in the depths of the sea.

At last the dreaded hour arrives, and you are a favored being indeed if you feel prepared, and are able at the right time to call to your standard thoughts that will aid you in that supreme effort. It happens too often that your trumpet call is unheeded. It is most perplexing and exasperating that just at the moment when you need your memory and a nice sense of discrimination, these faculties take to themselves wings and fly away. The facts you have garnered with such infinite trouble invariably fail you at a pinch.

"Give a brief account of Huss and his work." Huss? Who was he and what did he do? The name looks strangely familiar. You ransack your budget of historic facts much as you would hunt for a bit of silk in a rag bag. You are sure it is somewhere in your mind near the top—you saw it there the other day when you were looking up the beginnings of the Reformation. But where is it now? You fish out all manner of odds and ends of knowledge—revolutions, schisms, massacres, systems of government; but

Huss—where is he? You are amazed at all the things you know which are not on the examination paper. In desperation you seize the budget and dump everything out, and there in a corner is your man, serenely brooding on his own private thought, unconscious of the catastrophe which he has brought upon you.

Just then the proctor informs you that the time is up. With a feeling of intense disgust, you kick the mass of rubbish into a corner and go home, your head full of revolutionary schemes to abolish the divine right of professors to ask questions without the consent of the questioned.

It comes over me that in the last two or three pages of this chapter, I have used figures which will turn the laugh against me. Ah, here they are—the mixed metaphors mocking and strutting about before me, pointing to the bull in the china shop assailed by hailstones and the bugbears with pale looks, an unanalyzed species! Let them mock on. The words describe so exactly the atmosphere of jostling, tumbling ideas I live in that I will wink at them for once, and put on a deliberate air to say that my ideas of college have changed.

While my days at Radcliffe were still in the future, they were encircled with a halo of romance, which they have lost; but in the transition from romantic to actual I have learned many things I should never have known had I not tried the experiment. One of them is the precious science of patience, which teaches us that we should take our education as we would take a walk in the country, leisurely, our minds hospitably open to impressions of every sort. Such knowledge floods the soul unseen with a soundless tidal wave of deepening thought. "Knowledge is power." Rather, knowledge is happiness, because to have knowledge—broad, deep knowledge—is to know true ends from false, and lofty things from low. To know the thoughts and deeds that have marked man's progress is to feel the great heartthrobs of humanity through the centuries; and if one does not feel in these pulsations a heavenward striving, one must indeed be deaf to the harmonies of life.

CHAPTER 21

I HAVE THUS far sketched the events of my life, but I have not shown how much I have depended on books not only for pleasure and for the wisdom they bring to all who read, but also for that knowledge which comes to others through their eyes and their ears. Indeed, books have meant so much more in my education than in that of others, that I shall go back to the time when I began to read.

I read my first connected story in May 1887, when I was seven years old, and from that day to this I have devoured everything in the shape of a printed page that has come within the reach of my hungry finger tips. As I have said, I did not study regularly during the early years of my education; nor did I read according to rule.

At first I had only a few books in raised print—"readers" for beginners, a collection of stories for children, and a book about the earth called *Our World.* I think that was all; but I read them over and over, until the words were so worn and pressed I could scarcely make them out. Sometimes Miss Sullivan read to me, spelling into my hand little stories and poems that she knew I should understand; but I preferred reading myself to being read to, because I liked to read again and again the things that pleased me.

It was during my first visit to Boston that I really began to read in good earnest. I was permitted to spend a part of each day in the Institution library, and to wander from bookcase to bookcase, and take down whatever book my fingers lighted upon. And read I did, whether I understood one word in ten or two words on a page. The words themselves fascinated me; but I took no conscious account of what I read. My mind must, however, have been very impressionable at that period, for it retained many words and whole sentences, to the meaning of which I had not the faintest clue; and afterward, when I began to talk and write, these words and sentences would flash out quite naturally, so that my friends wondered at the richness of my vocabulary. I must have read parts of many books (in those early days I think I never read any one book through) and a great deal of poetry in this uncomprehending way, until I discovered *Little Lord Fauntleroy,* which was the first book of any consequence I read understandingly.

One day my teacher found me in a corner of the library poring over the pages of *The Scarlet Letter.* I was then about eight years old. I remember she asked me if I liked little Pearl, and explained some of the words that had puzzled me. Then she told me that she had a beautiful story about a little boy which she was sure I should like better than *The Scarlet Letter.* The name of the story was *Little Lord Fauntleroy,* and she promised to read it to me the following summer. But we did not begin the story until August; the first few weeks of my stay at the seashore were so full of discoveries and excitement that I forgot the very existence of books. Then my teacher went to visit some friends in Boston, leaving me for a short time.

When she returned almost the first thing we did was to begin the story of *Little Lord Fauntleroy.* I recall distinctly the time and place when we read the first chapters of the fascinating child's story. It was a warm afternoon in August. We were sitting together in a hammock which swung from two solemn pines at a short distance from the house. We had hurried through the dishwashing after luncheon, in order that we might have as long an afternoon as possible for the story. As we hastened through the long grass toward the hammock, the grasshoppers swarmed about us and fastened themselves on our clothes, and I remember that my teacher insisted upon picking them all off before we sat down, which seemed to me an unnecessary waste of time. The hammock was covered with pine needles, for it had not been used while my teacher was away. The warm sun shone on the pine trees and drew out all their fragrance. The air was balmy, with a tang of the sea in it. Before we began the story, Miss Sullivan explained to me the things that she knew I should not understand, and as we read on she explained the unfamiliar words. At first there were many words I did not know, and the reading was constantly interrupted; but as soon as I thoroughly comprehended the situation, I became too eagerly absorbed in the story to notice mere words, and I am afraid I listened impatiently to the explanations that Miss Sullivan felt to be necessary. When her fingers were too tired to spell another word, I had for the first time a keen sense of my deprivations. I took the book in my hands and tried to feel the letters with an intensity of longing that I can never forget.

Afterward, at my eager request, Mr. Anagnos had this story embossed, and I read it again and again, until I almost knew it by heart; and all through my childhood *Little Lord Fauntleroy* was my sweet and gentle companion. I have given these details at the risk of being tedious, because they are in such vivid contrast with my vague, mutable, and confused memories of earlier reading.

From *Little Lord Fauntleroy,* I date the beginning of my true interest in books. During the next two years, I read many books at my home and on my visits to Boston. I cannot remember what they all were, or in what order I read them; but I know that among them were *Greek Heroes*, La Fontaine's *Fables*, Hawthorne's *Wonder Book, Bible Stories,* Lamb's *Tales from Shakespeare, A Child's History of England* by Dickens, *The*

Arabian Nights, The Swiss Family Robinson, The Pilgrim's Progress, Robinson Crusoe, Little Women, and *Heidi*, a beautiful little story which I afterward read in German. I read them in the intervals between study and play with an ever-deepening sense of pleasure. I did not study nor analyze them—I did not know whether they were well written or not; I never thought about style or authorship. They laid their treasures at my feet, and I accepted them as we accept the sunshine and the love of our friends. I loved *Little Women* because it gave me a sense of kinship with girls and boys who could see and hear. Circumscribed as my life was in so many ways, I had to look between the covers of books for news of the world that lay outside my own.

I did not care especially for *The Pilgrim's Progress*, which I think I did not finish, or for *Fables*. I read La Fontaine's *Fables* first in an English translation, and enjoyed them only after a half-hearted fashion. Later I read the book again in French, and I found that, in spite of the vivid word pictures, and the wonderful mastery of language, I liked it no better. I do not know why it is, but stories in which animals are made to talk and act like human beings have never appealed to me very strongly. The ludicrous caricatures of the animals occupy my mind to the exclusion of the moral.

Then again, La Fontaine seldom, if ever, appeals to our highest moral sense. The highest chords he strikes are those of reason and self-love. Through all the fables, runs the thought that man's morality springs wholly from self-love, and that if that self-love is directed and restrained by reason, happiness must follow. Now, so far as I can judge, self-love is the root of all evil; but, of course, I may be wrong, for La Fontaine had greater opportunities of observing men than I am likely ever to have. I do not object so much to the cynical and satirical fables as to those in which momentous truths are taught by monkeys and foxes.

But I love *The Jungle Book* and *Wild Animals I Have Known*. I feel a genuine interest in the animals themselves, because they are real animals and not caricatures of men. One sympathizes with their loves and hatreds, laughs over their comedies, and weeps over their tragedies. And if they point a moral, it is so subtle that we are not conscious of it.

My mind opened naturally and joyously to a conception of antiquity. Greece, ancient Greece, exercised a mysterious fascination over me. In my fancy, the pagan gods and goddesses still walked on earth and talked face to face with men, and in my heart I secretly built shrines to those I loved best. I knew and loved the whole tribe of nymphs and heroes and demigods—no, not quite all, for the cruelty and greed of Medea and Jason were too monstrous to be forgiven, and I used to wonder why the gods permitted them to do wrong and then punished them for their wickedness. And the mystery is still unsolved.

> I often wonder how God can dumbness keep
> While Sin creeps grinning through His house of Time.

It was the *Iliad* that made Greece my paradise. I was familiar with the story of Troy before I read it in the original, and consequently I had little difficulty in making the Greek words surrender their treasures after I had passed the borderland of grammar. Great poetry, whether written in Greek or in English, needs no other interpreter than a responsive heart. Would that the host of those who make the great works of the poets odious by their analysis, impositions and laborious comments might learn this simple truth! It is not necessary that one should be able to define every word and give it its principal parts and its grammatical position in the sentence in order to understand and appreciate a fine poem. I know my learned professors have found greater riches in the *Iliad* than I shall ever find, but I am not avaricious. I am content that others should be wiser than I. But with all their wide and comprehensive knowledge, they cannot measure their enjoyment of that splendid epic, nor can I. When I read the finest passages of the *Iliad*, I am conscious of a soul sense that lifts me above the narrow, cramping circumstances of my life. My physical limitations are forgotten—my world lies upward, the length and the breadth and the sweep of the heavens are mine!

My admiration for the *Aeneid* is not so great, but it is nonetheless real. I read it as much as possible without the help of notes or dictionary, and I always like to translate the episodes that please me especially. The word painting of Virgil is wonderful sometimes; but his gods and men move through the scenes of passion and strife and pity and love like the graceful figures in an Elizabethan mask, whereas in the *Iliad* they give three leaps and go on singing. Virgil is serene and lovely like a marble Apollo in the moonlight; Homer is a beautiful, animated youth in the full sunlight with the wind in his hair.

How easy it is to fly on paper wings! From *Greek Heroes* to the *Iliad* was no day's journey, nor was it altogether pleasant. One could have traveled round the world many times while I trudged my weary way through the labyrinthine mazes of grammars and dictionaries, or fell into those dreadful pitfalls called examinations, set by schools and colleges for the confusion of those who seek after knowledge. I suppose this sort of "Pilgrim's Progress" was justified by the end; but it seemed interminable to me, in spite of the pleasant surprises that met me now and then at a turn in the road.

I began to read the Bible long before I could understand it. Now it seems strange to me that there should have been a time when my spirit was deaf to its wondrous harmonies; but I remember well a rainy Sunday morning when, having nothing else to do, I begged my cousin to read me a story out of the Bible. Although she did not think I should understand, she began to spell into my hand the story of Joseph and his brothers. Somehow it failed to interest me. The unusual language and repetition made the story seem unreal and far away in the land of Canaan, and I fell asleep and wandered off to the land of Nod, before the brothers came with the coat of many colors unto the tent of Jacob and told their wicked lie! I cannot understand why the stories of the Greeks should have been so full of charm for me, and those of the Bible so devoid of interest, unless it was that I had made the acquaintance of several Greeks in Boston and been inspired by their enthusiasm for the stories of their country; whereas I had not met a single Hebrew or Egyptian, and therefore concluded that they were nothing more than barbarians, and the stories about them were probably all made up, which hypothesis explained the repetitions and the queer names. Curiously enough, it never occurred to me to call Greek patronymics "queer."

But how shall I speak of the glories I have since discovered in the Bible? For years I have read it with an ever-broadening sense of joy and inspiration; and I love it as I love no other book. Still there is much in the Bible against which every instinct of my being rebels, so much that I regret the necessity which has compelled me to read it through from beginning to end. I do not think that the knowledge which I have gained of its history and sources compensates me for the unpleasant details it has forced upon my attention. For my part, I wish, with Mr. Howells, that the literature of the past might be purged of all that is ugly and barbarous in it, although I should object as much as anyone to having these great works weakened or falsified.

There is something impressive, awful, in the simplicity and terrible directness of the book of Esther. Could there be anything more dramatic than the scene in which Esther stands before her wicked lord? She knows her life is in his hands; there is no one to protect her from his wrath. Yet, conquering her woman's fear, she approaches him, animated by the noblest patriotism, having but one thought: "If I perish, I perish; but if I live, my people shall live."

The story of Ruth, too—how Oriental it is! Yet how different is the life of these simple country folks from that of the Persian capital! Ruth is so loyal and gentle hearted, we cannot help loving her, as she stands with the reapers amid the waving corn. Her beautiful, unselfish spirit shines out like a bright star in the night of a dark and cruel age. Love like Ruth's, love which can rise above conflicting creeds and deep-seated racial prejudices, is hard to find in all the world.

The Bible gives me a deep, comforting sense that "things seen are temporal, and things unseen are eternal."

I do not remember a time since I have been capable of loving books that I have not loved Shakespeare. I cannot tell exactly when I began Lamb's *Tales from Shakespeare*; but I know that I read them at first with a child's understanding and a child's wonder. *Macbeth* seems to have impressed me most. One reading was sufficient to stamp every detail of the story upon my memory forever. For a long time the ghosts and witches pursued me even into Dreamland. I could see, absolutely see, the dagger and Lady Macbeth's little white hand—the dreadful stain was as real to me as to the grief-stricken queen.

I read *King Lear* soon after *Macbeth*, and I shall never forget the feeling of horror when I came to the scene in which Gloster's eyes are put out. Anger seized me, my fingers refused to move, I sat rigid for one long moment, the blood throbbing in my temples, and all the hatred that a child can feel concentrated in my heart.

I must have made the acquaintance of Shylock and Satan about the same time, for the two characters were long associated in my mind. I remember that I was sorry for them. I felt vaguely that they could not be good even if they wished to, because no one seemed willing to help them or to give them a fair chance. Even now I cannot find it in my heart to condemn them utterly. There are moments when I feel that the Shylocks, the Judases, and even the Devil, are broken spokes in the great wheel of good which shall in due time be made whole.

It seems strange that my first reading of Shakespeare should have left me so many unpleasant memories. The bright, gentle, fanciful plays—the ones I like best now—appear not to have impressed me at first, perhaps because they reflected the habitual sunshine and gaiety of a child's life. But "there is nothing more capricious than the memory of a child: what it will hold, and what it will lose."

I have since read Shakespeare's plays many times and know parts of them by heart, but I cannot tell which of them I like best. My delight in them is as varied as my moods. The little songs and the sonnets have a meaning for me as fresh and wonderful as the dramas. But, with all my love for Shakespeare, it is often weary work to read all the meanings into his lines which critics and commentators have given them. I used to try to remember their interpretations, but they discouraged and vexed me; so I made a secret compact with myself not to try anymore. This compact I have only just broken in my study of Shakespeare under Professor Kittredge. I know there are many things in Shakespeare, and in the world, that I do not understand; and I am glad to see veil after veil lift gradually, revealing new realms of thought and beauty.

Next to poetry I love history. I have read every historical work that I have been able to lay my hands on, from a catalogue of dry facts and drier dates to Green's impartial, picturesque *History of the English People*; from Freeman's *History of Europe* to Emerton's *Middle Ages*. The first book that gave me any real sense of the value of history was Swinton's *World History,* which I received on my thirteenth birthday. Though I believe it is no longer considered valid, yet I have kept it ever since as one of my treasures. From it I learned how the races of men spread from land to land and built great cities, how a few great rulers, earthly Titans, put everything under their feet, and with a decisive word opened the gates of happiness for millions and closed them upon millions more: how different nations pioneered in art and knowledge and broke ground for the mightier growths of coming ages; how civilization underwent as it were, the holocaust of a degenerate age, and rose again, like the Phoenix, among the nobler sons of the North; and how by liberty, tolerance, and education the great and the wise have opened the way for the salvation of the whole world.

In my college reading, I have become somewhat familiar with French and German literature. The German puts strength before beauty, and truth before convention, both in life and in literature. There is a vehement, sledgehammer vigor about everything that he does. When he speaks, it is not to impress others, but because his heart would burst if he did not find an outlet for the thoughts that burn in his soul.

Then, too, there is in German literature a fine reserve which I like; but its chief glory is the recognition I find in it of the redeeming potency of woman's self-sacrificing love. This thought pervades all German literature and is mystically expressed in Goethe's *Faust*:

> All things transitory
> But as symbols are sent.
> Earth's insufficiency
> Here grows to event.
> The indescribable
> Here it is done.
> The Woman Soul leads us upward and on!

Of all the French writers that I have read, I like Moliere and Racine best. There are fine things in Balzac and passages in Merimee which strike one like a keen blast of sea air. Alfred de Musset is impossible! I admire Victor Hugo—I appreciate his genius, his brilliancy, his romanticism, though he is not one of my literary passions. But Hugo and Goethe and Schiller and all great poets of all great nations are interpreters of eternal things, and my spirit reverently follows them into the regions where Beauty and Truth and Goodness are one.

I am afraid I have written too much about my book friends, and yet I have mentioned only the authors I love most; and from this fact one might easily suppose that my circle of friends was very limited and undemocratic, which would be a very wrong impression. I like many writers for many reasons—Carlyle for his ruggedness and scorn of shams; Wordsworth, who teaches the oneness of man and nature; I find an exquisite pleasure in the oddities and surprises of Hood, in Herrick's quaintness and the palpable scent of lily and rose in his verses; I like Whittier for his enthusiasms and moral rectitude. I knew him, and the gentle remembrance of our friendship doubles the pleasure I have in reading his poems. I love Mark Twain—who does not? The gods, too, loved him and put into his heart all manner of wisdom; then, fearing lest he should become a pessimist, they spanned his mind with a rainbow of love and faith. I like Scott for his freshness, dash, and large honesty. I love all writers whose minds, like Lowell's, bubble up in the sunshine of optimism—fountains of joy and good will, with occasionally a splash of anger and here and there a healing spray of sympathy and pity.

In a word, literature is my Utopia. Here I am not disfranchised. No barrier of the senses shuts me out from the sweet, gracious discourse of my book friends. They talk to me without embarrassment or awkwardness. The things I have learned and the things I have been taught seem of ridiculously little importance compared with their "large loves and heavenly charities."

CHAPTER 22

I TRUST THAT my readers have not concluded from the preceding chapter on books that reading is my only pleasure; my pleasures and amusements are many and varied.

More than once in the course of my story, I have referred to my love of the country and out-of-door sports. When I was quite a little girl, I learned to row and swim, and during the summer, when I am at Wrentham, Massachusetts, I almost live in my boat. Nothing gives me greater pleasure than to take my friends out rowing when they visit me. Of course, I cannot guide the boat very well. Someone usually sits in the stern and manages the rudder while I row. Sometimes, however, I go rowing without the rudder. It is fun to try to steer by the scent of water grasses and lilies, and of bushes that grow on the shore. I use oars with leather bands, which keep them in position in the oarlocks, and I know by the resistance of the water when the oars are evenly poised. In the same manner, I can also tell when I am pulling against the current. I like to contend with wind and wave. What is more exhilarating than to make your staunch little boat, obedient to your will and muscle, go skimming lightly over glistening, tilting waves, and to feel the steady, imperious surge of the water!

I also enjoy canoeing, and I suppose you will smile when I say that I especially like it on moonlit nights. I cannot, it is true, see the moon climb up the sky behind the pines and steal softly across the heavens, making a shining path for us to follow; but I know she is there, and as I lie back among the pillows and put my hand in the water, I fancy that I feel the shimmer of her garments as she passes. Sometimes a daring little fish slips between my fingers, and often a pond lily presses shyly against my hand. Frequently, as we emerge from the shelter of a cove or inlet, I am suddenly conscious of the spaciousness of the air about me. A luminous warmth seems to enfold me. Whether it comes from the trees which have been heated by the sun, or from the water, I can never discover. I have had the same strange sensation even in the heart of the city. I have felt it on cold, stormy days and at night. It is like the kiss of warm lips on my face.

My favorite amusement is sailing. In the summer of 1901, I visited Nova Scotia, and had opportunities such as I had not enjoyed before to make the acquaintance of the ocean. After spending a few days in Evangeline's country, about which Longfellow's beautiful poem has woven a spell of enchantment, Miss Sullivan and I went to Halifax, where we remained the greater part of the summer. The harbor was our joy, our paradise. What glorious sails we had to Bedford Basin, to McNabb's Island, to York Redoubt, and to the Northwest Arm! And at night what soothing, wondrous hours we spent in the shadow of the great, silent men-of-war. Oh, it was all so interesting, so beautiful! The memory of it is a joy forever.

One day we had a thrilling experience. There was a regatta in the Northwest Arm, in which the boats from the different warships were engaged. We went in a sailboat along with many others to watch the races. Hundreds of little sailboats swung to and fro close by, and the sea was calm. When the races were over, and we turned our faces homeward, one of the party noticed a black cloud drifting in from the sea, which grew and spread and thickened until it covered the whole sky. The wind rose, and the waves chopped angrily at unseen barriers. Our little boat confronted the gale fearlessly; with sails spread and ropes taut, she seemed to sit upon the wind. Now she swirled in the billows, now she springs upward on a gigantic wave, only to be driven down with angry howl and hiss. Down came the mainsail. Tacking and jibbing, we wrestled with opposing winds that drove us from side to side with impetuous fury. Our hearts beat fast, and our hands trembled with excitement, not fear, for we had the hearts of Vikings, and we knew that our skipper was master of the situation. He had steered through many a storm with firm hand and sea-wise eye. As they passed us, the large craft and the gunboats in the harbor saluted and the seamen shouted applause for the master of the only little sailboat that ventured out into the storm. At last, cold, hungry and weary, we reached our pier.

Last summer I spent in one of the loveliest nooks of one of the most charming villages in New England. Wrentham, Massachusetts is associated with nearly all of my joys and sorrows. For many years Red Farm, by King Philip's Pond, the home of Mr. J.E. Chamberlin and his family, was my home. I remember with deepest gratitude the kindness of these dear friends and the happy days I spent with them. The sweet companionship of their children meant much to me. I joined in all their sports and rambles through the woods and frolics in the water. The prattle of the little ones and their pleasure in the stories I told them of elf and gnome, of hero and wily bear, are pleasant things to remember. Mr. Chamberlin initiated me into the mysteries of tree and wildflower, until with the little ear of love I heard the flow of sap in the oak, and saw the sun glint from leaf to leaf.

> Thus it is that
> Even as the roots, shut in the darksome earth,
> Share in the treetop's joyance, and conceive
> Of sunshine and wide air and winged things,
> By sympathy of nature, so do
> I give evidence of things unseen.

It seems to me that there is in each of us a capacity to comprehend the impressions and emotions which have been experienced by mankind from the beginning. Each individual has a subconscious memory of the green earth and murmuring waters, and blindness and deafness cannot rob him of this gift from past generations. This inherited capacity is a sort of sixth sense—a soul sense which sees, hears, feels, all in one.

I have many tree friends in Wrentham. One of them, a splendid oak, is the special pride of my heart. I take all my other friends to see this king tree. It stands on a bluff overlooking King Philip's Pond, and those who are wise in tree lore say it must have stood there eight hundred or a thousand years. There is a tradition that under this tree King Philip, the heroic Indian chief, gazed his last on earth and sky.

I had another tree friend, gentle and more approachable than the great oak—a linden that grew in the dooryard at Red Farm. One afternoon, during a terrible thunderstorm, I felt a tremendous crash against the side of the house and knew, even before they told me, that the linden had fallen. We went out to see the hero that had withstood so many tempests, and it wrung my heart to see him prostrate who had mightily striven and was now mightily fallen.

But I must not forget that I was going to write about last summer in particular. As soon as my examinations were over, Miss Sullivan and I hastened to this green nook, where we have a little cottage on one of the three lakes for which Wrentham is famous. Here the long, sunny days were mine, and all thoughts of work and college and the noisy city were thrust into the background. In Wrentham we caught echoes of what was happening in the world—war, alliance, social conflict. We heard of the cruel, unnecessary fighting in the faraway Pacific, and learned of the struggles going on between capital and labor. We knew that beyond the border of our Eden men were making history by the sweat of their brows when they might better make a holiday. But we little heeded these things. These things would pass away; here were lakes and woods and broad daisy-starred fields and sweet-breathed meadows, and they shall endure forever.

People who think that all sensations reach us through the eye and the ear have expressed surprise that I should notice any difference, except possibly the absence of pavements, between walking in city streets and in country roads. They forget that my whole body is alive to the conditions about me. The rumble and roar of the city smite the nerves of my face, and I feel the ceaseless tramp of an unseen multitude, and the dissonant tumult frets my spirit. The grinding of heavy wagons on hard pavements and the monotonous clangor of machinery are all the more torturing to the nerves if one's attention is not diverted by the panorama that is always present in the noisy streets to people who can see.

In the country one sees only Nature's fair works, and one's soul is not saddened by the cruel struggle for mere existence that goes on in the crowded city. Several times I have visited the narrow, dirty streets where the poor live, and I grow hot and indignant to think that good people should be content to live in fine houses and become strong and beautiful, while others are condemned to live in hideous, sunless tenements and grow ugly, withered and cringing. The children who crowd these grimy alleys, half-clad and underfed, shrink away from your outstretched hand as if from a blow. Dear little creatures, they crouch in my heart and haunt me with a constant sense of pain. There are men and women, too, all gnarled and bent out of shape. I have felt their hard, rough hands and realized what an endless struggle their existence must be—no more than a series of scrimmages, thwarted attempts to do something. Their life seems an immense disparity between effort and opportunity. The sun and the air are God's free gifts to all we say, but are they so? In yonder city's dingy alleys the sun shines not, and the air is foul. Oh, man, how dost thou forget and obstruct thy brother man, and say, "Give us this day our daily bread," when he has none! Oh, would that men would leave the city, its splendor and its tumult and its gold, and return to wood and field and simple, honest living! Then would their children grow stately as noble trees, and their thoughts sweet and pure as wayside flowers. It is impossible not to think of all this when I return to the country after a year of work in town.

What a joy it is to feel the soft, springy earth under my feet once more, to follow grassy roads that lead to ferny brooks where I can bathe my fingers in a cataract of rippling notes, or to clamber over a stone wall into green fields that tumble and roll and climb in riotous gladness!

Next to a leisurely walk, I enjoy a "spin" on my tandem bicycle. It is splendid to feel the wind blowing in my face and the springy motion of my iron steed. The rapid rush through the air gives me a delicious sense of strength and buoyancy, and the exercise makes my pulses dance and my heart sing.

Whenever it is possible, my dog accompanies me on a walk or ride or sail. I have had many dog friends—huge mastiffs, soft-eyed spaniels, wood-wise setters, and honest, homely bull terriers. At present the lord of my affections is one of these bull terriers. He has a long pedigree, a crooked tail, and the drollest "phiz" in dogdom. My dog friends seem to understand my limitations, and always keep close beside me when I am alone. I love their affectionate ways and the eloquent wag of their tails.

When a rainy day keeps me indoors, I amuse myself after the manner of other girls. I like to knit and crochet; I read in the happy-go-lucky way I love, here and there a line; or perhaps I play a game or two of checkers or chess with a friend. I have a special board on which I play these games. The squares are cut out, so that the men stand in them firmly. The black checkers are flat and the white ones curved on top. Each checker has a hole in the middle in which a brass knob can be placed to distinguish the king from the commons. The chessmen are of two sizes, the white larger than the black, so that I have no trouble in following my opponent's maneuvers by moving my hands lightly over the board after a play. The jar made by shifting the men from one hole to another tells me when it is my turn.

If I happen to be all alone and in an idle mood, I play a game of solitaire, of which I am very fond. I use playing cards marked in the upper right-hand corner with braille symbols which indicate the value of the card.

If there are children around, nothing pleases me so much as to frolic with them. I find even the smallest child excellent company, and I am glad to say that children usually like me. They lead me about and show me the things they are interested in. Of course the little ones cannot spell on their fingers; but I manage to read their lips. If I do not succeed they resort to dumb show. Sometimes I make a mistake and do the wrong thing. A burst of childish laughter greets my blunder, and the pantomime begins all over again. I often tell them stories or teach them a game, and the winged hours depart and leave us good and happy.

Museums and art stores are also sources of pleasure and inspiration. Doubtless it will seem strange to many that the hand unaided by sight can feel action, sentiment, beauty in the cold marble; and yet it is true that I derive genuine pleasure from touching great works of art.

As my finger tips trace line and curve, they discover the thought and emotion which the artist has portrayed. I can feel in the faces of gods and heroes hate, courage, and love, just as I can detect them in living faces I am permitted to touch. I feel in Diana's posture the grace and freedom of the forest and the spirit that tames the mountain lion and subdues the fiercest passions. My soul delights in the repose and gracious curves of the Venus; and in Barre's bronzes the secrets of the jungle are revealed to me.

A medallion of Homer hangs on the wall of my study, conveniently low, so that I can easily reach it and touch the beautiful, sad face with loving reverence. How well I know each line in that majestic brow—tracks of life and bitter evidences of struggle and sorrow; those sightless eyes seeking, even in the cold plaster, for the light and the blue skies of his beloved Hellas, but seeking in vain; that beautiful mouth, firm and true and tender. It is the face of a poet, and of a man acquainted with sorrow. Ah, how well I understand his deprivation—the perpetual night in which he dwelt—

> O dark, dark, amid the blaze of noon,
> Irrecoverably dark, total eclipse
> Without all hope of day!

In imagination I can hear Homer singing, as with unsteady, hesitating steps he gropes his way from camp to camp—singing of life, of love, of war, of the splendid achievements of a noble race. It was a wonderful, glorious song, and it won the blind poet an immortal crown, the admiration of all ages.

I sometimes wonder if the hand is not more sensitive to the beauties of sculpture than the eye. I should think the wonderful rhythmical flow of lines and curves could be more subtly felt than seen. Be this as it may, I know that I can feel the heartthrobs of the ancient Greeks in their marble gods and goddesses.

Another pleasure, which comes more rarely than the others, is going to the theatre. I enjoy having a play described to me while it is being acted on the stage far more than reading it, because then it seems as if I were living in the midst of stirring events. It has been my privilege to meet a few great actors and actresses who have the power of so bewitching you that you forget time and place and live again in the romantic past. I have been permitted to touch the face and costume of Miss Ellen Terry as she impersonated our ideal of a queen; and there was about her that divinity that hedges sublimest woe. Beside her stood Sir Henry Irving, wearing the symbols of kingship; and there was majesty of intellect in his every gesture and attitude and the royalty that subdues and overcomes in every line of his sensitive face. In the king's face, which he wore as a mask, there was a remoteness and inaccessibility of grief which I shall never forget.

I also know Mr. Jefferson. I am proud to count him among my friends. I go to see him whenever I happen to be where he is acting. The first time I saw him act was while at school in New York. He played Rip Van Winkle. I had often read the story, but I had never felt the charm of Rip's slow, quaint, kind ways as I did in the play. Mr. Jefferson's, beautiful, pathetic representation quite carried me away with delight. I have a picture of old Rip in my fingers which they will never lose. After the play Miss Sullivan took me to see him behind the scenes, and I felt of his curious garb and his flowing hair and beard. Mr. Jefferson let me touch his face so that I could imagine how he looked on waking from that strange sleep of twenty years, and he showed me how poor old Rip staggered to his feet.

I have also seen him in *The Rivals*. Once, while I was calling on him in Boston, he acted the most striking parts of *The Rivals* for me. The reception room where we sat served for a stage. He and his son seated themselves at the big table, and Bob Acres wrote his challenge. I followed all his movements with my hands, and caught the drollery of his blunders and gestures in a way that would have been impossible had it all been spelled to me. Then they rose to fight the duel, and I followed the swift thrusts and parries of the swords and the waverings of poor Bob as his courage oozed out at his finger ends. Then the great actor gave his coat a hitch and his mouth a twitch, and in an instant I was in the village of Falling Water and felt Schneider's shaggy head against my knee. Mr. Jefferson recited the best dialogues of *Rip Van Winkle*, in which the tear came close upon the smile. He asked me to indicate as far as I could the gestures and action that should go with the lines. Of course, I have no sense whatever of dramatic action, and could make only random guesses; but with masterful art he suited the action to the word. The sigh of Rip as he murmurs, "Is a man so soon forgotten when he is gone?" the dismay with which he searches for dog and gun after his long sleep, and his comical irresolution over signing the contract with Derrick—all these seem to be right out of life itself; that is, the ideal life, where things happen as we think they should.

I remember well the first time I went to the theatre. It was twelve years ago. Elsie Leslie, the little actress, was in Boston, and Miss Sullivan took me to see her in *The Prince and the Pauper*. I shall never forget the ripple of alternating joy and woe that ran through that beautiful little play, or the wonderful child who acted it. After the play I was permitted to go behind the scenes and meet her in her royal costume. It would have been hard to find a lovelier or more lovable child than Elsie, as she stood with a cloud of golden hair floating over her shoulders, smiling brightly, showing no signs of shyness or fatigue, though she had been playing to an immense audience. I was only just learning to speak, and had previously repeated her name until I could say it perfectly. Imagine my delight when she understood the few words I spoke to her and without hesitation stretched her hand to greet me.

Is it not true, then, that my life with all its limitations touches at many points the life of the World Beautiful? Everything has its wonders, even darkness and silence, and I learn, whatever state I may be in, therein to be content.

Sometimes, it is true, a sense of isolation enfolds me like a cold mist as I sit alone and wait at life's shut gate. Beyond there is light, and music, and sweet companionship; but I may not enter. Fate, silent, pitiless, bars the way. Fain would I question his imperious decree, for my heart is still undisciplined and passionate; but my tongue will not utter the bitter, futile words that rise to my lips, and they fall back into my heart like unshed tears. Silence sits immense upon my soul. Then comes hope with a smile and whispers, "There is joy in self-forgetfulness." So I try to make the light in others' eyes my sun, the music in others' ears my symphony, the smile on others' lips my happiness.

CHAPTER 23

WOULD THAT I could enrich this sketch with the names of all those who have ministered to my happiness! Some of them would be found written in our literature and dear to the hearts of many, while others would be wholly unknown to most of my readers. But their influence, though it escapes fame, shall live immortal in the lives that have been sweetened and ennobled by it. Those are red letter days in our lives when we meet people who thrill us like a fine poem, people whose handshake is brimful of unspoken sympathy, and whose sweet, rich natures impart to our eager, impatient spirits a wonderful restfulness which, in its essence, is divine. The perplexities, irritations, and worries that have absorbed us pass like unpleasant dreams, and we wake to see with new eyes and hear with new ears the beauty and harmony of God's real world. The solemn nothings that fill our everyday life blossom suddenly into bright possibilities. In a word, while such friends are near us we feel that all is well. Perhaps we never saw them before, and they may never cross our life's path again; but the influence of their calm, mellow natures is a libation poured upon our discontent, and we feel its healing touch, as the ocean feels the mountain stream freshening its brine.

I have often been asked, "Do not people bore you?" I do not understand quite what that means. I suppose the calls of the stupid and curious, especially of newspaper reporters, are always inopportune. I also dislike people who try to talk down to my understanding. They are like people who when walking with you try to shorten their steps to suit yours; the hypocrisy in both cases is equally exasperating.

The hands of those I meet are dumbly eloquent to me. The touch of some hands is an impertinence. I have met people so empty of joy, that when I clasped their frosty finger tips, it seemed as if I were shaking hands with a northeast storm. Others there are whose hands have sunbeams in them, so that their grasp warms my heart. It may be only the clinging touch of a child's hand; but there is as much potential sunshine in it for me as there is in a loving glance for others. A hearty handshake or a friendly letter gives me genuine pleasure.

I have many far-off friends whom I have never seen. Indeed they are so many that I have often been unable to reply to their letters; but I wish to say here that I am always grateful for their kind words, however insufficiently I acknowledge them.

I count it one of the sweetest privileges of my life to have known and conversed with many men of genius. Only those who knew Bishop Brooks can appreciate the joy his friendship was to those who possessed it. As a child I loved to sit on his knee and clasp his great hand with one of mine, while Miss Sullivan spelled into the other his beautiful words about God and the spiritual world. I heard him with a child's wonder and delight. My spirit could not reach up to his, but he gave me a real sense of joy in life, and I never left him without carrying away a fine thought that grew in beauty and depth of meaning as I grew. Once, when I was puzzled to know why there were so many religions, he said: "There is one universal religion, Helen—the religion of love. Love your Heavenly Father with your whole heart and soul, love every child of God as much as ever you can, and remember that the possibilities of good are greater than the possibilities of evil; and you have the key to Heaven." And his life was a happy illustration of this great truth. In his noble soul, love and widest knowledge were blended with faith that had become insight. He saw

> God in all that liberates and lifts;
> In all that humbles, sweetens and consoles.

Bishop Brooks taught me no special creed or dogma; but he impressed upon my mind two great ideas—the fatherhood of God and the brotherhood of man, and made me feel that these truths underlie all creeds and forms of worship. God is love, God is our Father, we are His children; therefore, the darkest clouds will break and though right be worsted, wrong shall not triumph.

I am too happy in this world to think much about the future, except to remember that I have cherished friends awaiting me there in God's beautiful Somewhere. In spite of the lapse of years, they seem so close to me that I should not think it strange if at any moment they should clasp my hand and speak words of endearment as they used to before they went away.

Since Bishop Brooks died, I have read the Bible through, also some philosophical works on religion, among them Swedenborg's *Heaven and Hell* and Drummond's *Ascent of Man*, and I have found no creed or system more soul satisfying than Bishop Brooks's creed of love. I knew Mr. Henry Drummond, and the memory of his strong, warm handclasp is like a benediction. He was the most sympathetic of companions. He knew so much and was so genial that it was impossible to feel dull in his presence.

I remember well the first time I saw Dr. Oliver Wendell Holmes. He had invited Miss Sullivan and me to call on him one Sunday afternoon. It was early in the spring, just after I had learned to speak. We were shown at once to his library where we found him seated in a big armchair by an open fire which glowed and crackled on the hearth, thinking, he said, of other days.

"And listening to the murmur of the River Charles," I suggested.

"Yes," he replied, "the Charles has many dear associations for me."

There was an odor of print and leather in the room which told me that it was full of books, and I stretched out my hand instinctively to find them. My fingers lighted upon a beautiful volume of Tennyson's poems, and when Miss Sullivan told me what it was I began to recite:

> Break, break, break
> On thy cold gray stones, O sea!

But I stopped suddenly. I felt tears on my hand. I had made my beloved poet weep, and I was greatly distressed. He made me sit in his armchair, while he brought different interesting things for me to examine, and at his request I recited *The Chambered Nautilus*, which was then my favorite poem. After that I saw Dr. Holmes many times and learned to love the man as well as the poet.

One beautiful summer day, not long after my meeting with Dr. Holmes, Miss Sullivan and I visited Whittier in his quiet home on the Merrimac. His gentle courtesy and quaint speech won my heart. He had a book of his poems in raised print from which I read *In School Days*. He was delighted that I could pronounce the words so well, and said that he had no difficulty in understanding me. Then I asked many questions about the poem, and read his answers by placing my fingers on his lips. He said he was the little boy in the poem, and that the girl's name was Sally, and more which I have forgotten. I also recited *Laus Deo*, and as I spoke the concluding verses, he placed in my hands a statue of a slave from whose crouching figure the fetters were falling, even as they fell from Peter's limbs when the angel led him forth out of prison. Afterward we went into his study, and he wrote his autograph for my teacher:

> *With great admiration of thy noble work in releasing from bondage the mind of thy dear pupil, I am truly thy friend.*
> *John J. Whittier.*

and expressed his admiration of her work, saying to me, "She is thy spiritual liberator." Then he led me to the gate and kissed me tenderly on my forehead. I promised to visit him again the following summer, but he died before the promise was fulfilled.

Dr. Edward Everett Hale is one of my very oldest friends. I have known him since I was eight, and my love for him has increased with my years. His wise, tender sympathy has been the support of Miss Sullivan and me in times of trial and sorrow, and his strong hand has helped us over many rough places; and what he has done for us he has done for thousands of those who have difficult tasks to accomplish. He has filled the old skins of dogma with the new wine of love, and shown men what it is to believe, live, and be free. What he has taught we have seen beautifully expressed in his own life—love of country, kindness to the least of his brethren, and a sincere desire to live upward and onward. He has been a prophet and an inspirer of men and a mighty doer of the Word, the friend of all his race—God bless him!

I have already written of my first meeting with Dr. Alexander Graham Bell. Since then I have spent many happy days with him at Washington and at his beautiful home in the heart of Cape Breton Island, near Baddeck, the village made famous by Charles Dudley Warner's book. Here in Dr. Bell's laboratory, or in the fields on the shore of the great Bras d'Or, I have spent many delightful hours listening to what he had to tell me about his experiments and helping him fly kites by means of which he expects to discover the laws that shall govern the future air ship. Dr. Bell is proficient in many fields of science, and has the art of making every subject he touches interesting, even the most abstruse theories.

He makes you feel that if you only had a little more time, you, too, might be an inventor. He has a humorous and poetic side, too. His dominating passion is his love for children. He is never quite so happy as when he has a little deaf child in his arms. His labors in behalf of the deaf will live on and bless generations of children yet to come; and we love him alike for what he himself has achieved and for what he has evoked from others.

During the two years I spent in New York, I had many opportunities to talk with distinguished people whose names I had often heard, but whom I had never expected to meet. Most of them I met first in the house of my good friend, Mr. Laurence Hutton. It was a great privilege to visit him and dear Mrs. Hutton in their lovely home, and see their library and read the beautiful sentiments and bright thoughts gifted friends had written for them. It has been truly said that Mr. Hutton has the faculty of bringing out in everyone the best thoughts and kindest sentiments. One does not need to read *A Boy I Knew* to understand him—the most generous, sweet-natured boy I ever knew, a good friend in all sorts of weather, who traces the footprints of love in the life of dogs as well as in that of his fellowmen.

Mrs. Hutton is a true and tried friend. Much that I hold sweetest, much that I hold most precious, I owe to her. She has oftenest advised and helped me in my progress through college. When I find my work particularly difficult and discouraging, she writes me letters that make me feel glad and brave; for she is one of those from whom we learn that one painful duty fulfilled makes the next plainer and easier.

Mr. Hutton introduced me to many of his literary friends, greatest of whom are Mr. William Dean Howells and Mark Twain. I also met Mr. Richard Watson Gilder and Mr. Edmund Clarence Stedman. I also knew Mr. Charles Dudley Warner, the most delightful of storytellers and the most beloved friend, whose sympathy was so broad that it may be truly said of him, he loved all living things and his neighbor as himself. Once Mr. Warner brought to see me the dear poet of the woodlands—Mr. John Burroughs.

They were all gentle and sympathetic, and I felt the charm of their manner as much as I had felt the brilliancy of their essays and poems. I could not keep pace with all these literary folk as they glanced from subject to subject and entered into deep dispute, or made conversation sparkle with epigrams and happy witticisms. I was like little Ascanius, who followed with unequal steps the heroic strides of Aeneas on his march toward mighty destinies. But they spoke many gracious words to me. Mr. Gilder told me about his moonlight journeys across the vast desert to the pyramids, and in a letter he wrote me he made his mark under his signature deep in the paper so that I could feel it. This reminds me that Dr. Hale used to give a personal touch to his letters to me by pricking his signature in braille. I read from Mark Twain's lips one or two of his good stories. He has his own way of thinking, saying, and doing everything. I feel the twinkle of his eye in his handshake. Even while he utters his cynical wisdom in an indescribably droll voice, he makes you feel that his heart is a tender Iliad of human sympathy.

There are a host of other interesting people I met in New York: Mrs. Mary Mapes Dodge, the beloved editor of *St. Nicholas*, and Mrs. Riggs (Kate Douglas Wiggin), the sweet author of *Patsy*. I received from them gifts that have the gentle concurrence of the heart, books containing their own thoughts, soul-illumined letters, and photographs that I love to have described again and again. But there is not space to mention all my friends, and indeed there are things about them hidden behind the wings of cherubim, things too sacred to set forth in cold print. It is with hesitancy that I have spoken even of Mrs. Laurence Hutton.

I shall mention only two other friends. One is Mrs. William Thaw, of Pittsburgh, whom I have often visited in her home, Lyndhurst. She is always doing something to make someone happy, and her generosity and wise counsel have never failed my teacher and me in all the years we have known her.

To the other friend I am also deeply indebted. He is well known for the powerful hand with which he guides vast enterprises, and his wonderful abilities have gained for him the respect of all.

Kind to everyone, he goes about doing good, silent and unseen. Again I touch upon the circle of honored names I must not mention; but I would fain acknowledge his generosity and affectionate interest which make it possible for me to go to college.

Thus it is that my friends have made the story of my life. In a thousand ways they have turned my limitations into beautiful privileges and enabled me to walk serene and happy in the shadow cast by my deprivation.